RISE!

A Girl's Struggle for More

Rise!

A GIRL'S STRUGGLE FOR MORE

Diann Floyd Boehm

OC
Publishing

RISE! A Girl's Struggle for More

First published in 2021 by

Halifax, NS, Canada
www.ocpublishing.ca

Cover and interior book design by David W. Edelstein
Cover background photo courtesy of the Drumright
Historical Museum

ISBN - 978-1-989833-11-7 (Paperback Edition)
ISBN - 978-1-989833-12-4 (eBook Edition)
ISBN – 978-1-989833-13-1 (Dyslexia-friendly Edition)

I want to dedicate my first novel to two special women in my life: my mom, Mabel Adella Harris Floyd, and my Grandma Ruby, Ruby Pearl Terrill Harris, who enriched my life even more with her stories and guidance.

CONTENTS

∽ *Part Three: Plan in Action* ∽

FOREWORD

I am dedicating my first novel to two special women in my life: my mom, Mabel Adella Harris Floyd, and my Grandma Ruby. Mom always shared family stories about grandmas, great-grandmas, and even great-great-grandmas and grandpas. How lucky our family is to have these stories to pass down the family line. My mom was a trailblazer in her own right. She worked hard as a wife and mother and was part of a team that developed the first hospice program for veterans in Hampton, Virginia.

My Grandma Ruby was very special to me and played a significant role in my life. Almost every week, my family would go to her house and have Sunday dinner. There were many weekends that some of my brothers and I would spend with Grandma. Being with her and having her exceptional guidance and love was priceless. There was a time when I was a young adult that I lived with my grandma, and she enriched my life even more with her stories and guidance.

Rise! A Girl's Struggle for More is a biographical, historical fiction based on my Grandma Ruby's life. Ruby was born in 1904 in a small town in Oklahoma, back when most Americans lived outside of cities, before any world war, when young ladies like Ruby were expected to continue the same way of life as their parents and grandparents and not stray too far.

As an adult, Grandma Ruby was a single parent and working woman, which was unheard of in the mid-1900s. She lived her faith and never said a bad word or spoke ill of anyone. Grandma Ruby always reached out and helped others. Her smile and giggle were contagious. I am sure she had faults, but through my eyes, she was the kindest person I knew, who did without so others could have more.

When Ruby came into the world, no one could imagine the changes that would occur in the next twenty years, much less during the rest of her life. Some changes were local and immediate—the oil boom in Oklahoma and the Black Wall Street Massacre in Tulsa. Some changes were nationwide or global—World War I, the 1918 flu epidemic, the Roaring Twenties, migrations within the country, the Great Depression . . . wave after wave of changes that shaped Ruby's life.

How did this young girl, my grandmother, decide

to leave home? To earn money for her "escape" by secretly entering and winning dance contests? To jump into the fast-moving current of big city life? Her experiences led her to teach her grandchildren, "As long as you can breathe you are meant to learn and be more than you were the last day. If you fall, that's OK. Just figure out what you learned and get up and keep going."

I hope that this book provides an enjoyable way to learn about some historical events and people, to gain insight into how people's thinking evolved during these times and how there were women who were breaking tradition. My grandma would come to look at the moon knowing astronauts had landed there and that she was able to rise above expectations and break through almost insurmountable barriers to become a well-educated, successful woman.

Diann Floyd Boehm

Part One

A DREAM

Chapter 1

PLUCK THE CHICKEN

"SERIOUSLY, RUBY PEARL, PUT THAT BOOK DOWN and help your sister get the chickens plucked for Sunday's dinner!" Ruby's momma yelled upstairs.

"Yes, Momma, I am coming," Ruby replied. Reluctantly, Ruby placed a marker in her book and left the upstairs landing alcove, her favorite reading spot. She loved it there because, as she read, she could look out the long window into the big back-yard and see her momma's garden. The alcove was the perfect place to gain composure, as some of Ruby's sisters would do, and for others, like Ruby, it was a place to read and let imagination run wild.

The alcove was inviting, with the built-in cherry wood chest with its soft cushions and the blankets tucked away inside just waiting for someone to pull them out. The window itself was like a picture of the day framed beautifully to match the chest. It was always hard to walk past the window and not be tempted to peek out and see what might be going on outside. Once more, Ruby had to give up her favorite reading spot, her escape coming to an abrupt halt as family duties called.

Ruby hated plucking the chickens. At times she would sit there looking at the headless bird, trying to figure out if she had named this one. No matter how Ruby's momma boiled the birds—just enough for easy plucking—it was not a chore any of the girls enjoyed doing. Though the bird was dead, Ruby could not help but imagine the bird alive, and with each feather she pulled, she would feel the pain of the defenseless, headless bird. Her momma would tell her not to be silly, but Ruby could not help it. She would imagine that just the day before, it had been clucking around, happily eating corn and not harming a fly. Today, Ruby was in for a real surprise when she went out back to meet up with her sister, Ida Jane.

Ruby's momma always called her sister by both names, and if Ruby or a sibling only called her Ida, her momma would say, "Her name is Ida Jane, period. End of story." Ruby always felt that Ida Jane was the princess of the family; after all, she did have her mother's middle name. Plus, Ida Jane was a momma's girl and did everything her momma told her to do without ever putting up a fuss. Ruby was glad that her momma had a few daughters, as they all enjoyed canning, cooking, and sewing, which pleased her momma very much.

On the other hand, Ruby did not want to have anything to do with these chores. On many occasions Ruby took advantage of her sisters to stall for time in the hope of not having to participate in whatever "girl chore" was going on at the time. Sometimes it worked! But today, Ida Jane was getting fed up with Ruby and her shenanigans.

Ruby loved all her sisters but was particularly close to Ida Jane. They had shared a room together ever since their big sister, Rilla, had married and moved to Seminole, which was not far from Oklahoma City. Ruby was three years older than Ida Jane, but even with the age difference, Ruby was interested in Ida Jane's thoughts on some matters, and most importantly, they had each other's back . . . well, most of the time.

Today would not be one of those days. Ida Jane was sitting in the green metal lawn chair, working away plucking feathers when Ruby opened the screen door.

"Ruby, why do you always have to be late when it is time to pluck the chickens? You know it is one of our Saturday morning chores."

As Ida Jane kept giving Ruby a piece of her mind, Ruby ignored Ida Jane and watched her mouth move in slow motion as she went to get her bucket for the feathers. Ruby wondered what her little brother, Henry, was up to. Chances were, it was no good.

Henry was the youngest boy, and he would do all sorts of things to get attention from his siblings. Henry also climbed like a monkey. He would be hiding up in a tree and then jump down and scare the living daylights out of his friends. Henry liked to catch baby frogs in the garden because their croak was quiet and the girls could not hear them. Henry would place them on the table when the girls came in to eat. Sometimes he would go so far as to drop the frogs down the backs of his sisters' dresses. Henry would roll over laughing as he watched them try and wiggle the frogs out of their clothes, and then, of course, a big chase would ensue, which is just what he wanted—to have fun with his sisters.

Henry did have a big heart and would cheer up his brothers and sisters when they were sad. He loved to give his momma big hugs, and he would always thank her for dinner, as he knew it made her feel good. "I don't know what I would do without you, you little monkey," Ruby often heard their momma say.

As she headed across the yard, Henry jumped out from behind the shed where he had been hiding, clutching the chicken around its neck. He waved the chicken under her nose, cut the head off, and let it chase Ruby all around the backyard. Ruby screamed bloody murder while the chicken ran around headless with blood spurting everywhere. When the nerves of the chicken finally died and it fell over, Ruby ran up to Henry to give him a whack, but his reflexes were quicker than a cat, and he caught her hand in midair. Luckily for Ruby, Momma was watching the whole thing from the kitchen window.

"Henry, you let Ruby go so she can get to work," she called out, startling both Ruby and Henry, "or you'll find yourself plucking feathers with the girls. Now, you mind your momma!"

Ruby pouted and stuck her tongue out at her brother as Henry quickly darted off to the front yard. She plunked herself down next to Ida Jane, who was trying to stifle her laughter so Momma didn't see.

"That's what you get for being late!" Ida Jane could hardly sputter out the words through her laughter. Ruby tried to explain that she was at a pivotal plot point in her book and just had to keep reading, but Ida Jane cut her off. "I don't care," she huffed. "I just want to get this done and go have some fun."

"OK, I am sorry, Ida Jane," Ruby said as she sat down to begin plucking.

At first the two girls sat in the lawn chairs in silence. Finally, Ruby could not take her sister being upset with her, so she gently nudged Ida Jane's leg with her foot.

"Stop it! Leave me alone." Ida Jane looked sideways at her sister and gave her a little push with her shoulder.

Ruby scrunched up her nose. "You can't stay mad at me forever; otherwise, this chore will be even more boring." Ruby went to kick Ida Jane, but Ida Jane was quick and moved her legs over, looked the other way, and kept filling her pail with feathers. Ruby put her hand on her sister's shoulder. "I am truly sorry," she said.

"OK. I forgive you this time." Ida Jane turned and smiled and gently kicked her sister back. They both gave each other a sisterly smile and continued pulling the feathers out one at a time.

The sisters talked about all sorts of things. Ida Jane did not understand Ruby's enthusiasm for burying her nose in a book to read about other people's experiences when she could have her very own adventures. Ruby tried to explain, but Ida Jane was not in the mood to listen. The fall day was a little chilly with an ever so light breeze. Their dad, James Adrian Dinsmore, was busy in the smokehouse, and Momma Zola was busy in the kitchen. Ruby loved to garden with her mother. Watermelons and cucumbers were Ruby's favorite things to grow. Her momma loved them too but did enjoy her blackberries as well. In the fall, the garden beds were filled with bright pink, red, and yellow stalks from the Swiss chard, and the green onions with their small white flowers were in bloom. The various fragrances of the garden filled the air, and the light breeze carried the aroma with it. Once Ruby adjusted to her plucking, she inhaled the smells of home. She would often imagine herself on various adventures . . . that is, unless she was busy sharing the day with one of her sisters, as she was that day with Ida Jane.

Ruby thought Ida Jane was one of the prettiest girls in her grade. Her blonde hair and blue eyes made her very popular, just like their brothers, Will and Robert, whom the girls in town were crazy over. Ida Jane was the only girl who looked like their momma. Zola's side of the family had been in America for several generations, but at one time, the McCoys lived in Northern Ireland. The rest of the brothers and sisters—Rilla, Zach, Thomas, Henry, and Ivy—all took after their dad James's side of the family, with their auburn hair and light brown eyes. The Dinsmores had made their way to America by way of Scotland and England.

Mr. Dinsmore would always remind his kids of their roots and tell them stories of how the Dinsmore clan were known for their loyalty. Ruby's daddy would sometimes proclaim that here in America, their family would make their ancestors proud.

As Ruby and Ida Jane plucked chickens, they talked about how their week had gone. Even though their school was connected, they were in different wings because they were in different grades. Ida Jane was boy crazy. All she wanted to do was talk about who liked whom and why she did not like so-and-so anymore because now she liked another boy while her best friend at that particular moment liked her old boyfriend.

Ruby would keep plucking the chicken, all the while staring at her sister wondering if there was anything else she wanted to talk about! But Ruby would act interested as Ida Jane carried on. Sometimes sisters just needed to be that way. When Ida Jane would finally stop to ask for Ruby's input, Ruby would share her opinion but then manage to change the subject in hopes Ida Jane might realize there was a big world out there to discover.

Ruby preferred to talk about life beyond their small town. The Great War had been over for three years. Life, music, and so much more was changing faster than ever before. People seemed happier as they worked hard and dreamed of the life to come with so many innovations.

Many Americans were now able to own a car and some even had a telephone. The Dinsmores and some of their friends were part of the few who enjoyed some of the new luxuries of life.

It was President Wilson's last year in office. His ideology was changing America's view of the world with his vision of what became known as the "Progressive Movement." High school students would debate the pros and cons and what they could do to improve the United States. Oklahoma had only been a state for a short while, and so there were many opinions—from the Indians on the reservations, the outlaws, and oilmen, to ideas around new ways of farming and preserving food that many Okies wanted to tackle as new Americans. Life was changing, and Ruby felt she and her siblings were destined to be part of the changes. Ruby admired the women whom she read about picketing in front of the White House for the right to vote.

Ruby knew she was just as smart, if not smarter, than her older brothers and could make intelligent decisions for herself and her country too. She got so carried away talking about it to her sister that she stood up with her featherless chicken in her hand, raised it high, and proclaimed, "One day, I will make Lucy Stone and Susan B. Anthony, and all other women who fought for the rights of women to vote, proud! Their efforts will not be in vain. Mark my words, I shall cast my vote with pride!"

Ida Jane was cracking up as Momma yelled from inside, "Until then, Ruby, can you clean up the chickens and bring them inside for me to prepare for Sunday dinner, please?"

Well, that took the wind out of Ruby's sails. The girls gathered up their chickens and finished their chores.

Ida Jane looked at her sister and smiled. "Don't worry, Ruby," she said. "I know one day you are going to do something grand."

Ruby blew her sister a kiss, and they giggled while they took the chickens to their momma.

"Finally, time to go have fun!" said Ida Jane.

"I am going to finish my book," said Ruby.

"Not so fast for you, young lady." Her momma raised her right eyebrow while speaking to Ruby. Ruby recognized that look. If the right eyebrow went up, Momma was not happy. Ruby knew something was coming.

"Yes, Ruby, reading is important. I am proud of you and your reading skills, but a girl's duty is first to her home. You were late with your chores, and Ida Jane was on time, so I need you to make up for the time you missed. It is only fair."

"What would you like me to do, Momma?" Ruby asked, knowing she was in the wrong.

Ruby loved her momma and would do anything for her. She really didn't like to disappoint her, especially since she knew her momma lost her own momma when she was just four years old.

Ruby couldn't even imagine what life would be like without her. Momma was everything to her.

"Well, I know you do not like to cook," began Momma. She stood with her hands on her hips and sighed. "Lord knows every girl needs to know how to cook, whether you like it or not. Now, I could use your help preparing the flour and spices to dredge the chicken in, and then we will put them in the icebox, so all I have to do is pop them in the fryer after church tomorrow." Zola wiped her hands on her favorite yellow cotton apron. "I realize you would rather be with your daddy watching him do business, but I also want you to help me prepare the dough for tomorrow's biscuits. Half the town is coming tomorrow for dinner, and I want to be able to enjoy some of the time with my friends. Now grab an apron."

Ruby's momma always made sure there were plenty of clean aprons hanging in the kitchen pantry, ready to wear. Zola enjoyed making aprons and always said one couldn't have enough with a family as large as theirs. Ruby grabbed the apron that her momma had sewn for her a while back. She threw it over her head and tied the sash in a big bow around her waist. The apron was a strawberry cotton print and white cotton lace with two pockets to hold cooking utensils, like measuring spoons. Momma told her girls it was essential to do everything they could to keep their clothes as clean as possible to save on the washing. Ruby still had to share her momma with her siblings, but with her oldest sister, Rilla, now married, there were moments like this that Ruby had her momma to herself, which meant she didn't mind being in the kitchen. As she thought about it, helping her momma prepare for tomorrow's dinner wasn't such a chore after all. Ruby was just happy those darn chickens were plucked!

Chapter 2

SUNDAY POTLUCK DINNER

THE LAST WEEKEND OF EACH FALL MONTH WAS always a busy time for the Dinsmore family, as all the townsfolk were invited over after church for dinner. The big Sunday meal was one that everyone looked forward to and enjoyed. The womenfolk cooked extra-large portions so when supper rolled around later that day, the family could just eat the leftovers.

The fourth Sunday of the month, Zola would have the house to herself to prepare for the neighbors, while Ruby's daddy escorted the rest of the family to church. The Dinsmore children dressed in their finest Sunday clothes made by their momma, as she was an accomplished seamstress. Many of the women who were not so talented in sewing wanted Zola to make their children's clothes, but, of course,

Zola had no time with nine children. While the Dinsmore family sang with the congregation and praised God in the newly built Baptist church, Zola would praise God by singing "Rock of Ages" or "The Old Rugged Cross" as she swept the carpets and dusted the furniture.

The Dinsmore family had an expansive side yard that was perfect for hosting a large Sunday dinner. Zola would have the older boys set up the tables for all the food, and then her daughters covered the food tables with red gingham tablecloths, and blue tablecloths went on those that held the drinks, spoons, and plates.

The women would let Zola know what they would be bringing to the potluck so that Zola could make sure there was plenty of variety as well as enough of a main course. James and Zola always provided some of the meat for the main meal as well as her biscuits.

The potluck dinner served many purposes, but there was an underlying one—the women had a chance to show off their cooking to the menfolk; it was sort of a woman's cooking competition. After all, women learned at an early age that the best way to a man's heart was through his stomach. This unofficial cooking competition was also a way for their unmarried daughters to demonstrate their cooking talents to the eligible boys in the crowd.

The men loved this friendly competition, as they knew there was going to be some delicious food on potluck Sunday. The preacher, Minister Cook, would cut his sermon short just because all he could think about was going to the Dinsmores' house to eat and enjoy being with friends for the rest of the day. There was excitement in the air as the families arrived, placed their dishes on the appropriate table, and set up their lawn chairs in various groupings of friends and family. There were always differences among the townsfolk, but they would set them aside on potluck Sunday.

During the Sunday gatherings, children were to be seen but not heard, which meant they ate at the "children's tables." Ruby had heard her momma and some of the other parents say, "Adulthood comes soon enough, and there's no reason for children to worry about adult things that are discussed over a meal."

The children welcomed this attitude, as they preferred not to have their parents listen in on their conversations either, and they could put their elbows on the table without getting lectured about table manners. After the meal, there was much fun to be had. Activities varied depending on what you were in the mood to do. The boys would go across the street and play football on a large piece of property owned by Ruby's family and the Rayhills. In the

Dinsmore backyard, some of the girls would play croquet, while others would sit on the porch tatting and gossiping.

Ruby and her friends sometimes made their way up to Ruby's room where the girls could enjoy some privacy. The year was 1921, and Ruby and her best friend, Bessie, had both just celebrated their sixteenth birthdays. The girls had been friends as far back as they could remember.

The girls would sit on the twin beds and talk about lots of things, especially if they were considered "taboo." Ruby loved these potluck Sundays for many reasons, but mostly she loved looking out the window and seeing her parents enjoying themselves with their friends. Often during the week, there would be so much whooping and hollering about daily events and chores that Ruby wondered how her parents had even stayed together, much less ended up with so many kids.

She also could not get over how practically a whole town would show up and set up for a townsfolk's potluck every single month. If someone did not make it, it usually meant a family member was sick, and someone would take a meal to them. Oilton townsfolk truly cared about their neighbors.

Most townsfolk in the West were known for taking care of one another, but this community had a special bond. They were there for one another no matter what. It was well-known that many neighboring towns wished they had the same neighborly connection.

The small town of Oilton was made up of people from all walks of life. It did not matter where you came from or what you looked like. The founders of the town wanted peace and prosperity. They believed in giving a neighbor a hand when help was needed. Most of them had left family back east, and the Oilton folks were their family now.

Ruby took in the scene outside her window, with all the adults enjoying the day. She tried to imagine what it must have been like in their day to be young and fall in love the way her generation dreamt of being in love.

She wondered about her father, James. She knew he took great pride in his family hosting the potlucks and was proud of Zola's fried chicken and biscuits. Like the other husbands, he always praised her for a job well done. When he did, Zola would look into her husband's big, dusty brown eyes, and hers would twinkle with delight as she smiled back at him.

Once everyone had finished, Ruby watched Momma and her friends place the food covers on the leftovers, ready to take home for a light supper. They would then enjoy catching up on the latest gossip while tatting away. For any child, it was a comforting, peaceful sight to see their parents happy and relaxed. Another reason Ruby enjoyed potluck Sunday was that her big sister Rilla would come, along with her husband, Gerald. Lastly, she enjoyed it because differences were set aside, especially when it came to James Adrian Dinsmore. He wore so many hats and seemed to be involved in many issues when it came to building the town. Ruby's daddy was respected and feared at the same time. He was a local politician, landowner, realtor, businessman, and most importantly, a Freemason. In other words, his network was extensive.

James Adrian was in Oilton one day in January of 1915 when Mr. Branigan was ready to sell some of the very first lots in the town. When the time came to purchase land in Oilton, James was among the large crowd waiting in line to acquire property. He saw this town as an investment for his family's future. He and Zola were excited to find the perfect place for their permanent family residence. No more moving around for them; Oilton was home. Ruby remembered it very clearly. She was nine in

1915 when they packed up and left Colbert, which was part of the Indian territory, to live in Oilton. Her parents built a bigger house than she and her brothers and sisters could ever have imagined. The house even had indoor plumbing! The Dinsmores called it "The Big Yellow House," as it was the only yellow house in town.

Ruby's dad purchased a total of eight lots—three for their home, three commercial lots, and two more lots that connected to his friend Mr. Rayhill's property. James had a written agreement with Mr. Branigan that the lots that butted up against Mr. Rayhill's property would stay an open area for the kids to play. James had met Mr. Branigan and Mr. Rayhill at a large Freemason meeting, about two years before the selling of the land to set up the town of Oilton. James, Mr. Branigan, and Mr. Rayhill all became quick buddies, as they seemed to see eye to eye on politics and shared some of the same values and experiences. They all fought in the Spanish–American War and, over the years, James became a great resource to Mr. Branigan and Mr. Rayhill. They appreciated that he knew whom to speak to concerning getting roads laid down for the new town. The three men met many times regarding the formation of the town. James would use his network of people who were involved in laying out the roads at the state level to make sure Oilton would have the roads needed for the new way of transportation—motorcars.

The town was growing and attracted people of many different religious denominations. Before they knew it, new churches were built: Baptist, Presbyterian, and Methodist. James Dinsmore's commercial building was soon leased out for new businesses, including a hardware store and a barbershop, followed by a furniture store and a dance hall. He got involved in state politics, as he could not imagine a better way to help a young state grow while representing the people of Oilton and watching out for their welfare.

James continued surveying roads in Oklahoma, making sure Oilton, Cushing, Shamrock, and Drumright were able to access Oklahoma City and Tulsa. He was also involved in making sure Oilton had fresh, clean water. Ruby had always thought her dad should be mayor, but then she learned about the ugly side of politics. "If you want to get something done, sometimes you have to upset the nest," he always told her. And her dad would do just that.

James did not believe in slavery, and he let it be known. He also did not agree that a handshake was all you needed for a deal to be made. He wanted signed, formal contracts in case there was a problem. Some men in those days were offended, as they felt their word was all that was needed, but the world was changing, and James believed a contract was the proper way to do business.

Having lived in Oilton for eight years, the Dinsmores were a well-respected family in town. Sunday was indeed a good day, as most folks saw it as the Lord's Day, and people did their best to set differences aside for one day and be cordial to one another. It was Ruby's favorite day.

Chapter 3

A DECISION

FRIDAY NIGHT WAS A BIG NIGHT IN EVERY SCHOOL district, and that meant everyone in Oilton went all out to support their football team, the Panthers. The townsfolk would talk about the upcoming game all week in anticipation of how their favorite players would perform. The Drumright versus Oilton game was considered a big deal in both towns. Drumright was just up the road from Oilton, and the game made for a friendly rivalry.

In the early days, Drumright was referred to as a "rag town" because most of the oil riggers built their houses from discarded boxcars, while others lived in large tents, but it was the discovery of oil in 1912 that made Drumright grow overnight.

It was a hard life, but the families did not mind,

as it was a job—the start of a new life. The one thing that had not changed was tempers flaring from a long, hard day's work, and disputes would erupt. Once a riot broke out, and the men locked up the police chief and the mayor.

The governor had to restore order by sending in six militia units. The rag town eventually grew into a respectable, vibrant city, with banks, hotels, dance halls, and even roadhouses, which provided a bar as well as rooms for travelers.

Drumright's population grew to over two thousand, and over time, it became the business center for the oilmen, and Oilton became the town where most of the oil rig workers lived. Oilton was known for being a rough town, and disagreements at times were settled with a gun.

It was wise not to be downtown at night, especially if any of the oil riggers had been enjoying one too many drinks. One never knew when a fight would break out, and it did not end well. The sheriff of the town was always busy. In spite of the nighttime disagreements, Oilton was also a place where hardworking men and women wanted to provide for their family. It was in this spirit that Oilton homeowners worked hard to turn Oilton into a legitimate town, competing with Drumright with hardware stores, hotels, restaurants, and a red-light district with a dance hall.

These new towns had something in common—they were small, and they counted on each other. Drumright and Oilton folks were kind to one another, and Zola said many times, "You can count on a woman from Oilton or Drumright to lend a hand when needed." People moved from all over the country, but they knew once they settled in either Drumright or Oilton, they had an extended family for life. Job opportunities in the oil fields made the towns a place to head to for work, and the population grew. Friday night became football night, a real crowd-pleaser, especially among the men.

Ruby could tell her father was daydreaming as she ran out to the car and brought him back to reality. He was probably thinking about the game that coming Friday and how his sons would play.

It was a beautiful morning with a clear blue sky. Every once in a while, another car would pass, and the drivers would honk at each other and give a wave. Ruby thought how the horn had its own language; at least, that was how she interpreted her dad's horn blasts and hand gestures. One honk plus a wave meant "hi"; two honks and a fist meant "you better move over"; and holding the horn down till her dad got what he wanted meant the person better get his car in gear. It was a new world, this language of a car. A horse—well, it seemed second nature. You pull the reins left if you want to go left; pull the reins right if you want to go right; hold straight and say, "Let's go, girl," and give a little nudge to get going; pull the reins hard and say, "Whoa" if you want to stop. Yes, the language of a car and naming your car was a big deal.

In Oilton, when someone purchased their first car in town and drove it around to show it off, the first thing people wanted to know was what they were going to name it. It was like a part of your identity, and it was not to be taken lightly. Ruby was very proud that her dad named their car "Lightning." She liked to think she had a quick wit that was lightning fast, and therefore, in her mind, the car was just like her—superfast!

Ruby's daddy pulled up to what had been a hitching post area, which was now the place to park your motorcar. Momma had stayed back home. She had things to do around the house. Ruby went with her father because Momma wanted Ruby to look at fabric for a new Sunday dress. The fabric shop was not far from the town hall where Ruby's daddy was going to meet some of his friends to discuss the various politics that were going on in both towns.

As Ruby and her daddy were making their way up the walkway, a man yelled out, "Hey, James, our

Tornadoes have been working hard for the big game! Your son better watch out. He just might want to sit this game out!"

James chuckled and replied as he and Ruby walked by. "Not on your life, Ed! See you on Friday!"

Ruby looked at her dad but did not say a word as they walked a little farther, to where one of Ruby's daddy's friends was sitting outside the barbershop, rocking slowly to and fro. James tipped his hat and wished him a good day as they walked on by.

Another friend stepped out of the barbershop just in time to be in earshot. "Say, James, the Panthers better get ready. We have a great team this year!"

James stopped and turned to face both gentlemen, and Ruby scooted on ahead so as not to be part of the menfolk giving each other a friendly "hard time." She paused and leaned against a horse post, just close enough to listen in.

James gave a big smirk. "Is that so? Well, that is excellent. It should make for a good game." He started to walk away but turned back. "Oh, by the way, in case you haven't heard, I have two boys on the team this year."

"Two?" The men outside the barbershop responded in a chorus.

"Yup, two!" James grinned. "Yes, sirree. The coach moved Thomas up to varsity." His grin grew wider as he watched the men's faces. They knew Thomas was a star junior varsity player. "What? Didn't you know? It is sure to be a good game." He tipped his hat. "See you there!"

James caught up with Ruby and they continued walking.

"Thanks for not getting those men too wound up," said Ruby.

Her daddy squeezed her shoulder. "Aw, it was just in fun. And they know better." He winked at her.

Ruby nodded. She knew there were times that the men could get a little feisty with one another, but today did not seem to be that type of day.

She was relieved because she wanted to see her best friend, Bessie, whose momma owned the Markey Fall Store. The store was known for having some of the prettiest fabric among the small towns in the area. Ruby hoped to get an idea for a new dress with the help of Bessie. The girls were going to look at the magazines with the new fashions all the girls were talking about in school. Things were changing, and in the big town of Tulsa, girls were purchasing ready-made dresses now instead of their mommas making them. Ruby knew that would not be the case for her, as momma could copy and whip up any dress she saw.

Ruby enjoyed going into the town of Drumright. It was busy with people hustling from one place to the other. Men talking oil and money. And people from up east coming to town to check on the progress of the oil production. You could see the oil fields just west of town if you were up on one of the Drumright hills. Ruby enjoyed looking out over the hilltops and thought about how this oil discovery was putting her state on the map. The oil wells brought jobs to all the surrounding towns, and she had learned in school that in 1919, Drumright began adding one new business after another.

Ruby also learned that the growth of the town was a welcome change from times past when one disaster seemed to follow another. Drumright had suffered from several huge fires, such as the oil well fire of 1914 and more fires in November 1916, caused by a blast in a rooming house in town. A gas explosion had led to the fires that wiped out two city blocks, as most of the buildings were made of wood. It was known as the "one-hundred-thousand-dollar fire."

The new Drumright business section was considered fancy for its time. Some of the buildings were two stories with larger storefront windows. Ruby's daddy walked into Drumright Derrick Newspaper, where he was going to talk business with some of his friends. From the sidewalk, Ruby watched him greet his buddies. He turned and waved at her, and she continued on to Bessie's momma's store.

Ruby stopped to gaze at the store window display before going in. She dreamed that one day, when she became a businesswoman in the big, wide world, she would wear some of the latest fashions the two mannequins in the window had on.

Edith, Bessie's momma, worked hard to make sure her window had something to catch a customer's eye. Each day she would do something a little different to spark interest and draw them inside, like adding hats, shoes, or gloves to complete an outfit on display.

The store was slowly turning into a ladies' dress shop with more women's merchandise being added all the time. When a customer walked into the store, a bell would ring to let Edith know someone was inside, in case she was in the back room.

Ruby liked coming to the store. She anticipated the moment she would enter to discover what was new. She would look around in awe at the rows of colored fabric, the dark wood shelves, and beaverboard walls. A long glass display cabinet housed the latest hats and gloves to keep them from getting dusty. The counter was always a place for customers to "ooh and aah."

Bessie's momma also had a little tea and coffee corner for women to sit, relax, and enjoy the latest news with friends. Ruby's momma always talked about how it was smart of Edith to add the tea and coffee corner, as the women would rarely walk out empty-handed; depending on where a customer sat, they would have a different view of the merchandise in the store. One customer could see the fabric and glass display, while another would have the eye-catching view of rows of shoes. The customer would sip her drink, and before she knew it, she would be thinking about how she needed the item that had caught her eye.

Just past the tea corner was the design room with tables and chairs to sit at and flip through the fashion magazines and the new ready-made dress patterns from Butterick. There was no need to make your own patterns from scratch anymore, which was a big time-saver. It also gave some women more confidence in developing their sewing skills.

The design room was also the place for cutting the fabrics and storing supplies.

Threads of all colors and weight were stored in a locked glass case and used as an art display. It was a clever way that Edith had found to sell more thread. Many of her customers wanted to have their own "thread of art" displays.

Ruby pushed open the door and, like clockwork, the bells chimed announcing her entrance into the store. Bessie's mom greeted her with a warm welcome, with Bessie not far behind.

Bessie had been expecting Ruby. She ran to her and grabbed her hand to lead her back to the design room where they flipped through the new catalogs and magazines, oohing and aahing over the latest fall fashions in *The Delineator* and *Vogue*.

"Oh, my goodness!" Ruby squealed and pointed to movie star Betty Compson modeling a stunning frock.

"Can you imagine what our mommas would say if we asked them to make that dress for us?" Bessie giggled.

"Well, I would not even get the words out of my mouth before my momma would say . . ." Ruby cleared her throat and raised the pitch of her voice, "Land sakes, Ruby, have you lost your mind? No daughter of mine is going to walk around town dressed like that!"

They both laughed. "You sound just like her." Bessie snorted, which made them laugh even harder.

Bessie closed the magazines and leaned forward to whisper in Ruby's ear. "Guess what? My momma has decided to order a few ready-made dresses for girls our age to see how they will do. Just regular church dresses and a few dance dresses." Bessie looked back into the shop to see if her mother could hear them then turned back to Ruby. "She is ordering only one size of each so that no one is wearing the same dress."

"Oh Bessie, that's the bee's knees! Your momma was so smart to be the first fabric store around here to offer ready-made dresses for ladies but now for us too." Ruby sighed. "I bet she'll sell them all to the oilmen's wives and daughters in town!"

"Exactly," Bessie nodded. "That is what my momma said to Daddy. He just rolled his eyes, but lucky for Momma, she ran her family's shop before she even met Daddy, so she has the final say."

"Wow! You don't hear many women 'having the final say' over a man out here." Ruby was impressed. "You know the law. When a woman marries, what is hers becomes her husband's property. Your momma is lucky."

"Yeah, Daddy doesn't know it, but Momma is teaching me how to make him think it's his idea so that he feels like he's in charge."

Ruby rolled her eyes. "I know just what you are talking about! My momma calls it the best-kept secret when she says, 'Now you know your father knows best.' Well, that is code for 'I will take care of it, don't you fret.'"

They both laughed again. They were always laughing when they were together. It was what made being together so much fun.

"OK, new topic!" Bessie said.

Ruby knew that Bessie meant she was ready to talk about something else. Ruby liked that about Bessie, as Bessie was not one to ramble on and on over a topic. Ruby also loved the confidence Bessie had about who she was. Bessie did not feel she needed people's approval. Either you liked how she did things or not. If you didn't, then you didn't have her as a friend. It was as simple as that.

Ruby enjoyed her frankness. They both agreed to use the phrase "new topic!" even if one of them did not want to change the subject. It made their friendship work.

Bessie looked again to see if her momma was in earshot then leaned over to whisper in Ruby's ear. "Did you know Arthur Woods is going to be at the game?"

"Well, I assumed he would be. Why?"

Bessie looked at her, puzzled. "What do you mean, why? You know he still likes you. Not just like but *likes* you!" Bessie squeezed Ruby's hand.

Ruby smiled and then quickly shifted and shrugged. "I don't know any such thing. I made it very clear to him that I needed to focus on my studies."

Bessie laughed. "You know, Ruby, boys love it when a girl plays hard to get. You just made it more fun for Arthur."

"Well, that's his problem, not mine. I don't play those silly games. I hear my brothers talking, and I have no intention of being one of the girls boys talk about in the locker room, or study hall, or anywhere else for that matter." Ruby crossed her arms and turned away from her friend.

"Goodness, Ruby, you don't have to get your fiery

auburn hair all in a tiff! Your Irish blood is starting to show, for heaven's sake!" Not to be out-pouted, Bessie crossed her arms too.

Then she smiled and reached out and tapped Ruby on the shoulder. "Truce?" She held out her hand.

"OK, truce," Ruby agreed and they shook hands, once up and once down.

"One thing is for sure—I am going to have fun at the big game," said Bessie. "Say, I know! At the half-time let's meet up. What do you say?"

"One condition, Bessie," Ruby warned. "You do not trick me and bring Arthur along. I certainly don't want to lead him on. Deal?" Ruby stuck out her hand.

Bessie shook it. "Deal, but you do beat all, Ruby."

They were still giggling when they heard the bells announce Ruby's daddy entering the shop. They both started laughing even harder but cupped their hands over their mouths, hoping he didn't hear them.

"Ruby, it's time to go," her daddy called out.

"I will be right there," she called back.

Ruby and Bessie put the magazines away and walked to the front of the store where Edith and James were exchanging pleasantries as they waited for their daughters.

"Did you find the dress pattern you wanted, Ruby?" Bessie's momma asked as the girls entered the main part of the store.

"Not yet, but I heard you will be selling ready-made dresses in a couple of days."

Bessie glared at Ruby, as she was not to have said anything. Ruby ignored her friend's stare and continued. "I think that is grand, Mrs. Scott."

Mrs. Scott chuckled. "I see Bessie let you in on our little secret." She shook her head and smiled. "It's really OK. It is time the word gets out."

Ruby looked at Bessie and saw she was relieved with her momma's reaction. "I will come back with Momma, and maybe she will let me have just one ready-made dress if I pick out material for her to make me one as well."

"Splendid! And thank you for being excited about our new venture. Be sure to tell all your friends."

"Oh, I will, first thing Monday morning!" Ruby promised. "Gosh, ready-made dresses . . . . It will be the big news at school for all the girls. And it sounds like you will have lots to choose from."

Mrs. Scott beamed at Ruby. They all knew word of mouth was the best advertisement. "See you at the game, Bessie!" Ruby called over her shoulder. Her father tipped his hat and wished them a good day as they walked out the door.

"Ah, Ruby, Friday evening's football game is going to be something else," he said as they approached the car.

"I know, Daddy, but I just wish they would not

play both of my brothers at the same time. When they tackle one of my friends' brothers, they give me a hard time." She paused before getting in the car. "Besides, I don't like how they call my brothers 'The Terrible Dinsmore Boys,' even though I know it is a compliment."

Her daddy cranked the car and they both climbed in. "Ruby, you should be proud of your brothers. If that is all you have to worry about in this town, consider yourself lucky."

Ruby recognized that his tone of voice meant business. "Yes, sir." Ruby knew there was no use trying to explain her feelings. Her daddy lived for Friday night football and had big dreams for his boys. He dreamed of them going on to university, playing football, and making it big in the world. Ruby also knew her daddy expected her to graduate from high school, marry, and have a load of kids. She shuddered at the thought.

"Men provide, and women take care of the men and babies; women are the nurturers of the family," he would say to his boys. "No discussion, just a fact!"

If Ruby was in earshot when something like this was stated, she would debate the issue. She was sure he would say it just to get her all worked up and then they would have a heated discussion on how the world was changing for women. Ruby knew she was falling into her daddy's trap, but she welcomed the challenge of speaking to him about politics and the world. She wanted him to remember she had a mind of her own and was just as intelligent, if not even more so, than some of her brothers. Today was not the day for debate. Football fever was in the air, and Ruby decided just to let it go.

The ride home was a reminder of how the world was changing and the State of Oklahoma was changing right along with it. These days, Ruby's daddy always drove his motorcar to and from the big city of Drumright, and as they made their way home, they passed men on horseback, horses and buggies, and the occasional motorcar as well. Ruby contemplated the various ways to travel and marveled at how far technology had brought the world—horse and buggy to motorcars. Drivers needed to be careful of the buggies and the men on horseback. They had to watch out for horses that might have gotten out of the barn and wandered onto the road too. It took some getting used to. Every once in a while, you would hear about a motorcar hitting a horse, and it was not a pretty sight to see, or to hear the gory details.

Yes, times are changing, Ruby thought to herself. *And I am going to be part of the change.*

Many of the roads were still dirt roads, but Ruby's daddy would point out when a new road was going to be built. He enjoyed surveying roads and being in the know. She was always proud of how her daddy was helping to shape the surrounding towns. Their small community was turning into a town on the map where people wanted to live. Of course, oil had almost everything to do with it.

Businessmen referred to the oil as "black gold." They would come from the northern states to visit the various boomtowns, set up companies, and work with people like her daddy, Mr. Rayhill, and Mr. Branigan. Ruby took note of some of the conversations and saw that it seemed to always come down to money.

Her daddy hit a big bump as he turned off the dirt road onto a new road that went all the way to Oilton.

"That road is next," her daddy said. He would say that every time he hit a bump. Ruby grabbed her hat to make sure it did not fly off. She smiled at her daddy and thought about how she wanted to be like him in so many ways. He was a well-respected community leader and innovator. Her brothers were lucky that they could be whatever they wanted to be. She wished for the same opportunity.

As the car bumped along the dirt road that was destined for smoother days, something occurred to her. It was her "light bulb" moment. Understanding numbers was the key to knowledge and success. *That is it! I am going to study math!* She smiled to herself and took in the beautiful day. How interesting that a trip to a fabric store could end up freeing her mind to discover a pivotal part of her plan. Ruby gazed at the puffy clouds that looked like ice cream cones and puppies as she daydreamed about being an independent businesswoman one day.

Chapter 4

THE UNEXPECTED SURPRISE

THE NEXT MORNING CAME FASTER THAN A THIRSTY cow could get to the water trough. That day the school was hosting a bake sale to help promote the football athletic club, which helped the club earn more awards. Ruby brought chocolate cupcakes, while others brought freshly baked cookies and brownies. Whatever the baked goods were, the girls made sure the football players knew who made what when they came over to the table to purchase a treat.

The pep squad decorated the hallways in the school colors of black and white. They made various banners saying "Go Panthers Go!" or "Panthers are Dynamite!" and taped them on the walls, with some continuing from one hallway to the next.

Some of the girls, people around town, and even

some of the school staff treated the football players like Greek gods. The cheerleaders made sure they were the ones who decorated the players' lockers. The girls who decorated her brothers' lockers always told Ruby they had done it, in hopes that Ruby would pass the information on to her brothers. In the cheerleaders' minds, this could possibly lead to getting together after the game. Ruby always rolled her eyes, but eventually she found the information worked to her advantage when she wanted something from her brothers, Zach and Thomas. It turned out there were some cheerleaders the boys tried to avoid. Ruby's information would give them a heads-up if they knew a particular girl had decorated their locker, and they could decide whether or not they wanted to avoid her. Ruby would tell them the girl's schedule, so they could make their plan to either run into her or be there at the appointed time to carry her books. Of course, Ruby only shared the information if she was able to get something in return. She decided it was their math textbooks. She wanted to borrow them because they were more advanced than hers. School officials had a bias and felt boys had more of a need for math. After all, they thought most girls would be at home taking care of the household. Ruby felt this was a good trade—math book for information. It worked to both of their advantages.

Ruby would walk down the halls between classes and instead of people genuinely saying hi to Ruby because they liked her, it was really all about her brothers. "Hey, Ruby, hope your brothers are ready for the game." Or "Hey, Ruby, can you wish Zach good luck for me?"

Even the teachers were all about the big game. When Oilton played Drumright, all tests for the end of the week were given on Wednesdays, so as not to ruin any player's week by causing them to worry about tests on Fridays. A Wednesday test gave the football players time to improve their grade by Friday so they wouldn't be benched for the game. Teachers never wanted to bench a player as there would be silent repercussions; football players were treated extra special.

That year, the town of Drumright was very excited about their new quarterback, Harry Peterson, who had moved from Arkansas and seemed ready to defend his new team, the Tornadoes. The folks in Drumright were buzzing about Peterson. The football team in Oilton had been known to win most of the games, and Oilton football fans wanted this game to be no different. This year, the Panthers had two of the Dinsmore boys on their team, and their coach, Jerry Geyer, felt they were ready to take on the Tornadoes and Peterson too. Friday night could not come soon enough.

Ruby arrived at the game and spied Bessie and waved. The friends hugged. Ruby stepped back and squinted at Bessie and scanned the crowd.

"Don't worry, Ruby, I have not even seen Arthur, so just relax," said Bessie. "See you at halftime."

"OK . . . see you then!" replied Ruby.

Ruby was relieved but maybe just a little disappointed. It might have been nifty to at least get a glance at Arthur. Ruby went up in the stands and sat with her parents. The Panthers came running out of the field house pumped, with their eyes fierce and hungry for their win.

Everyone in the stands stood up to cheer them on, and many of the townsfolk called out her brothers' names, which always made Ruby feel proud. The team looked up at the crowd and waved their leather head harnesses to say thank you as the other team ran onto the field.

The Drumright side went crazy, waving and cheering their players on as well. Once both teams were on the field, everyone quieted down for the national anthem, school song, and prayer. At the end of the prayer, both teams yelled in unison, "Let's play!" The crowd cheered and took their seats, ready for the referees and the team captains to do the coin toss. Drumright won the kickoff. The teams took their places on the field, and the referee's whistle blew.

Ruby's daddy never wanted to miss the first kick because in his mind, it set the tone for the game. The kick was a good one, and the game was off to a roaring start. The tension built as the evenly matched teams battled, and the coaches on both sides yelled at their players. Harry, the new quarterback for the Tornadoes, had a strong arm and liked to use the "forward pass" play, which became popular once it became legal in 1913. The forward pass was a favorite of many players, as they looked up to Knute Rockne and Gus Dorais, who won their game against Army using that play. Coach Geyer preferred the rougher side of football to gain yardage. He soon discovered they would have to change their strategy, with Harry throwing the pigskin farther than the Panthers had seen before.

"Get your head in the game!" Coach Geyer yelled.

Ruby never understood why her brothers thought being yelled at was encouraging in a game setting. But that was football, and it must have worked as the players began to "get their head in the game."

By halftime, everyone was on edge. The game was tied six to six. A tied game at halftime was a good thing in Ruby's mind. She loved the suspense. You could feel the anticipation of the crowd as they waited to see how the rest of the game would go.

As the teams and the coaches headed to the locker rooms, Ruby got up to make her way to see Bessie.

"Now, Ruby, mind your manners and always remember, the choices you make can change the direction of your life, so make good ones," her momma said.

"Yes, ma'am," Ruby dutifully replied.

It was a phrase she could recite in her sleep, as it wasn't the first time her mother had said that to her. Ruby sighed as she picked her way carefully down the bleachers. Her momma knew she was just going to see Bessie and talk, but everyone knew what some of her classmates did during halftime behind the gym. Her momma never really worried about Ruby, as she knew Ruby's brothers would beat up any boy that tried to lay a hand on her. Ruby knew it as well, and that is why the boys never bothered Ruby at school. Nevertheless, Ruby's momma felt it was her duty to remind her about choices.

Ruby was in a good mood and knew Bessie would be too because their team was not losing. She also knew that no matter what side of the field she was on, people would never be rude to her because they had high regard for her brothers and her father. Ruby spied her best friend peeking out from behind the bleachers, watching for her. Ruby walked a little faster.

She liked Bessie for many reasons, but the most important one was that Bessie wasn't her friend just to be close to her brothers. Many of the girls would come over to the house, pretending they wanted to see Ruby, but she was just an excuse for them to say hi to one of her brothers. Ruby would be mad and hurt all at the same time. Bessie had known Ruby's brothers for a long time, so she just never thought of them as possible boyfriends, and this made it easy for Ruby to have Bessie for a best friend.

"Ruby, over here!" yelled Bessie.

Ruby ran the last few yards and was a little out of breath. "How do those boys do that for a whole game?" she pondered out loud.

"I have no idea," Bessie laughed. "But more importantly, guess what? Hank wants to see me after the game." Bessie twirled and clapped her hands. "Do you want to join us at the ice cream shop?"

"Bessie, that is swell! Will your momma let you go?"

"I'm really not sure . . . but if you come, then for sure my momma would say yes. Please say you'll come!"

Ruby wanted to say yes, but she knew there was no way her parents would let her, so she gave a lame excuse that she had to go home after the game. As she was stumbling through her excuse, Bessie's eyes became huge, and Ruby could feel someone was coming up behind her.

Ruby looked at Bessie and mouthed, "Is it Arthur?"

Bessie's face said it all. "Gotta go, Ruby," she said loudly, then whispered, "I had nothing to do with this."

"Bessie!" Ruby grabbed her friend's arm.

"Oh, let her go," Arthur said as he joined the girls. "Bessie didn't know I was following her. I figured you two would meet up at halftime, and I really wanted to see you."

Ruby's tummy was doing flip-flops. It was bigger than butterflies, and deep down inside Ruby had to admit to herself that she really was happy to see Arthur. She just did not want to let on.

"Well, that is sweet of you, Arthur. What did you want to see me about?" She tried to control the jitters in her voice.

He gave a devious smile. "Come with me." He took her hand and led her behind the school gym.

Ruby always heard about what happened behind the gym but had never experienced it herself, and now her tummy was doing even more flip-flops. She could feel her face turn hot with the excitement of it all. She hoped it wasn't bright red.

"Ruby, I can't stop thinking about you. You know I care about you. I'd like to spend some time with you. Not like the old-fashioned courting our parents did. I want to take you on a date."

"A date?" Ruby asked. "Oh, I'm not sure. My

parents have reservations about that new 'dating' thing." She paused and took a deep breath. "But maybe . . ."

"OK, you graduate this year, right?" He paused and Ruby nodded. "And you'll be turning seventeen soon." Arthur squinted his eyes in thought. "Maybe I can just come and see you on your birthday. Then it's not really a date and we're not courting." He nodded as if they were both in agreement. "I want to spend time with you without anyone thinking we have to get married."

Ruby was touched that Arthur remembered her birthday. As much as she tried, she couldn't help but smile and inadvertently flutter her light brown eyes at him. Her mind raced back in time to her sweet sixteen birthday party, only a year ago.

In those days, the better-off families threw a party for their daughters when they turned sixteen. The parents invited their friends' daughters as well as eligible young men. There were towns in Oklahoma where the girls married at fourteen, but Ruby's parents believed courting should not start till sixteen—even if Ruby had no desire to be courted. There was etiquette to courting in the small towns in those days, as a young lady should never be seen unchaperoned with a man unless it was in the neighborhood; and then, of course, all eyes were watching. Ruby recalled her daddy announcing her name to the guests as she walked up to the platform in her grown-up dress, wearing her hair up off the neck. For a girl, this was a big moment, just as it was for boys to go from knickers to trousers. Ruby's parents gave her Grandma McCoy's comb for her hair, and Ruby felt like a grown-up wearing her hair up for the first time. As the guests were clapping and cheering for her, she smiled and looked at everyone as any princess would, and then her eyes met Arthur's. It took everything in her power not to give away how much she liked him. Ruby danced with lots of boys, as that was the custom, but she saved the last dance for Arthur. She knew if it were not for her dreams of the future, she would give in to tradition and marry him on the spot! Ruby had bigger plans, and she knew Arthur did as well. And just as Ruby's parents had plans for her, so did Arthur's parents for him. His dad wanted him to run their hardware store and have it passed down through the generations.

"That would be nice," Ruby heard herself saying before she could stop herself. In her mind she was going to say, *Sorry, I can't.* But her heart seemed to take over. "But right now, I need to go. Halftime is almost over and my parents will be looking for me. I do like you . . . really." The words continued to tumble out of her. "I am having a family dinner party, and I am inviting just a couple of friends. If you come, I will give you an answer." She smiled and lowered her eyes.

Arthur was so excited that he squeezed her shoulders, brought her in close, and kissed her right on the lips. Ruby was shocked, as she had never been kissed! She had never let a boy get that close to her, and now her belly had massive butterflies, like never before.

"Ruby, I have been waiting to do this ever since school started. I am nuts about you!"

Ruby stood there, dumbfounded for a moment, thinking she was in one of her romance novels that she had hidden away from her parents.

"Arthur, well, I . . . I . . ." Then, she gave him a quick peck on the cheek and went running back toward the Drumright stands.

She slowed down as she approached the Panther side before rounding the front of the bleachers so her parents wouldn't be suspicious. All the while, she was thinking about how confused she was and all the things she should have said to Arthur. At the same time, her body was having flushes of excitement as she relived the moment.

The game continued and, with her mind still on Arthur, Ruby responded like a mechanical doll. She would hear her brothers' names being yelled as well as Joe's, the linebacker for the Tornadoes. She glanced at her daddy and saw how proud he was of his boys, while her momma sat worrying about one of them getting hurt. The game was still neck and neck, and the Tornadoes had the ball. Harry, the Drumright's new quarterback, threw the ball, but Zach was ready for the play and intercepted it. He took off in hopes of a Panther touchdown. The crowd was screaming on both sides.

Everyone stood up to see if Zach would be tackled, but his teammates provided a perfect block. He ran with all his might and made the winning touchdown! The Panther side went wild, and the Tornadoes fans yelled in disbelief. The clock ran out, and the referee blew the whistle, announcing the end of the game. Coach Geyer greeted the boys coming off the field screaming, "Way to go!" People continued to cheer, and Ruby watched as everything seemed to move in slow motion, with people hugging one another in the excitement of it all. All she could think of was her first kiss.

Ruby was off in another world. Her mother brought her back to reality.

"Ruby, are you OK? We won the game. You seem distracted. Aren't you pleased?"

"What? Oh yes, of course I am. I was just thinking about how Bessie and some of my friends are going to give me a hard time about my brothers," Ruby said. "Oh, and Bessie wanted me to join her after the game, but I already told her I couldn't." Ruby coughed, hoping her mother couldn't hear her heart beating. She didn't need the extra scrutiny until she figured out what to do about Arthur.

Her momma smiled. "OK, grab the basket, will you? And let's head home."

Ruby picked up the basket and made her way down the bleachers with everyone still hooting and going on about the game. In the parking lot, everyone greeted their friends from both sides and swapped game stories. Sure, the Tornadoes players and their parents were disappointed to lose the game, but people knew it was a game and you didn't fight over it. Even Ruby's daddy took the high road, as it was not considered gentlemanly to brag. Ruby knew that her daddy was especially proud because "The Terrible Dinsmore Boys" had helped make the final play. She wondered if there would ever be a day when he would beam that way for her. The family might have seen this as a game that would go down in history. Ruby would never forget it either—but not for the reasons her family might have thought!

Chapter 5

NOT THE WEEK
ANYONE WANTS

MORNING CAME SO FAST THAT RUBY FELT LIKE she had not slept at all. One thing she knew for sure—she wanted to call Bessie without any ears around, which was almost impossible since she had such a big family. She needed to confide in Bessie and ask her to get a message to Arthur.

The day seemed to crawl by, and Ruby fidgeted and sighed. Finally, in the early afternoon everyone seemed to be busy at friends' homes or working outside. Ruby took another look around to make sure she was alone in the house and then ran to the telephone. She prayed the operator was not listening in. Ruby did not want her conversation with Bessie to be the new gossip for the quilting bees in town. Bessie, of course, said she wished they could meet in person, as it was all so mysterious, but they both were so busy with family obligations that details would have to wait. Bessie promised to get the message to Arthur. She would find time to quickly walk over to the hardware store.

When Bessie got back to the fabric store and her momma stepped out, she promptly called Ruby and said, "Message delivered." It was the code they had decided on in case the operator was listening.

"Wonderful, thanks. You are a gem!" Ruby said. She heard a faint clicking in the background and knew the operator was listening, which was always the case on weekends.

The girls figured the operator, Miss Fritz, would inform Zola about anything suspicious, and so they wanted her to have as little information as possible. Miss Fritz and Miss Burchman, the other operator in town, were the "little birdies" for most parents.

Ruby thanked Bessie again and hung up the telephone. She was still a bit nervous trusting her. Even though Bessie was her best friend, everyone in town knew that you could eventually break Bessie down to get a secret out of her.

Monday turned out to be a typical day. No one had seen Arthur and Ruby together even though quite a few couples were enjoying the pleasure of a full lip-lock during halftime at the game. Ruby was just glad they were so involved in their own romances that they did not pay attention to who was around them. Classes and teachers seemed to be in their regular daily rhythm of bell rings, teacher talks, and class dismissals. Everyday life was slightly boring and yet, at the same time, the routine gave a sense of stability for families.

Ruby and her siblings were lucky because they had their immediate family as well as an extended family in Oilton and surrounding towns. Ruby's uncle, her momma's brother Vernon McCoy, owned the dairy farm up the hill on the outskirts of town. His property spanned several acres, and most of the population of Oilton looked forward to his fresh milk delivered every day. Their brother Jim was in Oilton too. Their dad, Ruby's grandfather, had started the dairy farm. When he died, he left the farm to the boys. They could have sold it, but they decided to move to Oilton to be closer to their sisters. The boys were single, so they thought it was a sign for a change.

Ruby loved her Uncle Vernon very much, and sometimes he would come over in the evening with Uncle Jim. Jim lived closer to town, as he owned the grocery store, but he also helped Vernon a lot with the family dairy farm, and so sometimes they would come over to their sister's house for dinner with the family. Zola was always happy to have her brothers over. James enjoyed the brothers as well, and supper was a great time to catch up on the day's news. Zola's little sister, Issie McCoy, lived close by in Shamrock and often came too.

Some evenings they would have Ruby play the piano, and everyone would gather around and sing. Ruby loved to play the piano, and she had her momma's favorite gospel songs down. Ruby's uncles and her momma had performed in church and at some of the local fairs when they were growing up. Ruby would sometimes talk her uncles into singing, as she knew it would lead to them telling family stories, which gave Ruby a peek into her momma's childhood. They didn't come every night, and one particular evening, when they didn't come, no one thought much of it. Sometimes they just had evening chores that took longer than expected.

The Dinsmore family was relaxing in the living room one evening when the phone rang. Zola quietly answered with not a care in the world. James and all the kids were watching Zola, as they were always curious to know who was on the line. They saw the look on their momma's face turn from one of happiness to fright. Zola hung up and said it was Jim; he had told her to get to the farm as soon as possible. James sent everyone upstairs to prepare for bed and asked Ruby to take care of the household.

Ruby nodded and then watched her parents run out the door, hop in the car, and speed away down the street. She went back inside to calm Henry and the others down, as they were all worried.

Zola and James arrived at the farm to find Vernon lying on his bed with the doctor by his side. Vernon had suffered a heart attack earlier in the evening and had not woken since. The doctor was not sure if he ever would. Jim and one of the field hands were with him when it happened. Jim was able to revive Vernon by applying pressure on his chest and pumping his heart until help arrived. When the doctor felt it was safe, they moved Vernon inside. All they could do now was wait.

A few days went by, and Vernon seemed to be doing better. He woke up and was able to speak a little bit. The doctor was pleased but said he was not out of the woods yet. Vernon needed to stay in bed. Issie and Zola would take turns sitting with him while

Jim worked the dairy farm. Zach would watch the grocery store in the evening for Jim, while James covered the store during the day. The few times when Vernon was able to speak to whichever sibling was around were special moments for them. It gave hope that he was going to pull through. In the end that was not the case.

One evening, Vernon took a turn for the worse and died in the middle of the night. Jim found him in the morning and called the doctors and his sisters. Ruby couldn't grasp how her uncle had been getting better and talking to his sisters and then went and died. Issie and Zola went back to the Dinsmore house after Vernon's body was taken to Peck Funeral Home. Issie called her husband Abe so that he could make plans to come to Oilton.

Ruby and Ida Jane were upstairs in their bedroom when their momma came home. They heard her coming up the stairs. When she walked in the room, the girls ran and hugged her. Ida Jane kept saying it was not fair. She couldn't understand how he had been getting better and then he wasn't.

Zola sat on the bed with them, and she began to explain that the doctor calls the time near the end of life "a rally," where a patient musters enough strength to come back and share some things before they leave this world. Zola always thought of it as a blessing, one that her momma had not had. She kissed the girls and reminded them that life was just a journey and wasn't always meant to be fair.

The girls hugged their momma, who then gave them a kiss and told them to play quietly in their room, as she was going to be with her sister downstairs for a while. She blew them a kiss and closed the door. It was a very hard day in the Dinsmore home for sure.

The town was buzzing with talk about what would happen to the dairy farm. The rumor mill was cranking, and people were eager to see who was right. It was just the way small towns were. Thomas and Zach did not attend school, as they needed to help their Uncle Jim with milking the cows and then with deliveries. Each customer was a friend of the family and gave their condolences. The boys were exhausted by the time they were finished and made their way home. They had helped with the cows before, but this was the first time they had to do it several days in a row. Milking the cows at five o'clock every morning made them appreciate the milk they were drinking, and they now thought twice about guzzling it down when their momma served them breakfast.

Everyone from around the town came to Vernon's funeral. Afterward, at the Dinsmores' home, neighbors came to pay their respects and remember fun times with Vernon. Zola, Issie, and Jim appreciated the comfort the memories gave them. Eventually, everyone left, and Ruby and Ida Jane offered to clean up.

"Thank you, girls." Zola placed her hand on each of their cheeks. "But I will do it. I could use the time cleaning up to take my mind off everything."

So Ruby and Ida Jane made their way upstairs along with their brothers. Ruby hung back a bit and watched her Aunt Issie and her momma quietly pick up the family room, going through the motions to have a clean house once more. Ruby wanted to help but slowly turned around and headed up the stairs. She knew her momma would eventually retire to her room, and Issie and Abe would make their way to Robert and Zach's bedroom where they were sleeping. The boys would sleep on the couch and floor in the living room.

The window in her bedroom was open, and Ruby could hear her father and Uncle Jim out on the porch, rocking chairs creaking back and forth. She could imagine them looking up at the stars but couldn't quite make out what they were saying. She figured her Uncle Jim was not ready to go back to the empty house at the dairy farm or even to his home for that matter.

Ruby could not sleep. She looked over at her sister who could fall asleep in a matter of minutes. Ruby snuck out of her room and tiptoed to the bathroom and quietly opened the window. She was hoping to hear more clearly what her daddy and uncle were saying, but there was only the sound of the rockers keeping the same rhythm. With a heavy heart, Ruby moved away from the window and went back to her room.

Much to her surprise, Ida Jane was awake and sitting up in bed. Ruby did not speak but just shook her head to let her know there was no news. They both slid back under the covers without saying a word.

The next day the family had to go down to the lawyer's office to hear the reading of the will. No one even knew Vernon had made a will, but he had. There they were, in the midst of their grief, in a lawyer's office. Mr. Louie Sills was the lawyer in town, and his growing law firm handled both business and family law for all the townsfolk, including Vernon, it seemed.

Mr. Sills welcomed Vernon's family and asked them to take a seat around the table in the conference room. He poured each of them a glass of water, which was his way of making his clients feel somewhat comfortable under these trying circumstances.

"I'm so sorry for your loss," he said. "I liked Vernon very much—as a friend and client."

Mr. Sills went on to explain that Vernon had come to him wanting to draw up a formal will in case something was to ever happen to him. Vernon realized most of his family would expect him to give everything to Jim, but he had some other ideas. Mr. Sills then looked around and could see no one really understood what he was trying to say. Mr. Sills took a deep breath.

"Well, let's just read the will and it all will make sense."

Everyone looked at each other as the lawyer took a sip of water and picked up the will to read.

Clearing his throat, the attorney shuffled the papers and started reading. "I, Vernon McCoy, being of sound mind and body, leave my dairy farm to my sister Zola."

"What?" She looked at Jim and Issie in shock.

Mr. Sills paused a moment to let the shock fade. "Vernon told me you would be surprised so he left an additional note to Zola for me to read. I think this will soften the blow a bit."

Dear Zola,

Don't worry. Jim will be fine. We talked about this. Jim will tell you.

Mr. Sills paused, and Jim nodded yes, as Issie and the other family members looked on. Mr. Sills continued.

Dad would want you to have the farm as well. After all, it was only left to us boys because when Dad died we were the men of the family. When we sold our store in Bower, we moved up here to be closer to you and Issie. I know you're all thinking the farm is part Jim's, as it was the inheritance from Dad, but Jim and I talked about it. I bought him out a long time ago, and that's how Jim could have his grocery store. He just continued to help me with the farm, as it was something for both of us to do together. Issie and Abe already have a farm. But don't worry, Issie, I have something for you.

Jim nodded as Zola looked at Issie. Mr. Sills took a sip of water as everyone shifted in their chairs with the awkwardness of it all. The reading of the will continued.

"Vernon left Issie $200 and his motorcar, named Betsy. Daisy, the dairy truck, will remain on the farm for deliveries," continued the attorney.

Issie smiled. "Well, I can't imagine driving a car, but the thought is fascinating," she said. "What a lovely gesture."

Zola smiled and nodded as she watched her sister sink in her chair with embarrassment.

"Now for you, Jim. I believe Vernon has a little surprise for you too," Mr. Sills said with a slight grin.

It turned out Vernon was not a penny pincher but a saver. He never married, as he enjoyed the ladies way too much to settle down. Ruby recalled once hearing her Uncle Vernon express regret to her momma that he didn't marry the one girl he "let get away." Ruby had heard him say if he had married Margaret, he would have a slew of kids. He seemed to think because Margaret had eleven kids, that meant he would have had eleven too.

"Vernon, the choices we make determine our life!" Ruby had heard her momma say.

"I know, I know, Sis," he had said as he continued quietly rocking on the front porch.

The lawyer continued, "Before I go on with the formal part of the will, Vernon wanted Jim to have this letter."

Mr. Sills handed Jim a sealed envelope. Jim's hands began to shake as he opened it and unfolded the letter. He started reading silently but then stopped and handed it to the lawyer. He could not bring himself to continue.

"Please read it to everyone," he said to Mr. Sills.

When Mr. Sills finished reading the amount of cash Vernon had saved for Jim, everyone was dumbfounded.

"Can you read that last part one more time?" Jim asked.

Mr. Sills read it again.

> *Jim, if you're reading this, then I guess I have gone to the big house in the sky. I have been saving money, hoping one day you and I could move and enjoy life in the big city. We had great plans, but looks like Mom and Dad needed me up here with them. So now it is time for you to venture out and live for both of us. Who knows? Maybe you will finally catch a cute young thing.*

Everyone chuckled. It was so Vernon. He had always felt Jim devoted himself to his work and helping Vernon. Mr. Sills continued with the letter.

> *Issie and Zola will be fine. James and Abe are like brothers too, and they will always take good care of our sisters. So now it is your turn!*

I know it is not something most men say, but
since these are my last words, I reckon it will
be OK for a man to say to his little brother,
I love you. For that matter, I love my whole
blessed family! I will be watching you from up
here in the sky.

Yours truly,
Vernon

Silence filled the room as the words from the letter sunk in. Vernon's sisters had tears rolling down their cheeks, and the men passed their handkerchiefs to them. Everyone seemed to reach for their water at the same time, and the lawyer went back to read the final part of the formal document. Papers were signed and the legal work for the day was completed.

When they all arrived back at the Dinsmores' home, Ruby had lunch ready for them, which was an easy task with so much food brought over by the neighbors.

The grown-ups walked into the house to find the table set and iced tea poured, so all they had to do was freshen up and take a seat. The problem was that no one was really in the eating mood, but there it was, all ready, so they just went through the motions. Ruby and Ida Jane attended to all their needs and even cleaned up, as it was the least they could do for their momma.

Issie and Abe needed to get back home and told Jim they would call and arrange to get the motorcar back to their place. They all hugged goodbye. Zola walked Issie and Abe to the car, and Ruby waved from the porch as they drove off.

"I should stop by the store," said Jim. "I'm sure Zach's got everything under control, so I'll get on up to the farm after I check in with him. After all, life goes on whether we like it or not."

He kissed his sister and told James he would speak to him soon and gave Ruby an awkward hug. Zola returned to the house and went straight to bed without saying a word. Ruby would greet any ladies who came to check on her momma and pick up a plate that they had brought for the funeral. They had been thoughtful to also have left a few fresh dishes so that Zola could be free from cooking for a few days.

By nightfall, Ruby was in her favorite reading spot when a few of her daddy's buddies came over to hear how it went with the lawyer. Ruby's ears perked up, and she made her way to the upstairs bathroom. She gently opened the window and listened to her daddy telling them what had taken place.

James described how Zola had sat next to her siblings for the reading of the will, and the more they heard, the more Zola would tense up, and the more tears would stream down her face. Jim had just put his arms around her. James told the boys he had felt sorry for Jim, sandwiched between two sisters covered in tears.

"Abe and I sat there, wanting to help," he told his buddies, "but it was a sibling moment, indeed."

James continued with the part in which the men would be most interested. He shared how the lawyer had had them sign some papers and told them he would meet them at the bank first thing in the morning to finish the transfer of land and money. James told them how Vernon had surprised all of them.

"We had no clue that he was saving money for a dream," Jim said.

"A dream?" the men asked in unison.

"That's right—a dream. It seems he had been thinking about it for a good while and none of us had a clue, except the men at the bank and the attorney," James said.

Ruby could not wait to hear what her uncle's longtime dream was, as she had never really thought about grown-ups and their wishes. It never occurred to her that she and her uncle could possibly have a shared goal.

It would have to wait, though. The men had moved from the porch and the conversation had faded into the darkness as they walked down the laneway. Ruby strained to hear but to no avail.

Later in the week, Ruby's questions were answered. Her Uncle Jim came over and met with her parents. It turned out Uncle Jim had been wanting to sell his grocery store and move to Oklahoma City and open a store; why, he and Vernon had even discussed doing it together, he told her dad.

Vernon had left him enough money to do just that without selling the Oilton store. But Jim had an idea. He told Zola and James that with such a big family, the boys should help pay their way through college. Jim proposed, as they sat in their usual spot on the porch, that the boys could run his grocery store.

"And James, you could oversee it while I get my other store going in Oklahoma City," Jim finished, looking rather proud of himself.

Zola looked from her brother to her husband, her brows knit. Ruby held her breath, curious to see what her father would say. She sat very still, off to the side, not wanting them to notice she was listening and stop the adult conversation.

James stroked his chin, deep in thought as Zola looked on, waiting for him to reply.

"Well, Jim," he finally said, "maybe I could just buy the store, so you don't have to worry about two stores."

Jim looked at him, surprised, and after a lengthy discussion and a hearty meal, Jim agreed.

Ruby had a theory on why her father would just come up with the idea of buying his brother-in-law's store. Her dad was a self-made man. He was born in Searcy, Arkansas, and had a twin brother, Emmett, four more brothers, and three sisters. Agriculture was big those days, and large families were the norm, as you needed a big family to work the farms. Ruby never met her Grandpa Dinsmore, as he had lived in another state. It wasn't easy to get to. In spite of the distance, Ruby felt like she knew him, as her daddy would reference him quite a bit, especially when the boys would get out of line.

"Now boys," he would say, "don't be complaining. You know what my daddy, your Grandpa William, always said? 'Hard work means food on the table and keeps a man out of trouble.' Now get to work so you can learn to be a man."

The boys didn't like that saying too much, but they loved hearing about their Grandpa William Dinsmore.

Sometimes, on a cold night, the family would sit by the fire, and Ruby's daddy would tell stories about his childhood and life in Arkansas. Those were the times that Ruby's daddy let his guard down and was not the tough guy the rest of the town thought he was. Ruby would watch her daddy and know, somewhere deep down, he had a real soft heart. Ruby once asked her momma if her daddy was ever gentle like Minister Cook, the preacher. Her momma gave Ruby a sweet little grin with a twinkle in her eye.

"Of course," she said. "But one can't be gentle when out and about working in this neck of the woods, as you would not survive. Men need to be able to stand their ground, and other men need to know you are not afraid to stand your ground, especially in a town like Oilton."

Ruby's momma got a dreamy look in her eyes. "One of the things that attracted me to your daddy was his strong ways; besides, it took a tough guy like your daddy to be able to handle my stubbornness." She smiled, recalling her courting days.

"I am going to be like that," Ruby told her. "When I believe in something, I will stand my ground too."

Her momma laughed and said, "Honey, you already do. You are so much like your daddy in many ways."

Ruby smiled. "Oh, well that is a good thing if a girl wants to do things in a man's world."

Ruby's momma just shook her head. "I am sure you will handle the world just beautifully, dear."

James had learned a lot being with his brothers and working the family farm. He always figured he would live in Arkansas, work the farm, and raise kids, but then he felt the call to duty and signed up for the army. Soon after, he found himself preparing for the Spanish–American War. This was a pivotal point in his life. When James returned home, he no longer wanted to farm. There was a bigger world out there, and he was going to head to Oklahoma where one of his older brothers lived and see what life was like as a city man. James was not afraid of the West or outlaws. He had learned to shoot a gun by the time he was four. His sergeant in the army had taught his regiment many things, like strength, endurance, and focusing on goals.

The army gave James confidence in himself, and he knew after leaving he could achieve whatever goals he set out to accomplish. His dad still had plenty of boys to work the farm and somehow knew when James returned that he would not be a farm boy anymore.

James had made his way to Bower, Oklahoma, where his brother John lived, when it was still Indian territory. James could read and write, so his brother arranged for him to have a job reading legal contracts and looking for grammatical errors.

It did not pay much, but James didn't mind, as he was learning about law and how businessmen went about establishing towns.

It was a story Ruby loved hearing her daddy tell. James and his brother had come to realize that they were living in a time when they could help build a "great nation," and their work would have a lasting impact on the people who moved to Bower and surrounding towns. This was very appealing to a young man who was looking for his sense of purpose and destiny.

Now, nine kids later, James had a home of his own and a business, and he was a well-respected community leader with a strong voice in town politics. His family had contributed to building the church, helped develop the school, and dabbled in real estate. James also did land surveys for the government for laying out the newly paved roads for motorcars to go from town to town.

The oil in Oilton and surrounding towns made the men of power in Tulsa pay attention to the pioneers of these oil towns. These were tough men who could handle the roughness of the men who worked in the oil fields. They were frontiersmen, ready to tame a wild land and develop it into a prosperous, respectable town for the sake of the nation. It gave James a sense of purpose. He had arrived. He was a big fish in a little pond.

James was good at saving his money and watching for opportunities to make more money for the family. Ruby figured her daddy saw the grocery store as a great addition to his other enterprises.

By the night's end, Jim and James were drawing up contracts and making plans to have them signed in the morning with Mr. Sills. In less than a week, life had made some huge hairpin turns for Ruby's family. They had lost a family member, gained a dairy farm, and purchased a grocery store.

Practically overnight, the Dinsmore family became even bigger land and business owners in the small town of Oilton, and it set the town buzzing. No matter what people were saying, one thing they all could agree on was that the loss of a loved one was a sad way to gain property. Ruby was going to miss her Uncle Vernon, and now her Uncle Jim was going to move to the big city. The lesson Ruby learned from her beloved Uncle Vernon's death was that when you have a dream, figure out a way to make it happen before it is too late.

Well, Ruby did have a dream, and she had figured out in her mind a way to make it happen. She just needed to work a little harder to see that it came true.

Chapter 6

IT IS ALL IN THE DETAILS

SEVERAL DAYS HAD GONE BY SINCE RUBY'S FAMILY and friends had gathered at Highland Cemetery to lay Ruby's Uncle Vernon to rest. Things still seemed strange for Ruby's family as they readjusted priorities for the various family businesses. James was still doing surveys for new roads, which gave him a steady income. It also kept him "in the know" on politics in the surrounding towns. Oklahoma had only been part of the Union for fifteen years, but it was becoming a household name, being in the midst of the oil boom that brought jobs and a new life to many, putting small towns such as Cushing, Drumright, Oilton, and Shamrock on the map.

These boomtowns created a growing demand for more roads. Transporting the oil as well as getting the workers to the fields was a top priority for the newly formed oil companies like Devon/Dunning Petroleum Industry.

Ruby's momma missed her brother, knowing she would not be setting a place for him for supper ever again. It just didn't seem possible he was gone; and yet he was. They all knew life would go on. They were not the first to lose a loved one, nor was this the first person Zola had lost in her life. She was only six when her momma slipped and fell down the steep stairs in their family home in Mississippi, leaving behind her husband, two sons, and two daughters.

Zola sighed and returned to her chores. She enjoyed running her household and attending to her children's needs. There was always much to do, but Zola didn't mind. As a child, she had always wished her momma had been there to manage the household for her. Zola's duties as a wife and mother were the priority, but she did have other interests, including helping the community's family doctor when he needed to go out of town. Zola had a natural interest in medicine, and her instincts had saved premature newborns as well as children and adults in the area.

Ruby missed her Uncle Vernon too. She felt she was living in an altered reality. She was sad and thought she'd go crazy and lose her temper at her young siblings. All they did was chatter and slam the screen doors while she was trying to escape into one of her books.

Ruby tried not to scream and tell them to shut up and to stop slamming doors. She did not want to upset her momma who had enough on her mind. Ruby knew that whenever momma did extra baking, she needed to be by herself. Today was one of those days. So, Ruby tuned out the noise the best she could as she sat in her favorite place on the landing and let her imagination go. The book she was reading was *Rilla of Ingleside*. She could not seem to put it down, as each chapter made her want to find out more.

Before Ruby knew it, it was dinner time. She carefully slid a bookmark in to save her place and joined her family at the huge dinner table. All sat quietly eating and did not speak a word. They just pointed, nodded, and passed the peas.

Ruby finally spoke up. "Momma, Ida Jane and I will do the dishes and clean up the kitchen," she said. "You and Daddy can just relax."

Ruby and Ida Jane both took pride in finding ways they could give their momma a chance to rest, so they worked on making the kitchen sparkle.

It was a beautiful clear evening as the night sky took over and the stars began to shine brightly. It seemed to Zola like the perfect night to start getting back to her sewing projects. Zola called to Ruby to come into her room, as she was in the mood to fit her for her seventeenth birthday dress while her siblings were upstairs studying.

Zola and Ruby reflected on how quickly the year had gone and how incredible the previous year's birthday party had been with the whole town celebrating Ruby's sweet sixteen. Zola reminded her that not all girls had that luxury. In her generation, by the time a girl turned sixteen, most times she had a husband and one or two children.

"The world is changing for sure, Ruby," Zola said as she pinned the hem.

On days like this, Ruby's momma would share bits and pieces of her childhood. Her momma had Ruby's complete attention and would use this time to teach a lesson or two about life, even if Ruby was not in the mood to listen. Ruby had no choice; after all, her momma was working with pins while she fitted her into a new dress. Ruby loved having her momma all to herself; these were special moments. As Ruby was listening to her momma sharing a little insight into her life, they heard a pounding on the front door. They both froze for a moment.

"Stay here!" Zola told Ruby as she hurried into the hallway where she met Ruby's daddy, who grabbed his pistol out of the drawer by the entrance.

"Who is it?" he called out while motioning to Zola to get behind him.

"James, let us in! It's Mark and Paul!"

James recognized Mark's voice and put his gun down. He unlatched the screen and front doors, and Mark and Paul practically pushed their way in, looking back over their shoulders. The men quickly moved into the living room, and Zola followed them. She glanced up the stairs and saw the children watching from the alcove landing. She scowled at them so they would know to stay put.

Now, James had many friends, but enemies as well. He was a man of principle and believed that regardless of your skin color, all men were created in God's image and created equal. James was tough when he needed to be, but James also had a soft heart when it came to children. James knew children should not be going around barefoot, so if he saw a child, even as young as six, wandering aimlessly around, he would drag them by the ear all the while telling them how he was at school earlier and heard they had completed all their work for their teacher. James would sit them down in the shoe chair and look them in the eye and tell them to never take a handout. He would ask them if they understood, so the story would go, and they nodded yes, wondering what was going to happen next. He then would tell them, "Now since school is work and you had a good report for the week, then you earned a pair of shoes; therefore, this is not a handout. Do you understand?"

He would take other barefoot children into the shoe store and tell them he would purchase a pair of shoes for them if they were willing to work for them in exchange. Some of them would take care of his horse or shine his car, while others pulled weeds in the garden for Zola. He wanted to instill in them a sense of pride and encourage them to stand tall.

James would tell them, "Remember this day and start thinking of ways to earn money and help your family." He also told them to keep up their grades. He would assure them that one day they would turn around and help others as well. James would rub their heads, and the boys would grin from ear to ear. He only hoped the children would one day understand what he was trying to teach them. One thing he knew for sure—these children would have shoes on their feet. They would always thank him and run home to show their mommas, or so the story went around town. It was these acts of kindness that set the balance for James's toughness and sense of justice.

That night, Mark and Paul told James there were men in town who wanted to get even with him for some perceived slight around a property sale. The Dinsmores had acquired quite a bit of land

and several businesses over the years. Then they would sell some, which enabled them to purchase more. Part of the business sales came from Zola, who had acquired property from her late husband, Stuart Brinkman.

Zola had been considered a "great widow catch," as she owned property and lived in Bower in the home that she and Stuart had made for themselves. Stuart was a much older man—twenty years older, to be exact. He had married Zola when she was just fourteen, as he thought a lot of the McCoy family that had moved from Mississippi to Bower when Zola was eight years old. It was only six years later that Tom McCoy died after being thrown from his horse. He left his grocery store to his sons, and the boys had two sisters to support. As a family friend, Stuart knew the boys had more than they could handle, so he decided to ask the boys if he could marry Zola. Stuart saw himself as a father figure—nothing more and nothing less.

His wife had died a while back, and Stuart just wanted someone to cook, clean, and watch over the farmhouse and some of his other properties if he had to go out of town. He knew Zola had all those skills and was really smart. He saw this as a way of protecting her and teaching her how to manage more than just a house when she got older. Stuart made sure she would be aware that he would give her opportunities to learn. He just wanted to provide her with a home and make life a little easier for the boys. This way they would have only one sister to provide for until she came of age and could marry.

Zola accepted the proposal and became Mrs. Stuart Brinkman. She felt very lucky and at an early age started learning as much as she could about being a landowner. Zola took great care in determining how to run Stuart's properties and his household. She learned how to manage his affairs and took time to learn about medicine from her husband's best friend, the town doctor. Those years with Stuart Brinkman proved to be a blessing for Zola in years to come.

Mr. Brinkman caught the flu and did not recover. After a year of mourning had passed, men in town knew Zola was available. She was not interested, as she was free for the first time and was enjoying her independence. Zola, who was now twenty-two, discovered she was good at managing the farm and buildings that she rented out to men who came to town for business. Zola found time to volunteer at the doctor's office and had become very good at helping him with his practice. She was a natural when it came to working with the patients and understanding medicine, and he came to rely on her. She could even set a broken bone as well as he could. It was at this time that James Adrian

Dinsmore moved to Bower after returning home from the Spanish–American War.

As mentioned earlier, James returned to Arkansas and packed his things and moved to Bower where his older brother lived. James went to work with his brother and soaked up all the information he could from the seasoned businessman about the real estate business. After a few months, James purchased some commercial property in Bower and leased the building out to a newcomer who wanted to open up his own business.

James continued to invest wisely, and in time he was able to acquire even more buildings. James met the widow, Zola, through a mutual friend and courted her. She was not an easy catch, which made the chase even more exciting to James. He liked a woman who knew her own mind. Finally, he was able to get her down the aisle. They married on March 1, 1899. Zola was twenty-three years old, which was considered way past the marrying age.

Zola and James worked hard to build a comfortable life for themselves, but with the birth of each new child, the house seemed to be less and less adequate. They sold the farm but kept the Brinkman properties in town and moved to Colbert, Oklahoma, to a bigger home, where James began to make a reputation for himself as a shrewd, and sometimes ruthless, businessman.

James knew small towns and their politics and knew he had made business enemies along the way. Sometimes his involvement in swaying decision-makers on why one small town should have a new road over another left many disgruntled business-men who would have liked to see James "meet with an accident."

It was still the "Wild West," and hiring a killer was not unusual in those days. The boomtowns also attracted outlaws. Where there was oil, there were banks, which meant there was money. The outlaws knew James was an excellent shooter, and he had gained respect even from the wanted men.

James's Freemason connection with the various chapters around the state and beyond gave him a platform to communicate goals for the towns, morals for future leaders, and ways to achieve these shared goals. This bond between the Freemason chapters proved to be of great use when looking for outlaws as well other troublemakers.

James's gift of "not knowing a stranger," as well as his ability to negotiate and write contracts, made doing business easy for him. His deep voice and commanding nature led people to trust him, and they often didn't fully read the contracts. James didn't see it as his responsibility to tell people to read the fine print. It always seemed to work in his favor, and for some, that didn't sit well.

Ruby watched her momma sprint down the hall but wasn't worried. Her daddy was there and she knew her momma could handle a gun too. Women had to—not just to defend themselves but, depending on where they grew up, they might have to go out and shoot something for supper.

When Ruby was younger, she loved how her momma would tell stories of the outlaw Belle Star coming by her place in Bower and wanting to eat some of her momma's cooking. Belle was always amazed that her momma, who was so young, could cook the way she did. Belle would sometimes ask Ruby's momma for advice on her love life. Ruby was always bewildered that her momma would even have an opinion in that area, much less for an outlaw as famous as Belle Star.

Ruby's momma would tell her she didn't have much choice in the giving of advice, as the outlaws who came just wanted a little bit of a regular life while she was cooking a meal for them. Besides, they were also aware that she knew how to use a gun. The outlaws made sure they knew who they were up against in each town. Stories of who's who and their lives did get around from one small town to another; that was just a known fact. The outlaws who took a liking to Zola had their private reasons for never giving her trouble, and for that, Zola was happy to provide them with a little moment of peace and a home-cooked meal. The townsfolk were glad she could keep them happy.

The outlaws considered Oilton as the place to kick back and relax before they moved on. No one wanted to know or dared to ask where they were going. They kept quiet and made sure Zola had extra fixin's to keep them all happy. Knowing this particular little nugget of family history, Ruby wasn't worried that anything would happen at their house, but as her daddy got ready to go out, she had a feeling in her gut that it would not go well.

About the same time, some neighbors were upset about a particular group that had moved into their town. The Ku Klux Klan said they were there to help maintain law and order. It seemed Oilton had developed a reputation for its rowdy oil riggers, the red-light district, brawls, and regular shootouts.

For some, the gun was the way to solve a problem. The KKK used this as their excuse to move in, and of all people, they rented from James Dinsmore, the very same person who always preached to people at town meetings about equal rights for everyone. They would say to each other, "Look at him, taking money from the Klan—so much for him agreeing with President Harding and his civil rights beliefs!" They believed he must be on the side of former

President Wilson who executed many racist policies, like banning Blacks from the White House, and
supported federal agencies becoming segregated,
including the segregation of the civil service in 1913.
That same president prohibited Blacks from using
the same office areas, cafeterias, and restrooms as
whites—just a few of the racist policies of the Wilson
administration. Many of the townsfolk became very
upset with James Dinsmore. They could not understand why he would help the Klan and wondered if he
had forgotten what had just happened the previous
spring with the horrific fire on "Black Wall Street."

The community of Greenwood, near Tulsa, was
made up of some of the wealthiest, most well-
educated African Americans and many whites
who were jealous of their lifestyle and had it in for
them. A riot occurred, and people disagreed about
how it happened. But no doubt it was a devastat-
ing, massive race riot on a scale that no one had
ever heard of or witnessed before, according to the
newspapers. Bombs went off, and the town burned
as one business after another went up in flames. An
estimated three thousand African American lives
were lost. There were conflicting stories on how
it might have happened, but it was all speculation.
One thing was for sure: no one in Oilton wanted
trouble, and having the KKK in their town only
meant one thing—TROUBLE!

The town had people from all walks of life. There was a large number of hardworking Syrians that had made their way to this small town, and they added vastly to the community. They wanted nothing more than to provide for their families, just like anyone else. There were African American families who were well respected in town and were part of the community, lending a hand to their fellow neighbor when needed. They also enriched the community. James served under Teddy Roosevelt in the Spanish–American War, so he was influenced by this dynamic leader. Teddy would speak of freedom for all as he encouraged them to go to battle. It was Teddy's words that would help shape James's political beliefs regarding all human life.

James had a plan, but he played his cards close to his chest to ensure its success. He really didn't know who he could trust. So, he let people speak poorly of him for the good of the community. He couldn't even tell his best friend, Mr. Rayhill.

"What's gotten into you, James?" Rayhill asked him one day.

"You'll have to trust me, Ray," he told him.

Rayhill looked into his eyes and nodded.

James shook his friend's hand, knowing all would be well in the end. He had designed a contract that in the end would rid their town of the Klan and surrounding towns as well. James had included wording in the agreement that if they did not maintain the building to the level that James expected, then the lease would be null and void.

James believed the organization was oblivious to the fact that he did not like them moving into Oilton. When his Freemason buddies from several towns over gave him a heads-up that they were coming his way, he thought, I *will take care of that!*

He befriended them on their arrival and offered to rent them space above the post office. He even put "KKK" carved in stone on the upper part of the building, so people would know they were there and get ready to protect their town.

James accepted the ire of many of the towns-people, as it helped solidify his plan. It would only work if the Klan wasn't aware of his deception.

James let them settle in but kept his eyes and ears on where they were and what they were up to. Finally, when he felt the time was right, he did an inspection and, as he anticipated, they had not kept their end of the bargain. He informed them they would have to vacate and to leave town. Furthermore, they would not get their down payment or any of their money back from their month's rent. Was he a brave or a foolish man? When the white-hooded men found out that James had always intended to run them out of town, they vowed to kill him.

Mark began to fill James in. "It seems that evicting

the Klan was one thing, but one of the members saw you pick up Mr. Jackman and his wife walking home from the grocery store and give them a lift home. You know how they feel about a white man offering anyone of a different race a hand. Well, that just made them more determined that you needed to be taken care of."

"Yes, and Betty Lou heard about the plan," Paul added. "It seems one of the members had a bit too much to drink pretty early this evening, and he made his way over to"—Paul looked at Ruby's mom and said, "Pardon me, Miss Zola," then looked back at James and continued—"the red-light district. Betty Lou just happened to be the lucky lady for the evening. Well, the guy was so drunk that before he passed out, he told her the whole plan. As soon as she was free, she told us as we were coming out of the bar. When we heard what was going on, we came right over here."

"Miss Zola, the women have high respect for your family, as you are so good to them," Mark cut in. "You know, helping them when they are sick and all."

Zola just gave a soft smile as she waited to hear her husband's reaction. When James had heard all the news, he called up to his eldest boys, Robert and Thomas, to come down and grab their guns.

"Zola, call Zach at the grocery store." James was

in full command mode. "And Will too. Tell them what's happening and tell them all to come here."

While Zola was on the phone, James began working out a plan with his boys, and Mark and Paul, who knew where the shooter would be.

Only a few minutes later, Will entered the front room, having come through the back door.

"Did anyone see you?" James asked.

"No, I don't think so," Will answered and joined in the planning.

They all knew that there would be Klan members watching their every move, so they had to be smart about it and not all leave at once.

"OK, we need to get started." The muscles on James's jaw were twitching. "It'll take a while for you boys to sneak into town on foot. Stay in the shadows and stick to the back road so you're not spotted."

Will, Robert, and Thomas nodded and climbed out a back window.

The ringing phone startled Zola, whose nerves were already on end. It was one of her friends who wanted to get together in the morning. Zola tried to act natural, made an excuse and a promise for another time, and got off the phone as quickly as she could.

They all sat around, waiting for the phone to ring—and about a half hour later, it did. Zola answered.

"Hello? . . . Yes, he is. One moment, please." Her hand shook as she handed the phone to James.

"Yes? Uh huh . . . of course. Yes, I'll be right there. And, no hard feelings, right? This is just business." He hung up and turned to Zola.

"It was one of the Klan members." He took her by the shoulders and pulled her in for a hug then held her away again. "So, they've set the trap. Says he's having a problem with his horse. He also said the room was cleaned out, and they were out of the building, and that the others had left town, and he was just about to leave when it looked like his horse was having difficulties with one of his legs." James started gathering his things.

"Well, we know that's a lie and they're planning an ambush," said Zola.

"Yes, but we're ready for them."

Mark and Paul stayed at the Dinsmore home to protect Zola and the children.

James drove his car over to the hardware store—he no longer rode his horse to town once he had a car. He parked a safe distance away so as not to spook the horses. The Klansman walked toward the car, met James halfway, and they walked on over to his horse. Everything seemed normal. James knew his boys were ready for any sign of trouble, each one in his hiding place, with pistol out and cocked. Thomas was using his new Colt .45 semiautomatic; the others had the old pistols handed down from various uncles.

As James bent down to check the horse's shoe, the man kicked him in the ribs, and he fell to the ground.

"You damn traitor!" the man cursed and pulled a pistol out, aiming it at James's head. He pulled the trigger.

Fortunately, James had been ready for some trickery and rolled under the horse. The gun blast scared the horse, who stomped and tossed its head, pulling the reins tight against the hitching post. James got kicked but kept rolling. Before the man could shoot again, all three boys shot at him. He fell, clutching his leg. Years later, they would still argue about whose shot had hit its mark. When James rolled under the horse, the Klansman didn't have a clear shot. From his hiding place under the hardware store walkway, Will aimed carefully just in front of the man and fired his gun.

Dust and splinters flew, startling the man; his gun fell out of his hand as the bullet went clear through his shooting hand. The gunman bent over and grabbed the gun with his other hand.

Will quickly closed the gap, his gun at the ready.

"You dirt bag! Move and you die. Drop the damn gun!" Will demanded.

Just then, a shotgun roared, and a hot blast of buckshot caught Will in the side. His pistol fired wildly. A second gunman burst from the saloon and ran toward Will to finish him off, but Zach shot him dead in his tracks.

Thomas saw a third gunman hiding behind the post office building. The gunman had spotted Zach and was just about to shoot him when Thomas shot the gunman in the shoulder and put him out of commission. The gunman started to run, but the sheriff heard the commotion and came to see what was going on. He tackled the gunman to the ground as he tried to get away, hauled him to his feet, and handcuffed him.

Robert and Thomas ran over to Will, while Zach grabbed the first gunman who had been wounded in the leg and hand. Zach pushed the man, who was limping on his bleeding leg, straight to the sheriff and James. The sheriff handcuffed him as the doctor came running over. He checked Will over and had Zach and Robert carry him to his office. One dead man lay in the midst of the onlookers, who stared in disbelief. They all shared their version of what happened until, long after, the men came and took the body to the funeral home.

The sheriff and James took the others to jail. The

Klansmen struggled and swore, but they knew their time in Oilton was up.

James went to the doc's office to check on his sons. The doctor said that Will was lucky that the buckshot had just grazed his side. The doctor bandaged him up, said he wanted to see him in a couple of days, and sent him home with orders to change the bandage every day.

Ruby and her momma sat quietly in the living room, waiting for the boys and her father to return, while Mark and Paul were on watch at the front and back doors. Ruby's handkerchief was so twisted, she wasn't sure she'd ever get the wrinkles out. When James walked into the house, Ruby ran to her daddy and hugged him, so relieved he had made it back safely. As soon as Ruby let him go, Zola wrapped her arms around him and rested her forehead on his shoulder, sighing loudly.

The boys followed and Ruby reached out to hug Will, then, noticing the blood and dirt on his shirt, let out a scream.

"Oh my God. Are you OK?"

Will had been hiding behind his brothers so, at first, his momma hadn't seen him. She gasped and started toward him, but James stepped in between.

"He is OK, Zola."

"I will decide that for myself. Please . . ." Zola put her hand on James's arm and firmly moved him aside.

"Momma, I'm really OK. The doctor bandaged me," Will said.

Zola gave him a look and turned toward the other boys.

"Are any of you hurt too?" she asked.

"We're fine," Zach and Robert said in unison.

"Lord have mercy. James, you are all lucky. It could have been much worse." Zola gave her husband a look that meant business.

She gave each one of her boys a hug. "Now, go and sit." She waved them to the dining room table and went to the kitchen to get some glasses. Zola did not believe in liquor as a habit, as sometimes the menfolk would drink way too much. But they did keep a bottle on hand for visitors, and tonight was different. She quietly poured each of them a shot of whiskey to ease their mind after a rough night.

While her mother poured, Ruby took the younger ones upstairs to calm down. Once they were tucked into bed, she came back downstairs to help her momma in the kitchen. The men finally called it a night, and they all went to bed knowing there was peace once more in the town.

The last thing on Ruby's mind was her birthday, as it seemed so insignificant compared to the possibility of losing a family member. Ruby lay there thinking about a man's world, contracts, and pure survival in such a world. She concluded one should always read the fine print. She looked over at her sister soundly sleeping and then out her bedroom window.

It was a clear night, and the stars were shining brightly. Ruby smiled and gave thanks that all was well and went to sleep.

Later that week, the judge ruled that the men of the "organization" would go to trial for the attempted murder of James Dinsmore, unless they agreed to certain terms. They had to leave town and not move to any of the surrounding towns. The organization could never return, and if they agreed to the conditions, James Dinsmore would not press charges and there would be no trial. The men recognized it was a good deal and agreed to the terms. The sheriff had pictures taken of the men for identification purposes. What the men did not know was their pictures were given to the Freemasons and distributed to as many places as possible so they could be on the lookout for them. Oilton was free of the Klan, at least for a while.

The townsfolk were so thrilled at the outcome of

the deal that they threw a party. The townswomen even asked the "lady of the night," Betty Lou, to join in, as word had gotten out that she had played a significant role in the resolution of the town drama. Betty Lou came and she held her head high. She considered herself a businesswoman, providing a needed service.

Many townsfolk apologized to James for believing he was on the side of the Klan.

"You almost had me fooled," Ray told James.

James and his boys were the men of the hour. The girls made a fuss over Ruby's brothers, with a little extra for Will. The townsfolk had something new to talk about and would always remember to read the fine print.

Chapter 7

RUBY'S BIRTHDAY

SEVERAL DAYS HAD GONE BY SINCE THE DINSMORE shoot-out, and it was no longer the talk of the town. Gunfights were a pretty common occurrence when the oil rig workers had too much to drink; their hot tempers and habit of settling disputes with their guns gave Oilton a "rough town" reputation. Drumright, on the other hand, was considered a gentleman's town where polite business was conducted.

So, life went on in the Dinsmore household, and it was now time to concentrate on Ruby's big day on October 20.

Ruby's momma always felt proud that she and James could do a little extra for their children's birthdays. Ruby was turning seventeen, which, in Zola's generation, was over the marriage age. As parents, Zola's generation let their girls stay in school. They felt seventeen was a more appropriate age to consider marriage, as it would allow girls like Ruby to finish their schooling.

Ruby's sister, Rilla, had called her that morning before she left for her classes and wished her a happy birthday. Friends at school made Ruby cards wishing her warm birthday greetings as well. Even her glee and debate clubs made a point to recognize her birthday, which made Ruby feel very special all day long. The week's football game was on Saturday, so Ruby's family party was on Friday evening. When she arrived home from school, her momma would not let her in the kitchen so as not to ruin the surprise, but Ruby knew whatever the dinner menu was, it was going to be delicious.

She had finished her homework at school, so all she needed to do was to get ready for her birthday dinner celebration. Thinking of Arthur made her anxious to get extra dolled up, and so Ruby excitedly made her way upstairs. She looked in the mirror and smiled to herself as she recalled her amazing sweet sixteen party the year before. As she began fixing her hair in an updo, she remembered dancing with many of the local boys, especially Arthur. The boys knew she was a Dinsmore and knew never to get fresh with her or her sisters, as they would have to answer not only to James Dinsmore, but even worse, to the girls' brothers.

As Ruby placed her Grandmother McCoy's beautiful comb in her hair, she remembered the sweet moments on the dance floor with Arthur. She had explained to him that she had to focus on her studies to get high marks in school and accomplish her dream of going to college. He understood, as he had ambitions too. Arthur was impressed with how Ruby had tested for the college preparatory exam and passed with flying colors. Even though her parents had raised their eyebrows, they could not argue with her results.

In the 1920s, Oilton and Drumright schools were able to offer different study tracks, like most of the big cities. Students had a choice of college prep, commercial, or vocational studies, such as home economics or industrial arts. Ruby thought about how fast a year had gone by. She had been working hard and secretly saving money to put toward wherever and however she was going to make her dream come true; what the next step would be was still on the drawing board. In spite of her success at school, Ruby knew her parents were not prepared to have her attend college. They wanted a secure, traditional life for her.

Ruby came out of her daydream as she slipped into her shoes and prepared to go downstairs to greet her friends . . . and Arthur! She was a little nervous about his presence. Mixed emotions filled Ruby's mind as she thought about Arthur being at the family table. As excited as she was, she would not let her guard down with him.

Ruby had seen Arthur briefly at Vernon's funeral with his family, but she had not seen him alone since the night of the big game between Drumright and Oilton. Ruby kept reliving that moment over and over, and each time her face would turn red and sometimes her body would shiver just recalling their embrace. She loved all that a simple kiss could bring and yet, at the same time, knew giving in to her affection for Arthur could derail her plans for the future; yet, here she was about to enjoy his company.

She looked in the mirror. "Ruby, get your act together," she told herself. "It is not like an official date. You are just sharing a meal with friends and family." She then gave herself a nod and went downstairs to check on things and relax before her friends arrived.

Ruby kept thinking she had forgotten something, but for the life of her, she could not remember what it was. Ida Jane came out of the kitchen where she had been helping her momma.

"Wow, you look so grown up!" Ida Jane said. "I almost didn't recognize you with that sophisticated updo."

"Thank you, and also, thank you for letting me get ready for tonight in private. It was a thoughtful birthday present," Ruby said in a very grown-up manner and gave her sister a big hug.

Ida Jane pulled back from the embrace and called over Ruby's shoulder, "Momma, Ruby is downstairs."

Ruby glared at her and rubbed her ear. "Do you have to yell?"

"What! Momma told me to tell her. I am just doing what she said."

Ruby knew that Ida Jane yelled on purpose to get Ruby's goat, as younger sisters do. She rolled her eyes when their momma walked out of the kitchen, apron and all.

"Ah, Ruby, you look stunning," her momma said. "And your grandma's comb looks beautiful." She patted the comb and pushed it in gently. "I guess you really are seventeen." Her momma sighed and kissed her on the forehead.

The girls smiled as they saw their momma's eyes tear up. They both hugged her. Zola gave each one of them a quick kiss on the cheek.

"Now, Ida Jane, would you mind finishing setting the table for me while I spend some alone time with the birthday girl?"

"Happy to, Momma," Ida Jane said with a smile.

Ruby shot Ida Jane a look that asked: *What more can Momma tell me?*

Momma caught her in the act. "Get that look off your face, Ruby," she said. "It is not like I have anything embarrassing to say."

Ida Jane giggled, and Ruby marched behind her momma and into her parents' bedroom.

"Have a seat, Ruby." Zola motioned to the sitting area. "I just wanted some alone time with you before everyone arrives." She motioned Ruby toward "The Chair."

Ruby now remembered what she was forgetting—that little detail of the evening. She was in for one of her momma's "wisdom talks."

Her parents' room was in the front of the house, off to the left of the large living and dining areas. It was painted a soft eggshell white and had pictures of all their children on the wall. On her momma's vanity was a picture of her wedding day. Hanging above the dresser were wedding pictures of each set of grandparents. Ever since Ruby could remember, she had always enjoyed looking at their photos. She never knew them because they died before she was born, but she loved to imagine what they had been like. Ruby had heard they'd been happy, but she never understood why people looked so severe when they had their wedding pictures taken; Ruby thought they should be beaming with excitement on their wedding day.

Ruby's momma had a good-sized bedroom

compared to many of her friends in town. James made sure that Zola had a seating area for two where she rocked her babies and, when they were a little older, just held them when they needed comforting. The second chair was for whoever else was in the room.

Sometimes Momma used "The Chair" to speak to one of her children alone so she could find out what was bothering them, or to just calm them down after squabbling with a sibling. Today, Ruby knew it was her "special time" with Momma and, no matter what, Ruby needed to button her lip and just listen, which was a feat easier said than done.

Ruby sat in "The Chair" while Momma sat in her rocker. The room was tranquil.

"Make yourself comfortable, dear," Ruby's momma said as she stood up from the rocker and made her way over to the vanity.

"Yes, Momma," Ruby dutifully responded.

Zola opened one of the small drawers and took something out that looked like a present. Ruby noted her momma's creative work on the wrapping. Zola would take the brown paper that she used to make dress patterns and paint a design on it. No matter how small the gift, she would lovingly take the decorative paper and wrap it, then tie different-colored strings into a bow.

Zola smiled at Ruby and sat back down in her rocker.

"Now, Ruby," she began. "Our family tradition is to open birthday gifts after the cake and ice cream, right?" Ruby nodded. "Well, I want to do it a little differently this year." Momma smiled. "It will all make sense once you open it."

"Oh, Momma, you have given me so much already," Ruby said.

"Well, thank you, dear. You are always so kind and thoughtful, and that is why I decided to give you something else that belonged to my momma. I know you will treasure it. Now, open it!"

Ruby closed her eyes and made a wish as she began carefully unwrapping the gift. There really was only one thing she wanted.

It was a square box, and Ruby was not sure what it could be . . . a pendant? Not a watch, as it would not fit in the box. The anticipation was ever so exciting as she untied the beautiful blue bow her momma had made. Smiling, Ruby opened each side, all the while thanking her momma even before she saw it.

Ruby opened the box, and there it was—a beautiful necklace. The chain was made of tiny rectangles, connected by simple links with a clasp in the back. In the center of the necklace was a dollar-size flower that had tiny white rhinestones around it. The petals were hand-painted and in the center was a smaller, lovely pink flower.

"Oh Momma, it is exquisite!" She lifted it gently out of the box. "May I wear it?"

"Of course, dear, that is why I selected the pattern for your birthday dress, so it would match." Zola grinned and fastened the necklace behind Ruby's neck.

"Now, turn around so I can see."

It fell perfectly on Ruby's throat. Her momma turned her to face the full-length mirror by the vanity.

"It's beautiful." Ruby stroked the heirloom with a shaky hand. "I wish I had met her." Ruby turned to her momma, who was sitting back in her rocking chair.

"I do too, Ruby." Zola sighed. "Now, come sit with me."

Once again, Ruby sat in "The Chair" and smiled as she thought about all the times her momma had comforted her in this very chair when she was young. Now she was seventeen, and her momma still managed to find a reason to get her back in it.

"Now Ruby, I know you have heard the story a million times, but I just have to remind you exactly how much you mean to me."

Ruby smiled. She knew just what story her momma was going to tell her.

Zola began. "It was a Saturday morning, seventeen years ago today, and I had so many things to do, but I knew you were arriving. I told your daddy there would be no lunch for the men that day. He needed to get the doctor and stay home. We sent the other children to a neighbor's, as we did not want them to be frightened when my labor pains came. They didn't seem to mind; they saw it as extra fun times with friends. You know, Ruby, I never thought of it as pain in the sense of it being negative. I always thought of it as helping the little one work his way—or, in your case, her way—out of a long journey into a bright new world. It is a blessing to be a woman, to be part of the miracle of bringing new life into the world. You will understand once you become a momma." Zola scanned the baby photos of all her children on the wall. "You do not think you will change, but you do the moment you hold that baby for the first time."

She paused and took a long drink of iced tea. She set her glass down and continued.

"Ruby, the day you were born was a clear, cool day. It was cooler than most October days, and for that I was grateful. You were an easy delivery. I think you were so happy to get here. When I heard your first cry, I was relieved that you had a good, strong one. The doctor told me I had a little girl and he placed you in my arms, and you just looked up at me like you knew me even before you heard my voice. I called your daddy in, and he was so happy that I got my wish, as I was praying for another little girl! How could I be so lucky? I said, 'Look, James, have you ever seen such a beautiful baby!' He said, 'I can't say I have!' He couldn't take his eyes off you, and he told me, 'Zola, all our babies have been beautiful, but I think you are right; this baby is extra pretty!' And then he gave me the sweetest kiss on my forehead. We just looked at you, and you were so calm and happy. I rubbed your soft, light red hair and looked at your beautiful lily-white skin. At that very moment, I knew what we should name you. You were my jewel! My two favorite gems are rubies and pearls. So that day your daddy and I decided you would be Ruby Pearl, our beautiful jewel. I kissed you and said, 'I love you, Ruby Pearl.' Your daddy kissed both of us and went down to the neighbors to tell your siblings they had a new baby sister. They came home to meet you that night."

Ruby was trying hard not to tear up. It felt like she was hearing the story for the first time, as her momma was adding more detail. It made more sense to her now, how a mother bonds with her baby for the very first time. Ruby had never been keen on her name, but the more she heard the story and the older she got, the more she grew to cherish it. She even decided that being named a jewel made her extra special and destined to do great things in this changing world. Ruby got up and hugged and kissed her momma one more time.

"I love you so much, Momma." She felt the pendant at her throat. "I will treasure it just as I do my beautiful comb, and I will hopefully pass it down to my daughter one day."

With that, the two walked arm in arm out to the dining area. The house was spotless, the freshly polished woodwork sparkled, and her Grandma McCoy's silver candle holders, brought from Ireland, gleamed in the center of the table. Zola always used them on special occasions, and birthdays fell into that category.

There were several large homes in Oilton, and the Dinsmore home was one of them. Ruby was fortunate that her parents knew how to manage money and were able to provide for their children better than most people of that time. They had one of the first cars, one of the first phones, and their home had indoor plumbing. A person new to town could learn a lot about the people just by looking at the phone book. You could tell who the first people to purchase a phone were by their number. The Dinsmore number was 04; Ruby and her siblings were very proud to be one of the first to own a phone. When you entered the Dinsmore home, you saw to the right a larger room that served two purposes—a living area as well as the dining room. There was a long picture window on the wall for people to enjoy seeing the side yard while enjoying a meal or just relaxing on the sofa. The dining table was a large cherry wood table they had purchased from one of the furniture stores in Drumright. It was big enough to seat ten people. The whole family could not fit around the table, but children ate at a table in the kitchen, never with the adults.

Ida Jane had set the table, starting with her momma's best autumn tablecloth and good china that was a gift from James's family, sent all the way from Arkansas when Zola and James got married. People did not have large weddings or travel to distant weddings, as it was costly and much too complicated.

Ida Jane was admiring her sister's necklace when the doorbell rang. All of a sudden, Ruby's face flushed as the reality set in that a certain someone was coming over. She had almost forgotten with all the activity. Now she was all nervous again. Ruby's momma, who now had her apron off and was presentable, answered the door. Ruby waited by the china cabinet in case she wanted to make an entrance or check her hair once more in the mirror in the cabinet.

"Ruby, it is Bessie and her beau," announced Ida Jane.

Ruby stepped out to greet them. "Please let me take your coats." She took them, hung them up in the coat closet, escorted her guests into the living area, and offered them a seat on the sofa. The house began to fill with more guests, noise, and laughter. Ruby looked out the window and saw a car pull up, and her brothers Will and Robert got out. Everyone else was scattered. Zach and Thomas were out of town with their Uncle Jim. Henry was at a friend's house, and Ivy was with her cousin, Abigail.

The younger of Ruby's siblings had scattered so that she could have a grown-up family celebration. Will, Robert, and Ida Jane would be there representing the "adult" family members, along with Bessie, Hank, and Arthur. Zola made sure there was elbow room for the men. Robert could have gone with his Uncle Jim, but he had told Ruby that he was going to remind Arthur just who the Dinsmore boys were, and that he had better not break Ruby's heart. Having a boy over for dinner for the first time was a big deal to the family, no matter how much Ruby insisted it wasn't.

Zola came out of the kitchen with each ringing of the doorbell, in hopes it would be Arthur. She too was excited about his arrival. Zola and James were hoping Arthur would be the special someone that would remind Ruby that life was more than books and the philosophy of Elizabeth Cady Stanton.

Ruby needed to know that the men take care of the women, and the women take care of the men.

Zola peeked in the living room and saw that Arthur hadn't arrived yet. Ruby was over by the fireplace, showing Bessie a new glass candleholder. Their heads were together as they whispered, and Zola just knew they were talking about Arthur coming over.

The doorbell rang and Ruby dropped the glass candle holder, which hit the wrought iron fireplace cover, bounced, and hit the floor. Glass shattered everywhere. The girls gasped and stooped down to pick up the pieces.

Ida Jane scurried to open the door. "Come on in, Arthur," she giggled. "Ruby just dropped a candle holder when she heard the bell because she is so nervous about you being here."

Ruby turned blood red and glared at her sister. She quickly smiled, not wanting to show that side of herself to Arthur. Ida Jane was trying not to laugh, but Robert started laughing, and Will snickered behind his hand.

Zola hurried over to Arthur. "Hello, Arthur dear. Please come in." She guided him into the living room, looking over her shoulder at Ida Jane. "I think something needs tending to in the kitchen, Ida Jane. Please check and I'll be right there."

Zola took Arthur's coat, while Ruby straightened

herself up. The entrance was not quite what she envisioned, but it was what it was, and there was nothing to be done about it.

She walked over to her momma and Arthur and welcomed him. Arthur immediately commented on Ruby's necklace as if there had been no commotion at all, which eased Ruby's nerves. Ruby told him it was a gift from her momma and gave her a hug. With that, Zola excused herself to go and finish preparing dinner.

Chapter 8

DINNER IS SERVED

WHEN ZOLA PRETTY MUCH HAD SUPPER READY, she decided to check on James and make sure he had no plans to do anything that would embarrass Ruby. He could be quite a jokester. Zola walked into their room, and James was standing in front of the dresser, about to adjust his bow tie.

"Hello, dear, sure smells good out there!"

"Thank you, dear. I just popped in to see how you were doing and to let you know Ruby is nervous enough about Arthur being here, and if she thinks . . ."

James cut her off. "I know, Zola. Trust me, I am hoping Arthur is 'the man.' I don't want Ruby to be an old maid, and I want her to get it out of her head, the silly notion about college. She needs to settle down, and Arthur just might be the ticket. He comes from a good family. I couldn't have chosen any better myself."

"Oh James, what am I to do with you?" Zola remarked as she patted him on the chest and straightened his tie. She kissed him on the cheek and walked out of the bedroom.

Zola noticed Ida Jane, who wasn't part of any conversation, feeling a bit left out. She followed her momma into the kitchen.

"Momma, all they're doing is talking about the college game tomorrow, and they act like I am not even there. It is boring."

"Well, hon, you can help me with last minute things here in the kitchen."

"Gladly!" She put on her apron. "It's better than being invisible in the living room."

While the two put the finishing touches on the meal, the lively conversation continued in the other room.

Ruby was always pleased when both high school teams won their respective games. It put people in a good mood. It always took Saturday and Sunday for the boys on the losing side to cool down before the start of another week. With two Dinsmore boys being star players, Ruby could never have a party after any game. Good thing the game was the next night.

"Let's leave the boys to their discussion of the possibilities for the game tomorrow night," Ruby whispered to Bessie.

The girls headed into the kitchen to help Ruby's momma. It was perfect timing, as supper was ready to be served. The girls carried the beautifully prepared food out and placed it on the table. Delicious aromas wafted into the living room, making the boys even hungrier than before. Ida Jane rang the supper bell while Zola showed everyone to their places. They all stood behind their chairs and waited for Ruby's daddy to join them. As the head of the family, James always waited a few seconds until everyone was around the table before he made his entrance. He greeted everyone, and they replied politely and bowed their heads, as was customary, ready to say grace.

Ruby's dad began, "Dear Lord, we have so much to be grateful for today. First, thank you for our family and friends who join us on this special day. Second, thank you for giving us the ability to provide food for our family and our friends. Lastly, and most importantly, seventeen years ago today, you blessed us with the birth of our second daughter, Ruby. She has brought us much joy, and may she be blessed by you for a lifetime of happiness. Amen."

"Amen," everyone echoed.

"Now let's eat!" Ruby's daddy said with a big smile as everyone took their seats.

"Why, Mrs. Dinsmore, this is quite a feast!" Arthur complimented her.

"Oh, Arthur, you are too kind. It is a special day," said Zola.

Ruby gave a sweet smile of approval to her momma and to Arthur sitting across from her.

"James, start the meat, please," Ruby's momma said, and she started to pass around the side dishes. "I'm sure the boys are hungry after their football practice."

And thus, the meal commenced.

Now, Zola was big on table manners. No one could graduate to the adult table without knowing their table etiquette. She had her rules taped on the wall by the children's table, so they were sure to know how to behave. Zola did not have time for excuses such as "I didn't know." She had a household to run, and Zola needed it to move as smoothly as possible because each new day brought surprises. Zola had learned as a young girl, with the help of one of her aunts, how to run a house after her momma died. Therefore, posting the rules took care of the "ifs, ands, or buts" and helped to settle disputes before they even began.

Momma's Table Rules

1. Do not come to the dinner table dirty.
2. Dress for dinner or supper.
3. Always say grace before a meal.
4. Never speak to someone with your mouth full.
5. Always say, "Please pass _____."
6. Say thank you when you receive a dish.
7. Never reach across the table for food.
8. Use the proper utensils for your meal.
9. Cut your food into bite-sized pieces and chew your bite 36 times before swallowing, so you don't choke.
10. DO NOT burp at the table.
11. DO NOT guzzle your food like a hog.
12. Say thank you to the person who prepared the meal before asking to be excused from the table.
13. DO NOT leave the table until you have been formally excused.

With Zola's rules in place, a lovely dinner began: roast beef, mashed potatoes and gravy, green beans, carrots, Zola's famous biscuits, and iced tea to drink. The meal went off without a hitch. Will and Robert went down memory lane and told stories about

Ruby, but they were smart enough not to embarrass her since it was her birthday, and, of course, they did not want payback. They knew not to cross Ruby. She knew too much.

Then, of course, the topic of conversation changed back to college football. The Oklahoma Sooners were about to have a big game, and all the men could agree on which team they wanted to win—and it sure was not Kansas State. The table began to get a little rowdy discussing the possible plays.

Zola cleared her throat, and the men calmed down. She rarely had to say much. They knew her ways.

"Ida Jane, Bessie, would you be so kind as to help me take the plates to the kitchen?" Zola began clearing the table.

Ruby knew the rules. If you were the birthday sibling, then you didn't clear the table because the presentation of cake would be next, and her momma enjoyed a grand entrance with the birthday person in place to receive the cake.

Zola dimmed the lights and walked in with Ruby's cake all lit, began singing "Happy Birthday," and everyone joined in. She placed the cake in front of Ruby, who blushed. She wanted to act as if she was too big for this, but at the same time, she was enjoying all the attention a birthday brings.

Will nudged her. "Make a wish and blow out the candles before they melt." Ruby closed her eyes. She took her birthday wish seriously, and of course, she wished for the same thing every year . . . for her daddy to let her go to college. She took a deep breath and blew out all seventeen candles—and one extra to grow on! It meant her wish would come true, or so they said. Everyone cheered, and Ruby looked at her daddy.

In no time, everyone had a piece of chocolate cake with homemade vanilla ice cream. After they finished, Ruby and her friends went out to the porch to get some fresh air, and Ruby's brothers and Ida Jane went upstairs.

James had learned a long time ago not to help Zola clear the table, as she saw it as women's work, and she had no interest in having him anywhere near her kitchen. It always worked well for James, especially this time, as he wanted to eavesdrop on the conversations on the porch. Zola had a different plan.

"Well, James, times are changing," she stopped him as he was about to excuse himself. "I decided tonight would be a good night to implement a change in the household. I heard young men are helping their wives clear the table these days. Rilla has her husband helping her in the kitchen, so tonight I thought you could help me too."

It was Zola's excuse to keep James from eavesdropping on Ruby and her friends. He was taken aback but knew he couldn't make a fuss with guests over, so he found himself in the kitchen scraping plates, giving leftovers to their dog, Ralph, and taking out the kitchen garbage. Just when James was about to go to the bedroom, Zola asked him to help dry the dishes. It led to an interesting conversation in the kitchen, while things were developing on the porch as well.

While James was learning more about what it takes to clean up after a night's supper, Bessie and Hank had already said goodnight to give Ruby and Arthur extra time on the porch alone. So there the two were on the porch.

"Are you chilly, Ruby?" Arthur asked as he moved a little closer.

"No, but thank you. Oh, and thank you for coming to my family birthday party. It was nice of you." She smoothed out her dress.

"Aw shucks, Ruby, I am glad you asked me," Arthur said. "I have been thinking about you ever since . . ."

Ruby placed two fingers on his lips, stopping him.

She was afraid her daddy was listening. She had noticed when she came outside that he had cracked the window slightly. If he was inside, he would hear the conversation on the porch. She knew the trick well, since she did the same herself from the bathroom window.

She and her siblings knew their daddy was a skilled eavesdropper. So, she gave Arthur a look with her eyes toward the window so he might get the hint. He removed her hand but held on to it.

"Oh, I get it," he whispered as the porch swing gently swayed to and fro. "Have you thought about me since then?" he asked quietly.

"Of course," she said, remembering now more than ever. Just touching him with her two fingers made her body shudder, and all of a sudden, she wanted to kiss him again.

"Ruby, I have a little something for your birthday. It is not much, but I wanted to give you something. I know you have dreams for your future, but can we just think about this school year for now and make the most of it? I just want you to be my girl now. I am not saying we have to marry . . . yet." He laughed. "But just be my girl for the school year, and we can decide what to do after the year is over."

Ruby was not prepared for this logic, as it seemed to be a simple request, and she did like him more than any other boy in town. Still, she didn't want to detract from her goal. She knew she had to stay focused.

As she opened her mouth to reply, Arthur interrupted. "Don't say anything till you open your gift."

Ruby had read enough novels to know that the gift usually meant something big, yet the box was not small like a ring box, or even a necklace box for that matter. She smiled and began to open it, handing Arthur the ribbon and paper. She slowly lifted the cover to discover a beautiful blue and white silk scarf. Ruby was so touched and yet was hoping it would be a ring, as it would have been easy to say, "Go away." But instead, it was a lovely scarf that she could wear to school on Monday.

"Oh, Arthur, this is beautiful. And blue is my favorite color. You really shouldn't have."

"Of course, I should," he said as he took the scarf and tied it around her neck. "I remembered you telling me how blue was your favorite color."

He started to lean in to kiss her but paused. "I remember you told me about your hopes and dreams too. We are both graduating and want to leave here and do something bigger than this small town can provide. I get it. I just want to be part of your life now . . . this minute. I am not trying to tie you down for a lifetime—just for now. What do you say? Will you be my girl?"

Ruby twisted the scarf around her fingers. "Well,

I do like you. I mean, I like you a lot. And well, when we kissed, I knew I . . . really liked you. But . . ."

"But what?"

All Ruby saw were his big brown eyes looking ever so gently at her; actually, it was the way every girl dreams a guy would look at her. In the midst of everything going on, Ruby was thinking, *I am in one of my romance novels! Imagine, me on a porch swing with a boy.*

Arthur nudged her. "You look like you're off in dreamland." He took her hand and kissed it.

The chills in her body grew stronger. "Well, if it is just for the school year, and we are not engaged, and you're just my beau," Ruby said, "then OK."

"All right then. I am your beau, and you are my girl." He leaned in and gave her a big kiss.

Ruby sat back and her hand flew to her mouth. "Oh my! OK, can you do that again!"

Arthur smiled and embraced her. This time, he gave her a very long, tender kiss. When their lips parted, they gazed into each other's eyes.

"Ruby, I am so proud to be your beau."

"Me too." She sighed and put her head on his shoulder.

They sat there for a little while longer, but it was getting late, and Arthur still had to drive home to Drumright, which always seemed to be on the dark roads.

He got up to go but still held her hand. "So, we will be talking real soon."

"OK." Ruby stood up as the butterflies rallied for position in her stomach.

Arthur kissed her quickly one more time and headed for his car. Ruby waved goodbye. Once he was around the corner, she wiped her mouth as if it would make the kiss go away so her parents wouldn't see. She took a deep breath and casually walked in as if nothing had happened, knowing they would be waiting for her. Sure enough, they were sitting on the sofa pretending to be deep in conversation.

"Everyone has gone home. Thank you so much for making my birthday so special," Ruby said as she entered the living room.

"You are so welcome, dear. It was lovely to have your friends here as well," Ruby's momma said. "I hope they enjoyed themselves."

"Oh yes, Momma. You and Daddy always go all out for our birthdays. They were quite impressed," Ruby said. "They went home stuffed and happy. Bessie says she needs to take cooking lessons from you."

Ruby was hoping this would be enough information and she could go on upstairs.

"What a sweetheart," said Zola. "Her momma is an excellent cook too, but it was kind of her to say."

Her momma looked at her and raised an eyebrow.

Ruby should have known her momma's inquisitive mind wouldn't quit.

"Ruby, where did the scarf come from?"

Ruby had totally forgotten about the scarf as her lips still tingled after what had happened on the porch.

"Oh, this? It's a present from Arthur. Isn't it pretty?"

"It's beautiful. How sweet of him. And it seems like he had a nice time tonight as well," Zola said.

James sat quietly and listened.

"Oh, he did," Ruby said. "Arthur and Hank talked about you being a great cook as well. They even made a joke about how we girls will have to work hard to be as good a cook as you. That's when Bessie said she'd have to take lessons from you."

"You can always win the boys over by feeding them," said Zola. "I'm glad to see that hasn't changed."

James smirked but still stayed silent.

"Well, is there anything else you want to tell us, Ruby?" her mother asked.

"Uh, no, not really." Ruby turned to walk up the stairs. She stopped and turned back. "Well, actually, I suppose I should tell you before you find out from someone else. Arthur asked me to be his girl, and I said yes."

She turned and ran upstairs but paused as she heard her parents' reaction.

"Well, looks like my wish is coming true," said her daddy.

"What wish is that, James?" Momma asked.

"Well, the chickens are calling; it's time for bed, Zola."

And, on that note, they retired for the night, knowing Ruby Pearl had had an exceptional day. She felt the same as she continued up the stairs to her room.

Chapter 9

A NEW DAY

EARLY THE NEXT MORNING, RUBY WAS AWAKENED by the rooster, Red, as her daddy liked to call him. She usually slept straight through Red's announcement of a new day, but this day was not just any day. She woke up and stared at the ceiling. Ruby wanted to go back to sleep, but her mind began racing. She looked over at her sister Ida Jane, fast asleep, wishing she could do the same. She recalled the night before. The perfect birthday dinner and then how Arthur had caught her off guard. How she had blurted out to her parents that she was now Arthur's girl. With that last thought, Ruby pulled the covers up over her head, hoping it would erase the night before. She thought if she went back to sleep, she would wake up, and it would all have been a dream.

At first, it was all nice and toasty under the covers. Ruby closed her eyes and tried to go back to sleep. Momentarily, she had peace of mind, but once more, Arthur popped into her mind. The kiss . . . then how she had asked him to do it again. Her body turned warm, so Ruby threw the covers off over her head. *Oh my! Is this the beginning of love? Surely not.* The conversation inside her head continued. *Well, I need to let Arthur know this is a mistake. Yes, that is what I will do.*

She closed her eyes and then the kiss replayed in her mind. Once more Ruby's eyes opened and the argument in her head went on. *Well, it was nice. Maybe I won't tell him that. Wait . . . I have to. It wouldn't be fair. I have to stay focused and earn money for college. Yes, I will tell him it is a mistake for me to be his girl.* Ruby closed her eyes again, only to replay the kiss once more. She remembered how the kisses had made her feel all warm inside, how her body had ignited in the warmth of his caress, and how she had not wanted it to end. Ruby snapped out of it when she realized she was making a moaning sound. She quickly looked over to see if she had woken up her sister.

She stifled a giggle. *Yes, that was a nice feeling. I think I want to explore that further. After all, if I am going to go out into the big world, I should understand what my body is feeling so I don't make any mistakes.*

OK then, it is settled. Ruby snuggled deep into her covers, still thinking of Arthur. This time, she sighed and drifted back into a deep sleep, knowing that her parents would be pleased and Arthur would be happy he was her beau.

Ruby awoke to her momma calling, "Ruby, Ida Jane, time to get up."

She had let them both sleep in since it had been a late night for the two of them, especially Ruby. The younger kids were already happily playing on the porch.

"We'll be right down," Ida Jane called back.

"I need to tell you something before we go downstairs," whispered Ruby.

"OK, what is it?" Ida Jane asked as she looked in the closet for something to wear.

"Well, I kind of told Arthur I would be his girl."

"You what?" Ida Jane spun around. "No way!"

Ruby dashed over and cupped Ida Jane's mouth to muffle her words. "Yes, I did. Keep your voice down." Ruby removed her hands from her sister's mouth.

"Oh, my! Do Momma and Daddy know?" Ida Jane was paying full attention.

"Yes, I told them last night, and then I ran up to our room so they would not ask questions."

Ida Jane, now fully dressed, sat on Ruby's bed, eager to share her two cents' worth as well as hear even more details. "Oh, you know Momma is going to want to know what this means, you 'being his girl.' Tell me first! I never thought you would give in to a boy! This news is huge. Wait till I tell my friends!" Ida Jane paused. "Wait . . . I can't. I will lose a bet. No! OK, who cares, I will lose the bet. This news is huge!" Ida Jane had gotten lost in her own drama. She loved being the point person for the social news of the day.

"What? What do you mean, 'a bet'?"

"Oh, nothing, just a little something some of my friends and I agreed to."

"You mean your friends talked about whether or not I would have a beau?"

"Well, not exactly. We knew boys liked you. It was more like . . . You are very stubborn with your dreams and all. I told my friends that no one could catch you because you are incredibly hardheaded. It looks like I was wrong."

Ruby stood there in disbelief but knew there was zero time to argue. She needed Ida Jane's help.

"All right then, listen. I need you to do me a favor." Ruby waited until Ida Jane was listening. "Now, Momma is going to want to speak to me, and I don't want to talk about it. So, if she comes up with a chore for you that leaves me alone with her, you insist on having me help you, understand? I need some time to figure all this out."

"Sure, but you owe me." Ida Jane wagged her finger.

"Oh, I owe you." Ruby agreed. "Come on, we had better get downstairs, or Momma will know we are up to something."

The girls left the room, their plan at the ready if needed.

Their momma had prepared a fresh batch of pan-cakes with corn syrup, eggs, and hash browns. Ida Jane softly giggled with each bite. Ruby was glaring at her sister for the third time when the phone rang. They looked at each other, as they knew no one calls early on a Saturday. Their momma was startled as well and came out of the kitchen. When the phone rang at that hour of the day, it had to do with busi-ness, a baby coming before it's due, or some other lousy news. Ruby and her momma were both watch-ing Ida Jane as she ran to answer the phone.

"Ruby, it is for you." Ida Jane covered the phone and mouthed, "It's Arthur."

Ruby looked at her momma and then back at her sister and then walked over to take the phone. Her momma went back to the kitchen but stayed close to the door, while Ida Jane stood there soaking it all in. Ruby turned her back to her sister and spoke in a soft voice, hoping they wouldn't hear.

"Hello? Oh, hi, Arthur. . . . Yes, it is nice to hear from you as well. . . . Yes, I did. Well, I usually am. But . . . Well, let me ask my momma. Is it possible for you to call me in about half an hour? We slept in and are just having breakfast. . . . Oh, I see. OK. Bye." Ruby hung up and turned around to see her sister was still standing right behind her.

"Don't say a thing," Ruby commanded.

"Too bad, I am. It looks like Arthur knows how to handle you! I have never seen you so tongue-tied. So, what did he want?"

Ruby was flustered and didn't answer right away. She wanted to grow up to be a proud, independent, free-thinking woman. When she did marry, she and her husband would be equals. Ida Jane's comment had cut to the very bones of Ruby's existence.

"In no way, shape, or form was I 'handled.'" She narrowed her eyes at her sister and walked into the kitchen, where her momma had already moved to the sink to do the morning dishes. Ruby couldn't tell if she had overhead her conversation or not.

"So, Momma, as you heard, it was Arthur. He wants to know if . . ." Ruby cleared her throat. "Well, if . . . if he could come over later today and we could just sit on the porch and enjoy the afternoon. He likes to read too, so we might even read together."

Ruby's momma smiled and said, "Of course, dear. Will he be here for lunch?"

"No, he needs to have lunch with his family." Ruby smiled at her momma and walked out of the room before she could say anything else that might embarrass her.

Ida Jane had overheard everything. "Yes, indeed, Ruby—you have a beau! I can't wait to tell my friends. Maybe I will call them now."

Ruby looked horrified, and before she could respond, Momma interrupted. "No, you won't, young lady. Phones are not made for idle gossip; they are for emergencies."

"I know, Momma, and this is an emergency. This is the top social news," Ida Jane said, while Ruby gave her another look of death.

"You two finish your breakfast. It is almost time to begin your Saturday chores. Lucky for you two, there aren't any chickens to pluck!"

"Momma, you do not understand. A phone helps you be the first person with the best news of the day. It can make you popular at school."

Ruby stood there, in shock that her sister would want her to be the top news of the day and that she would back talk their momma. Ruby wanted to give Ida Jane a piece of her mind but had learned a long time ago to control the temper that her momma said matched her fiery red hair. She just wanted to be a person to spread sunshine and happiness, but

Ida Jane's reaction to the "situation" was about to bring back Ruby's childhood temper.

Ruby took a deep breath and wondered why her momma did not respond to Ida Jane's comment. But she followed her momma's lead. She kept quiet and began her chores . . . all the while thinking about Arthur's kisses.

Chapter 10

LOVE IS IN THE AIR

IT WAS A BEAUTIFUL, CRISP SATURDAY AFTERNOON. Most of the children had gone to visit friends, and James was busy in the smokehouse. It was just Ruby and her momma at home.

Ruby found herself watching from her brother's bedroom window, which was located on the south side of the house. She watched Arthur pull in and park his car in the side yard of their home. He did not park in the driveway, as that was for Ruby's daddy's car. Ruby was excited and yet nervous about this new situation she found herself in.

Her momma greeted Arthur, as it was not customary in the Dinsmore house for a girl to greet her beau upon his arrival. Ruby could hear Arthur pay his respects to her momma as she welcomed him inside. They had a proper exchange of pleasantries, and Zola invited Arthur to take a seat and wait for Ruby.

When Ruby finally came down, Arthur politely stood up and greeted her. Her face flushed. Arthur's hands stayed folded in front of him.

"Well, why don't you two visit out on the porch? It's a beautiful day," Zola said.

"Thank you, Momma. We will." Ruby blushed right to her roots.

Her momma hugged her, gave her a wink, and waved them out the front door.

Once outside, the air between the two of them seemed to lighten up as they took a seat on the porch swing. There was something about swinging that always made people relax. Arthur broke the silence.

"I hope you did not mind me calling you so early this morning."

"Oh no, not at all. I mean, it was a surprise, but a pleasant one." Ruby did not want to tell the whole truth, as it might hurt his feelings and she was new at having a beau. She knew she was his first too.

"Good." A long pause occurred, while they both watched the young children across the street playing kickball.

"Well, I am glad we could see each other."

"Me too," Ruby responded quietly, still watching the children.

"Ruby, I am so happy you are my girl." Arthur took her hand, kissed it, and then laid her hand down but kept holding it.

"Well . . ." Ruby began. She almost told him about the battle she had going on in her mind, but once more, her body began to tingle with delight. "Oh, I thought maybe we could enjoy reading our books since you mentioned you have to finish yours for school on Monday. I have to read two chapters for my English class as well. Did you bring your book?"

"I did."

"OK, so why don't we begin reading?"

Arthur shrugged and nodded. They took out their books, but Ruby could tell Arthur had more on his mind than reading. He placed his arm around her shoulder.

"Come closer," he said as he pulled her toward him.

"Oh, that won't work," Ruby said.

"Yes, it will. Just relax. You can easily turn your pages, and if you need help, I will turn them for you."

Ruby knew how her brothers were with girls, but she had never seen or heard of them making that particular move. She was curious to see how it worked. Much to her surprise, she found it to be quite comfy and melted into his chest more and more with each page. Before she knew it, she found herself reading with her head in his lap while he read and gently rocked the swing. They were both content taking in their stories like a young married couple when Ruby's mother opened the screen door to bring out some warm tea and cookies.

Ruby quickly jumped up, realizing the position she was in on the front porch. Her momma placed the items on the side table for them to enjoy and, without a word, went back inside.

"Oh . . . oh my, I . . . I did not mean to get so comfortable." Ruby stuttered as she spoke.

"I didn't mind. I quite enjoyed it," Arthur said as he took a bite of his cookie. "Did you get much reading done?"

"Oh, yes, I did. I was totally into . . ." Ruby started to share the whole chapter when Arthur placed his finger on her lips. "Oh . . . sorry." Ruby stopped her summary. "Did you get much reading done?"

"Yes and no," Arthur said with a grin.

"What does that mean?" Ruby asked.

"Oh, nothing. I was just a bit distracted." Arthur squirmed a bit and readjusted his tie.

"Ruby, it is not every day that a guy gets to sit on his girl's porch swing and try to study, all the while thinking how lucky he is to have someone kind, beautiful, and smart like you as his girl."

"Oh, Arthur, that is so sweet." Ruby poured them some tea and continued telling him how she was even a chapter ahead, seemingly missing his point. She looked up at him. "This just might work out . . . us being study buddies and . . . well, you know what I mean."

"I do," he agreed.

Arthur excused himself to the restroom, and when he came back out onto the porch, he invited Ruby to go for a walk. As they walked, he smiled at her and ran his fingers through her shoulder-length auburn hair that glistened in the sunlight.

They talked about all kinds of things but mostly her plans to escape Oilton. Arthur agreed to help her, especially if it meant spending more time with her.

Before long, they were back on the football field where their first kiss took place. Arthur led her around the bleachers, and next thing she knew, Ruby was up against the gym wall. Arthur leaned over her as he looked gently into her eyes.

"I have always loved you, Ruby."

Well, you would think she would have pulled away. This would have been the perfect opportunity to say it had all been a mistake. Instead, Ruby let him speak as she gazed back into his big, gorgeous brown eyes, noticing for the first time the bushy, dark eyebrows. He stroked her neck and gently gave her a soft peck on the lips. Ruby looked at him and could hardly catch her breath. Arthur stroked her hair, pulled her into him, and gave her a passionate kiss. It was long, and deep, and lasted a lifetime. When they both came up for air, they momentarily gazed at each other, and Arthur kissed her once more.

Ruby thought her body had done flip-flops before, but now it was on fire. She couldn't say he took advantage of her, because she was kissing him right back, wanting to discover more of this unfamiliar territory. She smiled at him. Now she understood what the girls at school meant when they said, "The bank is definitely open"—meaning, bring on the kissing!

They walked back hand in hand.

"Ruby, I need to head home and help my dad at the store to get ready for tomorrow's business," he said as they got to her driveway. "But I will call you every day and see you on the weekend."

The following weekend could not come soon enough. Ruby was on cloud nine. She happily agreed to help her momma in the kitchen instead of retreating to her favorite place to read. She soon learned that neighbors had taken note of her and Arthur walking alone in the neighborhood. Zola told Ruby that she was the topic of conversation at the quilting bee. Ruby did not care. For the first time in her life, she was delighted to have her very own beau or, as her generation called a boy they cared about, a "boyfriend." Love was in the air, and she didn't care who knew it. Her momma certainly did.

Chapter 11

THE TALK

ZOLA WAS WORRIED ABOUT RUBY GOING OUT WITH Arthur alone. Even though she and James approved of the boy, this was all so much to handle. It was times like this that Zola wished she had her momma to call. Zola had told the girls many times that she felt her momma watching over her and how that gave her comfort while she was growing up. Zola once told Rilla she would discover when she became a momma just how much a momma's wisdom would come in handy as her own daughter grew up.

Zola wondered what her momma would think of "The Chair." Zola recalled her daddy trying to give her "the talk" and wondered what her momma would have thought if she had heard her daddy stuttering his way through. Now, Zola found it hard to grasp that she was about to give that same talk to her baby girl. She felt it was necessary, and yet, she dreaded it. Zola loved how Ruby was growing into an amazing young lady and always told her she had a good head on her shoulders, just like her daddy. And smart as a whip. But oh, to hold her as a baby again . . . just for a moment. Zola snapped out of her daydreaming and realized she needed to get on with the business at hand.

"Ruby, I'd like to speak with you before you get ready to see Arthur," Zola called up the stairs. "Can you please come down?"

"Be right there, Momma," Ruby called back.

Ruby could not imagine what else her momma needed to speak with her about, as she had already lived through the "period talk." Ruby had been warned by her older sister Rilla that this day would come.

Ruby knew it meant a lot to her momma to have these conversations, but she found it a little uncomfortable. She only prayed that whatever her momma had to say, that it would be short and sweet. Ruby made her way downstairs and knocked on her momma's door. Zola told her to come in and take a seat. Ruby dutifully followed her momma's orders.

Ruby's momma was sitting in her rocker, tatting away, waiting for her. As many times as her momma had had these conversations with Ruby's older siblings, Ruby knew she still found it hard to discuss difficult topics with her children; and now it was Ruby's turn. Time was flying by in the blink of an eye. Her parents' "precious jewel" was going out alone with a boy.

Ruby sat and fidgeted, trying to be patient. Finally, Zola looked up and gave her daughter a gentle smile, and as always, she took a deep breath. The words came flowing out at such a nervous, rapid speed that Ruby listened and listened in horror at the direction this conversation was going. Ruby did not want "the talk" under any circumstances. She knew enough already and did not want to think that her momma and daddy even remembered that things like that took place.

Ruby squirmed as her momma continued nonstop, and finally Ruby interrupted.

"Momma, please," she stammered. "I appreciate you are worried about the concept of dating, but you do not have to worry about me." She leaned forward. "You know you can trust me, Momma. I have no desire to get myself into a complicated situation."

"Now, don't you try to worm your way out of hearing what I have to say. I did not give up with your siblings, and I am not finished with you yet. It's

a momma's job to make sure her daughters understand these facts of life."

Zola continued on till Ruby insisted that her
momma listen to her.

"Momma, really!" she implored. "I do not want
to be rude or disrespectful, but I promise you, Rilla
explained everything to me already."

"Everything?"

"Everything," Ruby replied.

"OK then," her momma said. "I suppose you can
go on and get ready for Arthur." Ruby hopped up,
gave her momma a kiss, and quickly made her way
to her room to get ready.

After she was dressed, Ruby stood in front of her
mirror and began pinching her cheeks to make sure
they were nice and rosy before putting on a different dress, when she heard the doorbell. Arthur was
on time, and now he would have to wait even longer
than usual for her to come down. Her parents had
probably planned it all along. She could hear her
momma invite him in.

She listened from the top of the stairs, picturing
her daddy, seated in his favorite chair.

"Have a seat, Arthur," she heard him say. "I'm sure
Ruby will be right down."

"I've got some things to take care of in the kitchen.
I'll leave you 'men' to talk." Zola excused herself.

"Arthur, my boy, Zola and I couldn't be more

pleased that you and Ruby are spending time together. You know, she is our little jewel. Of course, all our girls are special, and well, you know how great her brothers are. We're a very close family." James leaned forward. "So, I expect you to behave. Understand?"

"Oh, Mr. Dinsmore, I have the deepest respect for Ruby. Why, she is a fine girl," Arthur said. "I feel lucky to be able to take her out."

"Good, good, as you should. That pleases Mrs. Dinsmore and me," he said as Zola returned to the living room with the pot of tea.

"Here you go, boys. Have a cup of tea while you are waiting."

"Thank you, Mrs. Dinsmore," Arthur said as he took a sip of the warm black tea.

"Thank you, hon," James said to Zola as she returned to the kitchen. "Well, Arthur, let me just say one more thing. We are not used to our girls going out on dates in cars as young folk do now. We have no way of keeping an eye on the two of you."

Ruby could hear her daddy's spoon clink on the sides of his cup as he stirred his tea.

"So, just remember, as much as we like you, I will not tolerate any hanky-panky with my Ruby. If I get so much as an inkling . . . well, just remember one thing: she has me and plenty of brothers to take care of the situation. Do I make myself clear, son?"

"Oh, yes. Very clear, sir. You do not have to worry."

"Good. We understand each other then."

"Ruby, come on down, honey," he called up the stairs. "Don't keep Arthur waiting."

She quickly came down from her listening post at the top of the stairs and could not wait to get Arthur out of the house. She was wearing a new church dress that her momma had made for her. Ruby was known for having some of the prettiest dresses in town. This dress was a lovely blue cotton dress with a large white collar that complemented her neckline and made a V-shape to show a hint of her décolletage. The top part of the dress was a straight line with large buttons going down from the right shoulder to below the low waistline. The rest of the material was pleated just below the knee, which was a favorite style for the 1920s. The long sleeves had white cotton with lace around the seam, which complemented the white collar. It was a perfect choice for going out on her first date.

Arthur stood up as Ruby entered the living room. "Evening, Ruby. You look great!"

Ruby blushed and smiled. "Thank you!"

She heard a burst of giggles, and Ruby knew just what was going on. Henry and Ivy were hiding in the ironing closet under the stairs. They sure didn't want to miss anything when it came to their big sister. Ruby was sure it had taken everything for them to be quiet while their daddy was speaking to Arthur. Well, it was too late now. There would be no sneaking back upstairs without getting caught.

"Momma!" Ruby called. "Henry and Ivy are eavesdropping!"

"Kids, come out of there," their daddy ordered.

Ivy and Henry slowly opened the door and meekly walked out without saying a word. "Go to my room, you two, and wait for me. I will be there in a minute," their daddy said.

"Yes, sir," they both replied, and reluctantly scuffled off to their parents' bedroom, knowing full well what that meant.

Arthur looked at James and asked, "Will that be all, sir?"

"Yes," James replied. "Now you two go and have a good time."

"We will, Daddy. We will be home by ten, for sure," Ruby assured him.

Ruby grabbed Arthur's hand, gave it a tug, and out the door they went. Ruby had mixed emotions with everything her momma had said, and then listening to her daddy had helped calm her nerves, but all she could think about at that very moment was just getting out of the house . . . until she saw the car Arthur was driving. It turned out Arthur's daddy had let him drive his new 1923 Buick motorcar. *You girls in town, get ready to eat your heart out,* she thought to herself. Then she realized that she was already thinking impure thoughts, and it was not polite to make the girls in town jealous. Maybe her momma was right. The butterflies came back. Just seeing Arthur's car got her feeling the wildest things. *OK, stay calm, Ruby girl*, she told herself.

She shook her head and gave Arthur a gentle smile as he opened the door for her and then ran to the other side and hopped in. He started the car, and the engine almost purred. It was so different from her daddy's first car, which needed to be cranked. Ruby could not believe she was in a car that was newer than her daddy's even, though her daddy had traded his old motorcar in for a new model in 1921.

James was a Buick man as well, and she wondered what her daddy was thinking now about her being in a 1923 Buick. She knew he was watching out the bedroom window, and she just smiled thinking about it. All the way to the diner, people watched and whistled as Arthur and Ruby drove by. Arthur sat up and looked incredibly proud to be behind the wheel. *Seems Arthur's parents are just as interested in us getting hitched*, Ruby pondered. *No wonder they let him take the new Buick on our date.*

They pulled into Molly's Diner, where more eyebrows raised. The older townsfolk were probably thinking not only of the young couple being out unchaperoned—which was becoming more common but was still not the norm—but also, of Arthur driving a motorcar of such beauty!

Ruby knew that her momma had spies all over town, so the report would most likely reach Zola even before Ruby got back from her date. Zola had found the telephone to be just as useful as Ida Jane did for her own social networking "catch-up" news flashes.

When Ruby and Arthur entered the diner, they saw some friends having dinner as well, and they were invited to join the two other couples.

Molly, the owner of the diner, had realized that this "dating" thing could work in her favor. She quickly made her diner the place to be. She made sure she found out just what the dating crowd enjoyed eating and catered to their needs.

No matter what age the customer was, Eskimo Pie was a must. She always knew to have plenty on hand and would even run "teens only" specials. Over time, Molly's Diner became the hangout.

Ruby found herself having a wonderful time and was enjoying the company of these girls whom she knew from school but never had much to do with. Ruby thought, just perhaps, she should have started dating sooner. Her brothers had definitely misled her, most likely because they courted their girls. Ruby was now part of the generation that started "the dating scene."

Ruby and Arthur made sure they were back at the Dinsmores' home a little before ten so as not to worry her parents. She knew they would be up waiting.

She opened the front door and called inside, "Momma, Daddy . . . I'm home! We're just going to sit on the porch for a bit, OK?"

"That's fine, dear, but don't be too long," her daddy called from the bedroom.

"OK, good night then," she called back, hoping they would stay put and not come out.

Ruby and Arthur settled on the porch swing and listened to the sounds of the night. The crickets were chirping and the night owls called. Every so often, Arthur would lift her hand to his lips for a light kiss as they rocked back and forth. Ruby would smile at him with each kiss and then say something silly about the stars, and Arthur would play along.

When Arthur finally leaned in to make his move, Ruby's momma called her inside. Ruby sighed, looked into his eyes, and lifted her chin. He pulled her close and gave her a deep kiss. Ruby responded to his embrace, leaning into him and parting her lips. He had her heart, so completely.

Arthur stroked her hair and whispered, "Till next weekend, my beautiful Ruby." He gave her a peck on the forehead and went to his car. In a daze, Ruby watched him walk away, still vibrating from his kiss.

She came out of her trance and waved goodbye and stood on the porch for a moment, taking it all in. She gazed at the sky and took in the quiet street, imagining the birds resting in their nests. She was lost in her thoughts when her momma called out to her once more. Ruby blinked and shrugged her shoulders, reentering reality. She realized she'd better get inside and subconsciously wiped her mouth. She tried to look as innocent as a fresh new flower. But she knew her flushed face gave her away as she said goodnight to her parents.

Ruby tiptoed up the stairs and quietly prepared for bed, reliving the highlights of the night. She tried not to disturb Ida Jane, who was fast asleep, and crawled into bed. As she lay there, she thought about the beautiful, safe life she could have with Arthur, but then she came to what she liked to call "her right mind."

Ruby knew she would eventually hate him for getting her off track and leaving behind her dreams of going to college. As she snuggled under her warm covers, Ruby began thinking of her big dreams of being a businesswoman and discovering other places and meeting new people. These thoughts made her happy, and she drifted off to sleep as she remembered Arthur had big dreams too.

Part Two

A PLAN

Chapter 12

CHRISTMAS BREAK
AND THE PLAN

THE REST OF THE SEMESTER SEEMED TO DISAP-
pear into thin air. Ruby was busy with school, and
when time permitted, she would find time to enjoy
the alcove, her special place, to read and escape to
new worlds. Arthur had become a regular part of
Ruby's life, and they settled into a routine. Arthur
and Ruby had an understanding. They were a couple
but did not need to speak every day. They needed
to concentrate on their studies, which would only
strengthen their relationship. They decided weekends were for catching up with one another, and in
both of their minds, the weekend could not come
soon enough.

The more time Ruby and Arthur spent together,

the more they discovered they had in common, especially their dreams for the future. Arthur admired how Ruby wanted to further her education and that she had the determination to do so. Ruby was amazed at Arthur's progressive attitude toward women's issues, such as working and women's right to vote. They would have interesting conversations about politics and the changing dynamics going on not only in their state, but across the entire country as well. Ruby soon found herself looking forward to seeing Arthur and getting his take on the changing world.

Ruby knew her parents read more into their dating than just friendship. They were still in the mindset of the courting days, with Arthur being her suitor. They were still not comfortable with this new concept of "dating." Even though her parents were open-minded most of the time, they still believed that they knew best who was a good match for their daughters, and once you were no longer a child (having gone through puberty), it was time to marry and start your own family.

Ruby discovered that having her parents think she was following a more traditional route made life more comfortable at home and allowed her to continue working on her plan. Ruby even enjoyed being with her momma in the kitchen and learning cooking tips from her, like how to make the perfect biscuits and rhubarb pie.

Zola and James felt this was going to be an extra special Christmas, as Ruby had asked if Arthur could help with decorating the tree. This new development only raised the anticipation of the couple getting serious. The Dinsmore family was growing with the arrival of their first granddaughter, Abigail. The Dinsmores wanted to go all out in decorating the house, as Rilla's family would be spending Christmas with them. They had added a new bedroom for their expanding family, and it was complete with a private bathroom. The addition made it possible for Abigail to spend more time with her grandma and give Rilla a little break. Rilla had missed her family and wanted to catch up with them, and Christmas was the perfect time.

As always, it was a busy time of year, and the traditions were such that Santa had to work double time on Christmas Eve. Santa not only brought gifts and filled the stockings, but he also brought the Christmas tree and decorated it. James and Zola were happy to pass the baton of the "magic of Christmas" on to the older kids—Rilla and her husband, Gerald, along with Arthur and Ruby. They knew the two couples would develop a more mature friendship while bonding over this tradition. So off to bed they went.

Rilla tucked Abigail into bed while Ruby watched for Arthur's arrival. Gerald popped into the kitchen as he saw Arthur make his way to the back of the house, and Gerald and Ruby quietly let Arthur into the kitchen. Before long, Arthur and Gerald had gotten the tree from out of the storm shelter and brought it into the living room. Ruby and Rilla joined them as well.

"Shh," Ruby put her finger to her lips. "We don't want to wake the little ones."

She pointed to the space she and Rilla had made for the tree, and the men, following orders, set the tree in front of the large living room window. The tree was already in a stand that Robert had made, so all Arthur and Gerald would have to do is place the tree in its allocated space. The girls were quite pleased with the tree and wrapped the skirt around the stand and stood back to admire it. They opened the boxes filled with tree ornaments and started trimming the tree.

The two couples had become quite comfortable with each other, and Gerald openly gave Rilla a peck on the lips. Ruby giggled from her perch on the ladder and placed an ornament high on the tree while Arthur held the ladder to keep it steady. He snuck in a kiss as she made her way down. Before you knew it, the couples had made a game of creating ways to steal a kiss. One would think the tree was never going to get decorated, but it did, and the angel was eventually placed on top.

The appointed Santas, Arthur and Gerald, enjoyed the cookies and left extra tinsel so the children could put the finishing touches on the tree. Arthur grabbed one more kiss and then went to his car that was parked down the road so as not to wake up Abigail and give away any secrets.

Christmas morning arrived, and even though Abigail still did not understand the full meaning of Santa and gifts, she did recognize that the house was different; it had a tree in the living room, all lit up.

Abigail gasped and yelled, "A tree is in the house, Grandma!" She ran toward the tree and looked way up. "Look—it has lights!"

Everyone laughed, but luckily Grandpa James was ready, and he grabbed her before she knocked the tree and all the ornaments to the floor.

Abigail's reaction was what everyone had been waiting for: a little one to see the "magic of Christmas." A tree all lit up sparked happiness throughout the Dinsmore family. Henry laughed along with "the adults." He was especially happy, as he was no longer considered the baby of the family. Christmas Day was an extended celebration, so the gifts would have to wait.

"First things first," said Zola. "Time for a family breakfast and then off to church to celebrate the birth of Jesus."

Later that day, as the adult Dinsmores prepared for the Christmas feast, Ruby's brother Will and his new wife, Dorthea, arrived, bringing more gifts.

While they were all enjoying each other's company and opening gifts, Rilla and Gerald announced a new grandbaby was on the way. Everyone whooped and hollered and gave hugs all around. The biggest hugs came from Grandma and Grandpa. Abigail didn't quite understand what the fuss was about, but she was all for receiving presents.

Once they all settled down, Rilla turned to Abigail. "Santa brought a special gift for you." She reached to the very back of the tree and pulled out a beautifully wrapped gift. Everyone quieted down and watched.

Abigail held the gift and looked up at her. "Momma . . . help."

Rilla started the corner and handed the package back to Abigail to tear open the rest. Abigail tossed the paper aside, opened the box, and pulled out a beautiful doll. She squealed with delight.

"Abigail, I have a special gift for you too," said Grandma Zola.

The little girl reached for the parcel and opened it. It just so happened that Grandma had made some doll clothes that fit Abigail's new doll perfectly.

"Wow! Christmas is magical, just like you told me!" She giggled.

Everyone was thrilled with the baby news, especially Ruby, as she knew this would distract her parents from worrying about her plans. She could not wait to tell Arthur.

"Ruby, what did Arthur give you for Christmas?" Her mother's question brought her back from her thoughts.

Ruby knew they were hoping it would be something that would lead to marriage, even though Arthur had not brought up the topic to Ruby's dad and it was customary to ask the father for his daughter's hand in marriage.

"Oh yes, I will go get it and show all of you."

Ruby caught her parents' puzzled look before she turned to dash upstairs. She could hear everyone buzzing while waiting for her to return. When she returned, they all became quiet and waited. Ruby proudly showed them a picture frame that Arthur had made in school and a picture of the two of them. Will turned around to stifle a laugh. Ruby smirked too. The looks on everyone's faces as they tried to cover their feelings—either shock, laughter, or disappointment—made Ruby realize they all had her walking down the aisle.

"Isn't it a thoughtful gift?" She smiled and handed it to her mother to have a closer look. "Not only the lovely picture but a frame that he made himself. Truly thoughtful, don't you agree?"

Everyone nodded and made comments on how beautiful it was.

"That's a fine photo of the two of you," Ruby's daddy said, handing it to Rilla.

"What did you give him?" Ruby's momma asked.

"Well, we had agreed to make things for one another," Ruby replied. "So, I wrote a poem."

"A poem?" Thomas asked. "Wow, I would never want that." He rolled his eyes. "Then the girl would probably expect me to write one too. Don't want to give anyone the wrong idea!"

"Silly, it was not mushy. It had nothing to do with romance. It had to do with the world." She glared at her siblings. "And before any of you say anything, Arthur liked it."

"Of course he did," Momma said. "Now, let's see what Abigail is up to."

Abigail was busily stacking her blocks, seemingly bored of the adult conversation.

"What a smart girl," said Zola. "You've stacked them perfectly."

Everyone's attention turned to the little one, and the Christmas celebration continued, creating treasured memories for all.

"Thank you, Momma," Ruby mouthed. Her momma smiled back. She understood.

For the rest of the Christmas break, Arthur and Ruby talked about how to make sure Ruby could go to college. Ruby shared most but not all of her plan with him because she did not want to put him in a difficult situation when the time came. So for now, it was just crucial for Arthur to assume that Ruby wanted to go to the same university as he did. They figured out how much money they needed, and Ruby was not sure how on earth she would pay for it. She already knew that her dad would never allow her to go to college, because in his mind it was not necessary. James felt a women's work was at home. He wasn't being mean; it was just the way it was.

Ruby saw the world differently than her daddy. She wanted to be part of the women's movement and knew she was up to the challenge. One weekend, Ruby invited Arthur over for lunch, as she knew it would please her parents, and more importantly, they would approve of them taking a stroll after lunch.

That afternoon, Ruby and Arthur walked to the football field and sat in the bleachers. Ruby laid out her plan, and the more she spoke, the more Arthur tried to make suggestions, but she would not have it and kept shushing him to let her finish.

Finally, after much chattering, Ruby said, "OK, it's your turn. What do you think?"

"Are you nuts?" was the first thing that sputtered out of his mouth.

Ruby was not pleased at his reaction, but he insisted it was his time to speak, as he had waited patiently when she had shared her plans. So, she sat and listened to him but could not understand why he was not immediately on board with the idea.

"Let me get this straight," he began. "You want me and my friends to help you climb out your window three nights a week, including Saturday. Then you are going to go to the red-light district and enter a dance contest. Are you off your rocker?" He stared at Ruby and shook his head. "Your dad has a gun, and both he and your momma know how to use it! Besides, when did you learn to dance? How did you get away with dancing in your house? It does not make sense. When did you feel comfortable enough to dance in front of people? How do you know these dances? You know our pastor frowns on these dances! And the red-light district? Do you know what kind of ladies are there?"

"Stop acting like it is preposterous," Ruby hissed. "I have always liked music. I am in the glee club, you know, and even if we sing traditional songs, it doesn't mean I do not like all types of music. Besides, when I am at Bessie's and her mom is out, we dance. She learned the Charleston from her cousin, and she taught me. I would practice when no one was looking at home. So there." Ruby stomped her foot.

Then she took a deep breath and her gaze softened as she took his hand.

"Look, I know we might be taking a chance, but I think I can take care of that." She batted her eyes. "Let's just give it a try. Please? You find out if the boys can help, and I will take it from there."

"Ruby, did you hear what you just said? You 'think'! That is not good enough. I sure don't fancy getting shot." Arthur dropped her hand and stood up. He started pacing. "I know! Why don't you and I both ask your dad about going to college? Maybe if he knows we are going to the same school, then he might have a different opinion. What do you say?"

Ruby thought for a moment. "You know, Arthur, that could actually work," she said. "But you also know that speaking to my daddy is not that easy. And he would expect us to marry, and we would both lose control of our future."

Arthur sighed and nodded.

"I will tell you what." Ruby touched his arm. "You speak to the boys, and I will put more thought into making sure no one is caught. How is that?"

Reluctantly, Arthur agreed.

A couple of weeks passed, and everyone was ready to put the plan into action. The first few times were scary, but with each successful outing, Ruby got braver, and then it became a game. Ruby's parents did not drink regularly, so she was not able to spike their drinks, which would have been the obvious thing to do to get them to sleep soundly. So, she just made their bed extra comfortable by telling her momma they should sleep on the super soft cotton sheets instead of just saving them for guests, and her momma agreed. Arthur got a fan from his dad to give as a gift to Ruby's parents, and in return, the Dinsmores would spread the word about how a fan can help one sleep more soundly at night. Little did they know, the real purpose of the fan was to hide the noise when Ruby came down the ladder.

Lucky for Ruby, Zola and James had moved their room to the new addition and made the front bedroom the guest room, which meant it was usually empty. The family dog was given a bone by the boys to keep him occupied. Her brothers' and sister's rooms were in the back of the house, and thankfully, they were all hard sleepers. Even Ida Jane, whom she still shared a room with, could sleep through a stampede.

The mission became a successful one. The wool was firmly pulled over the Dinsmores' eyes . . . and Ruby regularly won the dance contests.

Often, on a Sunday morning, the Dinsmore family would be walking to church, and one or more of the boys would see Ruby and her dad, and would greet them. She could tell the boys were bursting to spill the beans, just to see the look on his face. But they kept quiet, as it meant so much to Ruby to go to college. Even the women at the dance hall would never let Ruby's dad in on what she was up to. They felt like they were part of her dream too. Ruby learned a lot from the women in the dance hall . . . their hopes and dreams and how life had brought them to where they were.

The experience gave her even more conviction to help fight for women's rights. Yes, Ruby was more determined than ever, and even though she had a boyfriend, Arthur wanted to go to college too, so it was all working out. To make extra money, she also babysat and helped her momma with canning and baking bread to sell. Ruby even occasionally worked at the family dairy farm with her uncle.

She just told her parents she wanted to save money for a rainy day, and that was enough to make them happy. Yes, Ruby had a plan, and it seemed to be on schedule.

Chapter 13

A NIGHT TO REMEMBER

THE WEEKEND STARTED OUT JUST LIKE ANY OTHER weekend, except the doctor was out of town, and that meant Ruby's momma was on call if there was a medical emergency. If that happened and her momma was needed, Ruby was expected to stay close to home to mind the house and her younger brothers and sisters. Zola was not a doctor by any means, but she had the respect of the town doctor, and he knew of her earlier experience with the doctor in Oklahoma. He always told people to call Zola if they could not reach him, especially if it was time to have a baby. She would know just what to do. The women in town agreed, and there were quite a few children running around town that Zola had delivered. They even called her Aunt Zola, which pleased Ruby's momma so much. Zola felt lucky that the doctor trusted her with some of his cases while he had to be away.

Everyone in the Dinsmore family had duties that aided in making the household run smoothly, especially if Zola was called away. The one skill Ruby never really picked up was her momma's gift for sewing. Her momma did try to teach her, but Ruby just couldn't seem to make things as beautiful as her momma. Cooking was not something Ruby cared about either, but she decided she would learn the basics; it seemed a necessary skill to know, even if you were going to live in the city. So, Ruby would follow directions and cook a meal to give her momma extra time to sew. Ruby was never interested in learning about medicine. She knew the basics—how to take a temperature, how to bring a fever down, how to treat someone with a bad cold—in case one of the younger Dinsmores got sick. She would rather be lost in a new adventure taking place in whatever novel she was reading. The other thing that would take her away from books was spending time with her daddy.

James Dinsmore was good with numbers, and since Ruby had a knack for numbers as well, sometimes when they were enjoying time together, he would teach her a thing or two about accounting. Ruby found these rare moments with her daddy very meaningful, as he would also talk about various jobs, like being a surveyor or managing bills for the family businesses. Her favorite was when he let her read a contract that he had written for purchasing land or buildings.

James, for the most part, did not see the need for girls to be knowledgeable in business matters, but since Ruby was dating Arthur, who would one day inherit his family's business, he felt it was appropriate and would come in handy when Arthur and Ruby were married. Now, no one had mentioned the word "marriage," but for James, it was a given. Arthur was around all the time. The two were often out alone on "dates," so it was only natural to assume marriage was in the cards for Ruby and Arthur. It was the only reason he allowed it.

Zola and Ruby were in the kitchen cleaning, and Zola noticed a full moon was out, even though it was the middle of the day.

"Ruby, it is going to be a beautiful full moon tonight. It is already out now."

Ruby looked out the kitchen window and spotted the moon as she dried off her hands on the fresh, clean hand towel. "I think you are right, Momma. It looks so pretty and bright already."

"That full moon can only mean one thing—a lot of babies will be born tonight," Zola said. "I bet for sure I will be getting a call, so please don't plan on going out."

"I was planning to go to Bessie's, but can I have her over here for the night instead?"

"That will be fine, dear," Zola replied as she finished the last chore in the kitchen.

Bessie and Ruby had not spent much time together lately, what with schoolwork and boyfriends. They had decided earlier in the week that on Saturday night, they would catch up and have a girls' night. Ruby called over to Bessie's and made plans for Bessie to come over to Ruby's house.

Evening came lickety-split, and before long, the girls were upstairs comparing notes about boys, life, and other girl stuff, while Zola and James were happily relaxing on the porch, each in their rockers. Ida Jane had become the mentor for their little sister, Ivy, as Ruby was never around. The boys were out with their busy schedules, except Henry, who was upstairs with his big sisters, playing.

The phone rang, and Ruby ran downstairs to answer it. Her parents were now used to the older children answering the phone, as it was most likely for them anyway. Ruby thought it might be Arthur or Hank wanting to come over and see them, as Bessie had made sure the guys knew where they would be.

Instead, it was a neighbor down the street telling Ruby to get her momma to quickly come, with her medical bag, to Mrs. Sullivan's house.

Ruby frantically ran outside and told her momma.

Zola looked at James. "She is not due for another month!" She quickly went inside and grabbed her supplies for delivering babies, and James drove her down the street to Mrs. Sullivan's home.

When James returned to the house, the girls asked if everything was OK. He nodded his head yes but didn't go into details. Ruby looked at Bessie and shrugged.

"Daddy, since everything is fine, can Arthur and Hank come over and sit with us on the porch?" she asked. "They called while you were taking Momma to Mrs. Sullivan's."

James looked at Ruby, and then at the phone, and back at Ruby. Ruby knew what he was thinking. He had often said that the phone made it easier for kids to meet up more often and ignore their chores. She also knew he felt things were getting out of his control, and he did not like it. Not one bit.

"OK, they can come," James told Ruby. "But make sure the boys come in and say hello first." He paused. "Ruby, just how is Arthur going to know he can come over?"

"Don't worry, Daddy. I know the rule: 'Nice girls do not call boys.' I asked Arthur to call back in about fifteen minutes, as I figured you would be back home, and, sure enough, you are."

"Well, Ruby, I hope you told him that is the family phone rule."

"Oh, I sure did," said Ruby. "And thanks, Daddy. You are the bee's knees!"

And with that, the girls ran upstairs to fix their hair quickly and straighten their clothes for the boys' arrival.

"Girls, take your time getting ready," James yelled up the stairs. "I will answer the phone when Arthur calls and then let the boys in and speak to them a bit. Maybe I will have my pistol handy just for grins." He chuckled.

"Daddy, you better not!" Ruby said, knowing her daddy expected that reaction. It was his way of teasing that meant, "I love you." James was not one who said it very often. You were just expected to know it by his actions.

Ruby had learned over the years how to read her daddy and the twinkle he would get in his eyes when he was pleased about something, or when he was trying to be mad, but his lips would quiver as he was trying not to laugh when her little brother pulled a prank. Yes, rough old James Dinsmore did have a soft side, and Ruby enjoyed the rare occasions when the soft side came out.

About ten minutes after the second phone call,

the doorbell rang. Ruby could hear her father open the door as he welcomed the boys into the house.

"How is it going, boys?" James asked.

They both replied, "Fine, sir."

"Hmmm . . . Well, good. You boys are welcome at any time. Just remember when you are on the porch, no hanky-panky. The neighbors' eyes are everywhere."

"Of course, sir," both boys answered. "We would never take advantage of the girls."

"Well, good." James stood up to his full height. "I would hate to put my old pistol to work." He opened the drawer in the table by the wall so they could see it.

"No, sir!" They stood perfectly still waiting for the girls.

James called them downstairs and then went in the living room and sat in his favorite chair. Ruby and Bessie politely greeted the boys and then led them to the door.

"We will be on the porch, Daddy," Ruby called over her shoulder.

"I will be right here if you need me," James replied.

Ruby turned around and looked at her friends as she rolled her eyes and whispered, "Mrs. Grundy," which was a popular expression, meaning uptight and straightlaced. Her friends giggled as Bessie and Hank took the porch swing. Ruby started to ask them to switch. She was not going to let Arthur sit in her dad's rocker. She didn't think he'd like it. But before she could, her dad called out.

"Ruby, let Arthur sit in my rocker."

"Ah . . . Oh, thank you, Daddy," she said, surprised, and waved Arthur to the bigger rocker while she lowered herself onto her momma's identical, only smaller, version right beside her daddy's.

"Wow, that is nice of your dad. I feel very special." Arthur smiled and reached out to hold Ruby's hand.

With that, Ruby and Arthur pulled the two rockers close to the swinging chair so they could speak in low voices and have a little privacy. A quiet yet lively conversation ensued on the Dinsmore porch, which was built extra wide for many reasons. It wasn't just for entertaining friends; it was also great for rainy days. The children were always able to run around on the porch so that their momma would not have them in the house all day. It was big enough that they could even pull up a card table if they wanted. On many summer nights, mattresses were brought out and it became a "sleeping porch" in order to catch a summer night's breeze.

Ruby hoped that even if her daddy could hear them, he wouldn't understand some of the new slang of the 1920s. It was sort of a code, and many times parents had no idea what their children were saying. Youngsters countywide and beyond learned the modern slang by listening to the radio. Tea was now "noodle juice," "mazuma" referred to dollar bills, but one of Ruby's favorites was "let's blouse," which meant "let's leave this place."

The evening was going very well, and the two couples snuck in kisses when the coast was clear. They could see James take a peek once in a while through the living room curtains.

It seemed like the perfect romantic night, like in one of Ruby's novels, with the full moon watching over them. Each couple wished on a star, but then the phone rang and broke the mood.

"Who could be calling so late?" Ruby wondered.

"I hope it's not my momma," Bessie said. "My grandma is at my house with a cold, and Momma said she might call me to come home early if she needs help with her."

Ruby could hear her daddy speaking to whomever it was but could not make out anything clearly. She heard him hang up and come down the hall.

"Ruby, I hate to cut your evening with your friends short, but your momma needs you."

"That is strange. Why would Momma need me?" she asked.

"I don't know, but she said to put on old clothes and bring an apron and more of her towels for deliveries—and for me to bring you right away." James looked at Ruby's company. "Sorry, boys, looks like your evening is over. You best be leaving. Bessie, of course, you can stay and wait for Ruby if you like."

Ruby looked at Bessie turned to her daddy. "Can she come with me? I am sure Momma could use an extra hand."

"Sure, I think that would be all right."

Hank and Arthur said their goodbyes, and Ruby ran upstairs to change her clothes. She grabbed her momma's things, a new apron, and an old, long T-shirt for Bessie just in case she needed it.

James told Ida Jane to watch the house and that he would be right back. Then, the two girls and James hurried to the car and were around the corner at Mrs. Sullivan's in no time at all. The girls hustled into the house where, to their surprise, they were greeted by Mrs. Sullivan.

"Ruby, oh, Bessie, uh . . . you're here too. Well, I guess that's OK. Now, before you go in, I need to tell you something. . . . Well, I do not know how to say this. . . . Oh . . . well . . . Myrtle's daughter up the street, well, she is having a baby. Her momma and daddy are out of town, and she is spending the weekend with me."

The girls' eyes grew big with surprise. Myrtle's daughter, Gail, was only fourteen. They did not respond but just listened as Mrs. Sullivan continued.

"I did not know she was expecting. I thought she

was just having gas pains, which is why I called your momma, but then she admitted that she had been hiding that she was going to have a baby."

At that moment, Gail let out a long, spine-chilling moan. The girls looked toward the moaning and then back at Mrs. Sullivan, who continued.

"With all that is going on, it is a wonder I am not going into labor myself." She mopped the sweat off her brow. "Anyway, Ruby, your momma needs you in there. Bessie, you can keep me company, and we will boil more water."

Ruby glanced at Bessie, shrugged her shoulders, turned around to open the door, and walked into the room where her mother was waiting for her. She closed the door behind her.

"Good, I'm so glad you're here, Ruby. Did you bring everything I asked for?"

"Yes, ma'am," Ruby replied.

"Ruby, you remember Gail, Myrtle's daughter. Gail, this is Ruby. She is going to help me. Now, I know you are scared, but it is going to be OK," Zola said, trying her best to soothe the frightened girl.

"Ruby . . ." Zola motioned for her to come over to her. "Wash your hands in the basin with clean water and then come stand beside me." She waited for Ruby to do as she was told. "Now, I know you have never helped me before, but there's no need to be nervous. I've done this a hundred times, so just follow my lead. No need to frighten Gail any more than she already is. Do you understand?"

"Yes, ma'am."

"Good. Now no matter what I ask you to do, you may not question or tell me you do not know how. Just do it, OK?" Zola was firm but calm.

Ruby nodded her head. She had never seen her momma with the doctor hat on before. She never really gave it much thought. Her momma was her momma; she never thought of her as really doing medical work. This new momma was exciting to Ruby and, at the same time, puzzling. Did she really know who her momma was? Ruby's mind raced with questions. Was her momma actually a progressive woman? Did she not even realize it herself?

"Ruby, come over here."

Ruby snapped out of it and quickly moved to her momma's side. Zola stroked Gail's forehead while explaining to Gail that she was going to help her have this baby, that she needed to listen very carefully to her instructions, and that no matter how much it hurt, it was important she do everything she said. Ruby could tell how frightened Gail was by the wild look in her eyes and how furiously she nodded her head and bit her upper lip. Gail screamed again, and Zola moved to see how the baby was doing.

"The baby is beginning to crown," said Zola. "Ruby, come see what is happening."

Ruby took a quick look and then moved back to Gail's side and held her hand.

"Gail, I think you are just about . . ."

"AHHHHH," Gail started screaming and pushing with all her might. She held Ruby's hand so tight that Ruby thought it was going to break.

"Keep pushing, Gail. You can do it," Zola kept saying.

Finally, the baby was out! Ruby couldn't believe how focused she was and how she was not freaking out. Later, it would hit her what had taken place.

Zola held the baby in a towel as she gently cut the cord, cleaned the baby, and then gave it a whack on its bottom to make it cry and take its first breath.

"Congratulations, honey." She held the baby up for Gail to see. "You are now a momma to a beautiful little girl."

Gail looked at the baby as Zola placed her on her tummy. "She is so tiny." At the sound of her momma's voice, the baby looked up at her. "She looked at me." A tear rolled down Gail's cheek, and she kissed the baby's forehead.

Everyone watched as Gail and her baby were bonding.

Zola began to clean up Gail and the baby, and Ruby was asked to throw the rest of the afterbirth into the garden outside. Her momma always said, "The afterbirth makes the soil fertile."

Zola taught Gail how to nurse the baby and then left the room once they were both sleeping. The baby seemed very happy in a clothes drawer Mrs. Sullivan had turned into a baby bed. Bessie made everyone hot tea to relax and unwind.

"Well, Ruby, you're certainly a natural," said Zola as she raised her teacup. "You might want to consider being a midwife."

"That thought had never really entered my mind," said Ruby.

She had only seen her daddy's world of business and her momma's world of women's work. Ruby loved getting a compliment from her momma, but she was still thinking how impressed she was with the other side of her momma that she had discovered that evening. Ruby had always been proud of her, but now she was even more so. In her mind, her momma should have been a doctor; had life been kinder to her, perhaps her momma would have been one of the first women doctors in the county.

Ruby's thoughts were interrupted when her momma spoke again. "Now girls, Mrs. Sullivan needs to speak to you about something."

Mrs. Sullivan looked at the girls with knit eyebrows and shook her head.

"OK . . . Well, girls, what a night it has been. Thank you so much for helping out." She sighed and continued. "Now, as you can see, Gail has herself in quite a pickle. She was in denial the whole time she was pregnant, but I think she knew in her heart that she was with child. But she didn't tell anyone. So, it seems her parents do not even know. They just thought she was getting heavy. Easy enough to hide it, I suppose, with these new low waistline dresses." Ruby and Bessie nodded. "Girls, I need to ask a favor of you. You must not speak of this night to anyone. We need to protect Gail because we just do not know how her parents will react, and they need to find out from us, not from town gossip. May I count on you girls?"

"Of course," they both replied.

Zola, Bessie, and Ruby finished their tea, and all three decided they would walk home to have time to process what had happened. Not a word was spoken as they made their way home. There was dead silence. Not even the crickets were chirping— just the dead silence of the moonlit night.

The next morning, Ruby and Bessie were allowed to sleep in and miss church. They woke up to the smell of Ruby's momma starting the dinner preparation for when the rest of the family would gather later that day.

Ruby's momma had saved them breakfast and

served them a lovely meal fit for two princesses. No one mentioned the night before. It was as if it had never taken place. When the girls went back upstairs, Ruby could not help but whisper to Bessie how strange it was not to talk about it. They both agreed it was sad that the boy would never know he was a dad, and his parents would never know they were grandparents. Yet they knew that for the sake of Gail, it was better to keep quiet, as the town was too small to let Gail become the subject of gossip. Ruby now had a deeper understanding of what her momma was trying to teach her when they had "the talk." Ruby never forgot that night.

Chapter 14

THE DEBATE

EARLY ON IN RUBY'S HIGH SCHOOL CAREER, SHE
had decided that she needed to join some clubs to
have an impressive résumé for college; hence, she
added the debate team to her activities, in addition
to the glee club. There was only one other girl on
the team, and Ruby figured this would perfectly
demonstrate to college professors that she was
ready for a man's world.

Ruby discovered she was a natural when it came
to debating, as it was a place to disagree and not
get into trouble! *What more could you ask for?* Ruby
thought. At first, the boys on the team were not
very welcoming, but Ruby proved to be a keen
researcher and came up with good arguments to
defend a position. The boys soon found themselves

asking Ruby for her opinion, which was very pleasing to Mr. Payton, the debate coach. Mr. Payton liked the way Ruby thought as well and would even give her more opportunities to build her debate skills. That year, there would be four debates between schools, and Ruby looked forward to the challenge. She enjoyed debating in front of an audience. It seemed to make her team do better, and it was good for Ruby's competitive nature, as she always wanted to win.

Mr. Payton worked hard at teaching the students how to research current events, which led them to his highest goal: a paradigm shift in looking at life. The team studied what was going on in local, state, and federal politics and how it shaped their lives. They took hard issues that people were passionate about and had to figure out what the pros and cons were in order to defend each side. They practiced by debating each other.

From that time on, Ruby loved to look deeper into current affairs. She kept up with the issues that impacted women but realized she also needed to look at how politics in general was going to affect her life and the lives of others around her. Ruby's dedication to studying current events made the team appreciate her, and the debate coach could see something extra special in her. The team went up against other schools and came home victorious.

It was the first year the school had made it to the district runoffs.

Mr. Payton was thrilled and wanted to take home the win, so he decided for the first time to have a debate in front of the school as extra practice to prepare for the competition. That morning, while Ruby was dressing for school, she wondered what the surprise question would be. Ruby didn't worry about it, as she felt she was ready for any issue.

That morning, the students filed into the auditorium, and the two teams took their places onstage. There was one girl on each side, and in this case, on the other side was Adella Rhodes. Ruby and Adella smiled at each other as they took their places along with their teammates. The girls hung out only during debate period and extra practice; otherwise, they had never found much in common over the years growing up. Both girls had mutual respect for each other since they were both on the debate team and never seemed to have a problem. Going to the debate was not like getting ready for a pep rally, but it did take students out of class, so they were all happy to sit there rather than listen to a boring lecture. The principal introduced Mr. Payton, who then explained what the two teams had been preparing for in the district debates. He introduced the two teams amidst lackluster applause.

The first debate question dealt with immigration;

Ruby argued the pro-immigration side and Adella took the negative side of the immigration debate. The debate lasted for five minutes, and the girls tied. They rested, and their teammates took up the rest of the debate time on the same topic, with the pro-immigration side winning.

The second debate question dealt with the new passage of the Fordney–McCumber Tariff Act: Was this protectionism good for the United States in dealing with foreign relations? The debate team enthusiastically presented both sides of the issue exceptionally well, oblivious to the audience's lack of attention. Several teachers were the judges, and they would decide which team had provided the best case based on a set of debate rules. The judges announced in favor of the pro-tariff argument, and the applause was so light that Ruby wondered if anyone in the audience had understood. Her mind started to wander as she looked out over the audience, but she jumped back in to focus once she heard Mr. Payton's voice at the podium. It was time for the surprise debate question, and the teacher called both girls to the microphones to prepare for their debate. Some boys in the audience snickered and quietly heckled as the two girls prepared to face off.

Ruby heard a few of the comments, mostly about how girls belonged in the kitchen and should leave the politics to the men. Ruby wasn't going to let some immature teasing bother her, and Adella did not seem fazed either. They were used to the heckling from earlier debates at other schools. One thing Ruby and Adella agreed on was that they were the pioneers for young girls in debate clubs who would follow them in the years to come.

Each one stepped forward, proud of her performance thus far. Ruby felt she was ready to handle any question thrown at her and would go home a winner. Mr. Payton explained to the audience how the bonus question worked. He then turned to the girls and had them draw from a box, which would determine if they would be in favor of or against the topic.

Adella stepped to her microphone and stated that she drew "for," and then Ruby went to her microphone and stated, "I am against." The air in the room had changed; the audience was interested in the face-off between a Dinsmore and a Rhodes, as they were both familiar names in politics in the local town. The teacher then read the question. All the students were now engaged and leaned forward to hear it.

Mr. Payton looked at each girl and said, "Can a person be both honest and a politician?" A gasp came from a few in the audience, and a cold silence filled the room in anticipation of what would happen next. Adella was to argue that yes, you can be honest and be a politician, while Ruby was to state all the reasons why a person can't be honest and be a politician. Everyone, including the teachers, watched to see how Adella would answer the question, as her dad and James Dinsmore had their differences, but the classmates were more interested in Ruby's response.

Ruby could feel the air in the auditorium change to dense and hot. She was nervous for the first time, as she realized the topic really hit home. She had never had to deal with the feelings that suddenly welled up in her. You could hear a pin drop in the auditorium as the audience waited to hear the responses.

Adella stood tall and turned toward the microphone. With all the confidence in the world, she began to answer the question.

"Yes, you can be honest and be a politician. Just because James Dinsmore is a crook doesn't mean that others can't be honest."

Everyone gasped in horror that Adella would say such a thing about Ruby's daddy. Ruby had been ready to politely listen to her opponent, but after this comment about her daddy, she turned from a young lady to a fireball. She jumped up and ran toward Adella, and the audience gasped again. Ruby drew her fist and punched Adella in the stomach.

Shocked, Adella leaned over and head-butted Ruby in the stomach, causing Ruby to lose her footing. Before anyone knew what was happening, both girls were rolling on the floor. The students began cheering for their favorite friend and yelling, "Fight, fight, fight!" Teachers were trying to calm everyone down and remove them from the auditorium. Adella did not have brothers, so fighting was not her forte, but Ruby had no problem hitting back. Mr. Payton had trouble separating the two, but, with the help of the principal, the girls were pulled apart. Their teammates looked on but stayed out of it, as Mr. Payton had ordered.

Adella had to go to the nurse's office escorted by a friend while she held a handkerchief to her bloody nose. Ruby, on the other hand, had to go to the principal's office, where her dad was called to come to the school.

Now, Mr. Dinsmore was also the vice-president of the school board, so when he arrived and heard what had happened, he said, "Ruby, I can't believe you did this. I am going to take you home. Thank you, Principal Wilson. I am sorry for the trouble."

When Ruby and her dad got outside of the schoolhouse, Ruby's dad laughed. "Now, Ruby, as your dad I should tell you that girls should not be fighting. But in this case," he chuckled, "I say, good for you! Always stand up for the family." He then looked at her and shook his head. "So, you gave her a bloody nose. I suppose it could be worse!" Then they quietly walked home.

The next day, Ruby had to apologize to Adella so that she could stay on the debate team. Mr. Payton did not want to lose Ruby when they were about to go to the district competition. Adella had to apologize for bringing Ruby's dad into the debate. Both girls accepted the other's apology, just so they could remain on the team. Ruby never wanted to be friends with Adella after that, but she was cordial for the sake of the team. One thing the students learned . . . never mess with Ruby!

Chapter 15

MOMMAS JOIN FORCES

ONE MORNING, THE WOMEN OF THE QUILTING bees in town gathered at Zola's while their children were at school. They were all abuzz, sharing stories about the way their children were now dating instead of courting.

"It's so hard to have a say when they're not sitting in the parlor anymore," lamented one momma. "Heck, they're not even within earshot."

The mommas had their ears to the ground and watched out for each other's kids, but they were still worried. Times sure had changed compared to the days when they were growing up and their parents followed many Victorian era traditions and rules that children would never question. There was a sense that children "these days" had silly notions and wild thoughts, but now it had reached a boiling point.

"I had dreams when I was a child too," she continued. "But those ideas disappeared with the harsh reality of life."

Most of them had married by fourteen and had their first baby by fifteen. Childhood for girls ended with menstruation; courting began with their parents' matchmaking, and marriage followed, along with adult responsibilities. There was nothing in between childhood and adulthood.

"Our daughters of 'courting' age will not even call us 'Momma' and 'Daddy' anymore," bemoaned another momma. "Mine insists on calling us 'Father' and 'Mother.'"

"My son calls us 'Dad' and 'Mom,'" agreed another. "They might as well just put a knife in a momma's back! It sounds so cold. Not the warm and loving way they should refer to their parents, who sacrifice everything to raise them properly."

"And the slang words they are using that they hear on the radio . . . Well, I just cannot keep up!"

The list didn't stop there as the women continued sharing their woes.

Some women were upset that now their sons wanted to borrow their parents' prized possession . . . the car! Others were upset about jazz music and dancing an outrageous dance called "the Charleston."

The women felt they had given in to their daughters enough by allowing them to wear some of the new fashions, which showed most of their legs! But now the girls wanted to cut their hair instead of keeping it long and putting it in, what the mommas considered, beautiful updos. The mommas decided they were going to stop this nonsense and protect their children from the evils of the changing world. They wanted them to realize it was not right to date around and "experiment" with the opposite sex. They needed to understand the facts of life; when you start your period, you are ready to get married and have children. You are first a child, then an adult, ready to take on adult responsibilities. And it was high time they realized it.

The mommas were cackling like a bunch of hens in Zola's living room, talking and eating at the same time. One of them almost choked on the banana nut bread Zola had served, but that did not keep them from going on and on. Zola tried to calm them down by making a joke, but she knew the women were just venting their frustrations.

Finally, Luetta, who was one of the top quilters in the town, settled everyone down and took the lead.

"Ladies, I have an idea for how to tackle this monumental issue," she began. "Each bee can share what is bothering them most, and then we will write it down for each group to discuss a way to resolve the problem. Once each group finishes their assignment, they will select a speaker for their bee."

All agreed, and when they were done, Luetta called on each speaker, and Thelma wrote down what each team had in common. Zola moved from serving banana nut bread to sugar and butter cookies, as the meeting went on for several hours.

It was an exciting debate, but in the end, they all agreed on the community rules:

1. Daughters and their parents would agree on one weekend day to be a car date.

2. A second date must take place at the house, but they could be alone on the porch.

3. Girls were not to use the telephone to call a boy.

4. "Courting age" sons and daughters would refer to their parents as "Momma" and "Daddy."

5. Proper English would be used; slang was not allowed.

The next day, Zola sat Ruby down in "The Chair" and told her the new rules and how there would be no debate. Ruby protested, but not about the one car date night; she found that to be a relief. It gave her the perfect excuse to not go out both nights. On the other hand, she told her momma that she found it odd that Zach was not presented with these rules just because he was a boy. Ruby felt they both were going on car dates; therefore, they should both have to hear the rules. Zola explained that since the girls were given the dating rules, the mommas saw no need to tell their sons, since they would automatically have to follow the rules based on the girls they dated. This explanation meant nothing to Ruby; she said her brothers still had to hear the rules so that both the boys and girls in the family were treated equally.

Zola just shook her head and made her way to the kitchen to prepare supper, and Ruby stomped upstairs. She passed her brothers' bedroom, and they pointed at her and covered their mouths to stifle their laughter, but burst out laughing even louder.

Zola yelled up to the boys to quit laughing at Ruby or they would find themselves in "The Chair."

"Yes, Momma!" they yelled back.

Ruby knew where her momma was coming from, but she saw this as a way to stand up for women's rights. Couldn't her momma and the others see that girls were being singled out due to their gender? Her momma did not hold that opinion. Zola had been ready for Ruby to protest, but her main point was to inform Ruby that she would be spending less time alone with Arthur. Ruby knew her momma may find it odd that she protested more about her brother Zach not being told all the new rules, but being equal was important to Ruby.

Her momma said that of course there were different rules for girls and boys . . . life is different for each.

Zola had never dreamed Ruby would use the word "sex" in front of her, much less the term "sexist," which Zola had never heard before. She watched Ruby stomp upstairs. It was Ruby's way of having the last word. Ruby also informed whomever was listening as she made her way upstairs that she would be in charge of the radio and the channels.

Zola was looking forward to James returning home from work so that she could share the news of the day. He would be very pleased. The phones were ringing throughout the town with friends calling one another to see if the "dating rules" had been imposed on them. The phone rang at their house, and it was Bessie. Zola could hear Ruby tell her the new rules regarding dating. Friday would be a car date night, and Saturday would be at the house if they wanted to see each other, but Arthur would have to leave at ten.

Zola was quite pleased to hear that the news had spread to Drumright, and the mommas there decided they wanted to impose the women's rules as well. She thought about how two towns sharing the same standards for their courting age children was going to make life much more comfortable.

At their quilting bees, the women told stories of their children's reactions. They were all very pleased with themselves and felt they had regained control of their children once more. Zola was delighted to hear from Ruby that Bessie's car date night would be the same as Ruby's.

Over time, the rules were adopted, but not without debate in some homes. Zola felt lucky that her daughter did not complain. She had overheard a conversation between Ruby and Bessie, so she knew that, deep down inside, Ruby was relieved to use her momma as an excuse not to have to go out. Zola had learned some other tidbits—how much Ruby liked Arthur and that Bessie might have found herself a husband, which was great news to Zola. Zola was very excited about the thought of Bessie possibly getting married; maybe this could influence Ruby to settle down too.

Ruby really didn't mind the new rules. Now, with extra time to herself, she could sneak in some reading for fun. She had been so busy with her chores, tutoring, clandestine dance contests, and studying. Ruby had also agreed not to refer to her momma as "Mom" or "Mother." She had never started, though she wanted to; she felt it was not worth hurting her momma's feelings. Ruby just wanted peace and for her parents to believe all was copacetic.

Ruby's friends were all talking about the new rules at school and on their dates. Talking about it only made them want to break the rules even more and drag their parents into the twentieth century.

Ruby loved silent movies. They always made for a fun date. Films like *Her Own Money* starring Ethel Clayton had all the girls talking, but it was *Beyond the Rocks* with Rudolf Valentino that had ruffled the mommas' feathers. The young girls were going crazy for the movie stars, and this particular movie put wild ideas in their heads, such as "French kissing."

Ruby found herself wanting to experiment with her sexual side but would then remember Gail's baby and come to her senses. She told Arthur that they would just have to make do with kissing. For some of Ruby's friends, the open fields and parked cars replaced haystacks for sexual discoveries.

Yes, there had been a good reason to call the meeting of mommas. It was high time to get a handle on their children, but, as they were discovering, they were not children anymore. They were a new generation with new ideas about life and how to live it.

Chapter 16

DANCE THE NIGHT AWAY

THE NEW RULES FOR DATING REALLY DID TURN out to work in Ruby's favor. She used Friday date night as the night she would enter the dance contests. It was easy for Arthur to take her, and most importantly, there was no need to sneak around. Ruby never allowed him to watch her. If he did, she would become self-conscious and lose focus. Ruby had the Charleston down perfectly, and she wore a wig and used the fake name "Ada Mae" in some of the small towns where she felt they might know her daddy.

Ruby had saved quite a bit of money, but she knew she was still short. When she left town for college, she would need money to live on until she found a job, but she was running out of competitions to enter and needed to figure out how to beat the other girls. They were all doing the Charleston, and you needed to be willing to do more than just dance to win the vote. Ruby knew she had to spice it up but had no desire to become a red-light girl. It was out of the question to go that far, but what could she do?

One Saturday night, as Ruby was listening to the phonograph, an idea popped into her head. Off she went to her momma's room where she started going through her chest. Lots of hand-me-down clothes were stored there for her siblings to wear as they each grew in and out of them. Ruby was hoping that Rilla's old swimsuit was still there, as she remembered seeing it a long time ago. Sure enough, it was, but it was not the time to take it out. She did not want anyone to notice it was missing. When Ruby came out of the bedroom, her momma asked her why she was rummaging about in the chest.

"I was hoping to find some things of Rilla's there that I might like to wear to school," Ruby said as she breezed by, hoping her momma wouldn't ask anything further. Zola just looked at her, puzzled, but did not say anything more. They all went back to enjoying the music and a quiet evening.

Sunday was a regular day with not much going on, so Ruby grabbed the swimsuit from the chest and ran upstairs to try it on. Sure enough, it fit, and her dress covered it up, which was extremely important. She quickly changed before anyone saw her, tucked the swimsuit into the bottom of her dresser drawer, and went on with her day.

She had the first part of her new plan checked off, and now it was on to the next phase: when and where? Ruby would really need to give this a great deal of thought. She had read that there was going to be a big dance contest at the cabaret in Shamrock where Ruby Darby had performed. The oilmen were infatuated with Ruby Darby, so much so that if they struck oil big, they would call it a "Real Darby." If a young girl heard her boyfriend call her a "Real Darby," she would give him the biggest kiss ever, as that was considered a huge compliment.

Ruby decided this contest just might be the one that would top off her savings. The rules stated they were looking for a "unique Charleston." Ruby had already done a creative version of the dance that had won her one competition. She was beginning to enjoy her alter ego, the free-spirited Ada Mae. This new identity was giving her more and more confidence with each prize she won. Now she needed to really think outside of the box—something new and daring but not enough to land her in jail. She was still a lady deep down inside. She decided to sleep on it.

The week before the dance competition, Ruby was sitting on the porch with Arthur and speaking softly about the upcoming event.

"Arthur, next week I would like you and Hank to do something for me. I need you to be there to watch me this time. I do not want to tell you what I am going to do, but just in case anything goes wrong, I need you there, ready to jump in."

"Ruby, you have never let me watch you dance before." Arthur's eyebrows raised. "You said I would make you nervous, but now I am worried, and I don't even know what you are up to."

"Well, I would rather not tell you. Let's just say I want you to be surprised, and I want your honest opinion. And I want to be able to leave as soon as it is over. OK?"

Arthur reluctantly agreed, and Ruby told him the plan.

The following Friday, Hank and Bessie joined them on their date. It always pleased both girls' parents when they were in a group of four, and they even allowed the girls to stay out until eleven o'clock. Bessie would spend the night with Ruby when it was a group date so that they could make the most of their extra time with the boys. Ruby had her costume on under her loose, low-waisted dress, and her wig was tucked into her brassiere. Hank did as instructed and brought with him some of his little brother's clothes for Bessie. Girls were not allowed in the audience, so the disguise was essential. No way did Bessie want to miss seeing Ruby in action, so dressing like a boy was not a problem. Arthur pulled over once they were out of sight so that Hank and Ruby could trade places. Ruby needed to be in the back seat to help Bessie put on her boy clothes.

Bessie had taken an old mannequin wig that her momma wasn't using anymore and cut it into a boy's hairstyle just for this occasion. Bessie's boy wig was the hardest thing to put on, but, lucky for her, she had recently cut her hair in the latest fashion, which made it fit more comfortably.

"You look cute as a boy, Bessie." Ruby laughed, pleased with Bessie's transformation. "Now I need to focus on the prize." Ruby went into silent mode.

Her friends knew that when she was concentrating, she was to be called Ada Mae. It was crucial that she recognize her name. If by chance someone in the crowd called out, "Hey, Ada Mae!" while she was dancing, she would know they meant her.

The car was quiet now as the three tried not to stare at Ruby, who was deep in thought. Ruby tapped her feet as she practiced the dance steps. She was determined to win, and her friends wanted it just as badly for her.

"Why the change of heart?" Hank whispered to

Arthur. "Ruby never wanted us to watch before . . . guess she has a plan."

"Shh!" Bessie shushed him from the back seat as Ruby shot the boys a look.

"I'm not too sure I want to see," Hank replied and slunk down low in the front seat.

"Shh!" Bessie and Ruby both hissed.

Ruby was getting more nervous and had gone from toe-tapping to drumming her fingers to a rhythm. Arthur finally pulled up to the cabaret. The blond Ada Mae got out of the car and sashayed toward the entrance, accompanied by her entourage.

Ada Mae signed up for the dance, and the owner of the cabaret took her backstage. She would be the last dance of the night. The woman looked at her as if Ada Mae did not have a chance, but little did she know what was in store. Ada Mae went into the changing room and began putting on makeup; she drew on big, pouty red lips and a mole just above the tiny dimple on her left cheek. As she was getting dressed, Ada Mae looked at her competition and, much to her surprise, saw that two other girls had on swimsuits. Ruby gasped but quickly turned it into a fake cough and smiled at the girls. They just shrugged their shoulders and kept preparing for the dance-off. As the girls were all finishing up, Ruby was thinking, *Now what? My idea is not that different.* Then it hit her. The girls left to line up, but Ruby stayed in the dressing room since she knew she was on last. She grabbed the scissors someone had left on the dressing table and cut a hole on each side of her one-piece swimsuit from above the waistline down to the lower hips in an oval shape to show skin. Then she cut the round top into a V-shape down the middle to show cleavage and quickly removed the binding that flattened her bust for the flapper look. Tonight was the night to let a little more show. Then Ruby put on a robe. She did not want to be kicked out of the contest for showing too much skin.

Ruby finally got in line, and the girls scowled at her because she had missed watching several of the dancers compete. Ruby knew it was a tight-knit group of girls that all supported one another. She did not have time for such silliness. Once she had saved enough, she would never see them again anyway. So, she just smiled at them. *Ada Mae, the actress, can do this over and over and over again,* she said to herself. Through the curtains, Ruby saw her friends in the front row. Finally, she was up. Ruby heard her stage name being called. The music started, and she dropped the robe and danced her way onto the stage. The gasp from the stage director was just the reaction Ruby needed to give her the confidence to sell her dance and win the contest. The men in the audience whooped and hollered with delight as the robe fell; their imaginations were already running wild. Hearing the whistles, it took everything for Ruby to stay focused. Arthur stood there in shock, and all the while Hank was making wisecracks about how Arthur had never told him that Ruby was a wild one.

"Maybe I should learn to move like that," Bessie yelled to Hank. Hank just shook his head—no way!

Despite their disbelief at watching their friend dancing, they too had to clap and holler so as not to look like oddballs in the dance hall. Ada Mae could move her hips in a way that made the Charleston so seductive. She used her pouty red lips to entice the men even more.

When Ruby had finished, she ran offstage, but the crowd wanted more. She quickly got back in line with the rest of the girls, ready to return to the stage for the results.

The other girls were not happy, and they elbowed her as she made her way to the end of the line, as they were to come out in order of appearance.

The owner had been watching from backstage. "Kid, I never thought you had it in you," she said. "Who would have ever thought to cut up a swimsuit? Now if you want a regular gig, I have a job waiting for you."

"Thank you," Ada Mae said. "That's very kind." She tried to be polite, but in her mind, she was thinking about the money she was saving to go to college. She would never make a career of being an exotic dancer.

The contestants all came out from backstage and lined up. The winner would be chosen by applause. There was loud applause and whistles for all the dancers, but Ada Mae won hands down. That night, she was handed a one-hundred-dollar bill, more than she ever imagined she could win by just dancing.

Arthur, Hank, and Bessie were in shock and now understood why Ruby had needed them to watch her dance; they were going to have to get her out of there quickly, as Ada Mae had brought out the wolf in the men in the audience that night. Arthur was not sure he liked what he saw, and he certainly didn't like all those men ogling his girl.

While the other contestants made their way to the bar to flirt, Ruby took the opportunity to make a run for it. She recovered her robe from the stage manager, quickly took off her wig and swimsuit and stuffed them into a bag, wiped off the red lipstick, and put on her own clothes.

She walked out the backstage door as Ruby. No one gave her a second look. They were all waiting for the blond bombshell to go out to the bar. Ruby quickly hopped in the car, and she and her friends took off. The boys were quiet as Bessie's mouth was going a hundred miles a minute talking about her best friend dancing with hardly anything on! All the while, she was in the back seat changing out of the boy clothes and back into her own.

Ruby started laughing, and Bessie, realizing how absurd she was being, started laughing too. The boys, who were sitting up front, joined in. They took the girls back to Ruby's house, and the last thing anyone wanted to do was say goodnight, but it was late, and the boys needed to get home. Arthur told Ruby he wanted to come over the next day if her parents agreed. "Of course," Ruby said, as he had been the key to making her plan work, but she was not too excited about his tone and what he might be thinking.

The girls whispered and giggled pretty late into the night. Ida Jane slept in the guest room so that she wouldn't be disturbed. Finally, Bessie fell asleep, and Ruby lay in bed, overwhelmed by what had just happened. She thought to herself, *I do not know who did the dancing, but whoever did it danced the night away.* She smiled at that thought and then silently thanked her angels for giving her the strength to pull it off. *Now I have the money to make my dreams come true.* She fell into a deep sleep, which was very much needed.

As it turned out, Arthur was not able to come on Saturday, as he needed to help his dad pick up some supplies in Tulsa. So, Ruby's parents invited him to go to church with them on Sunday instead.

As the Dinsmore family walked up to the church, everyone greeted them as usual. Arthur found it hard to look Mr. Dinsmore in the eye, but somehow he managed. Ruby sat next to her momma, and Arthur sat next to Ruby's daddy. Ruby managed to smile at Arthur, but he just turned to the minister and did not react to her smile at all. As they walked out of the church and were greeted by the minister, it seemed Arthur saw Ruby in a different light. There she was: the sweet girl thanking the minister for the thoughtful sermon and then walking down the steps to speak to a few of her girlfriends. Arthur stood there with the menfolk, just watching.

James slapped Arthur on the back, bringing him out of his daydream. "I see you looking at Ruby, and I must say, I am very pleased with you two courting," he said.

Arthur looked at him, puzzled, then realized what he had said. "Oh, um, thank you, sir. Ruby is something else, that is for sure."

Ruby overheard this as she and her momma finally joined the men, and they all headed home.

"Now, Ruby and Arthur, you can make yourselves comfortable on the porch," Zola said as they came up the front walkway. "I am going to get the young ones their dinner first." She waved them to the porch swing. "I'll let you know when I'm ready for everyone else."

The two did as they were told and took their usual places on the porch swing. When everyone was out of earshot, Ruby turned to Arthur.

"I want to thank you so much for the other night," she began, still unsure of what he wanted to say to her. "It meant so much to me." She paused, and when he didn't say anything, she lowered her voice to a whisper. "I finally have enough money for college."

Arthur just kept staring. Ruby could tell he was upset and decided not to say anything else until he spoke.

Several minutes passed. Finally, Arthur whispered, "Wow, Ruby, is that what you have been doing all this time, dancing half-naked in front of men?"

"No, of course not," she gritted her teeth, not used to being chastised by him. "I have been dancing in dresses; I just needed to do something dramatic to win this contest."

Arthur was not happy, and he began peppering her with one question after another without even letting her answer the first one. What did the men think of her? What would their parents do if they had seen her? How would the community react? What was he supposed to do? Ruby was finally able to calm him down and told him to think of it as acting and that Ada Mae was now retired. She promised him over and over until, finally, he believed her. And, with that, they made up.

The air was still a little tense as they quietly sat on the porch swing. Finally, Ruby got Arthur to laugh when she said, "Just think—Daddy has no idea he is a 'dapper.'" With that, they agreed on one thing for sure: Ruby's daddy had no idea that he was the dad of a flapper girl—if he even knew what a "dapper" was!

Chapter 17

GRADUATION

GRADUATION DAY FINALLY ARRIVED. RUBY FELT excitement as she approached the school for her last day. It was a day of saying goodbye and signing yearbooks. Many girls had received their engagement rings at the end-of-year school dance. Ruby's parents were disappointed that Ruby's finger still had no ring. Ruby's dad didn't press the issue, as he had learned through the grapevine that Arthur was planning to attend the University of Oklahoma. Zola and James were preparing for Ruby's heartbreak and wondered when it would come. They had already disappointed her by telling her she could not go to college.

As Ruby collected her yearbook, she looked around and envisioned how her friends' lives and her own would change. Ruby wondered for a moment if she was making a mistake by not going to the same university as Arthur, but she knew in reality that would never happen. Ruby had to stick to her plan. She left school and headed home to prepare for the afternoon graduation. The whole town would be involved in preparing for the ceremony. The townspeople were always so proud of their youth and their ability to attend high school, much less graduate. For many parents and grandparents, wars, harvest time, and life in general had robbed them of their opportunity to complete their high school studies. When someone in the family or town was graduating, it was the closest thing to feeling what it must be like, so the whole town celebrated the accomplishments of their young graduates.

The bakery donated the cakes and cookies for after the ceremony. The various churches set up tables with a variety of foods and sweets for the townspeople to enjoy, as well as multiple fruit punches to quench their thirst. The hardware store donated the materials to make decorations and to build a stage for the students to walk across. The school courtyard took on a whole new look, with rows of chairs for the graduates and their families. The stage had a podium for the guest speakers to address the families and friends, and there were chairs for the teachers, honored guests, and, of course, the valedictorian. Everything was all set.

The time had come for the ceremony, and parents of the soon-to-be graduates sat close to the front in the row of seats marked for them, while the rest of the town filled in the rows behind. James looked around to see where Arthur and his family were sitting, as he knew they were coming, and he wanted to be sure to see them. He was interested in getting a feeling of whether Arthur was possibly waiting until after graduation to pop the question.

"Pomp and Circumstance" began to play, and Ruby felt butterflies thinking of what the future would bring. She could feel the high emotions of her classmates as they all fidgeted and whispered to one another. Their English teacher, Mrs. Posey, had taught them how to walk slowly, with dignity, and how to hold their head high. The time had arrived, and each student stood tall with pride as they walked down the aisle. The fears of being in front of an audience disappeared, and only a sense of accomplishment showed on their faces as they saw their families, teachers, friends, and neighbors watching with admiration.

The graduates walked in, girls first and then the boys, filling in the rows. The girls wore white Sunday dresses, while the boys dressed in their Sunday suits. It was Ruby's turn to walk up the aisle, and she scanned the crowd to see where her parents were. She found them. Her momma was looking on with a big smile, and her daddy looked like he was about to burst with pride. Ruby's heart filled with love, and at that moment she wanted to turn the clock back and be their little jewel again. For so long she had been in a hurry to grow up, and now that she was becoming a grown-up, seeing her parents gave her this warm, secure feeling that she never wanted to lose. She came out of her trance as she passed by them.

The twenty-one students in her graduating class filed into the saved section. The teachers then followed and sat in their assigned seats. The principal took the stage, along with the mayor, and the ministers from the local Methodist, Baptist, and Presbyterian churches. Mayor Peterson gave welcome remarks.

"Good afternoon, Principal Shaw, ministers, teachers, parents, graduates, and everyone else who has come to support the class of 1923. It is customary in Oilton to have the town greet the graduates, as many of you will be leaders here, in the very town you grew up in. Why, one of you just might be mayor yourself one day." He paused as everyone chuckled. "Therefore, when the town gathers together on such an occasion as this, it only seems fitting that I, your mayor, welcome you and be the first to congratulate you. Well done. With that, I turn it over to our distinguished principal of the high school, Principal Carl Shaw."

Principal Shaw walked up to the podium where Mayor Peterson was standing. They shook hands before the mayor took his seat, and the principal began his address.

"Welcome, everyone, to the graduation of the class of 1923," he began. He continued with his welcome and then invited Reverend Cook to open the ceremony with a prayer.

The minister stepped up to the podium. "Please bow your heads," he began. "Dear God, we give thanks for this beautiful spring day you have blessed us with. We give thanks for our town and all the wonderful families who help to make it a great place to live. We especially give thanks today to our young graduates. They have worked hard and will now receive their high school diplomas. I ask you to watch over them as they go out into the world as adults ready to begin a new life. Please give them the guidance they need to make smart choices. In the name of Jesus Christ, our Lord. Amen."

"Amen," everyone responded.

The Eagle Scouts stood to present the stars and stripes as everyone placed their hands over their hearts to prepare for the Pledge of Allegiance. They said the pledge with such fervor that it made the graduates, parents, and neighbors stand straight and proud to recite it together.

The Eagle Scouts placed the flag on the stand and marched back to their seats.

The ceremony went off without a hitch. Everyone remembered their parts, beginning with Stella Thrift, who had a voice like an angel. She stepped up to the microphone, and when the music began to play, she sang the national anthem for the last time as a high school student.

What a voice, Ruby thought. *Too bad she is not even going to try to go to the big city and see how she can use it.* Ruby liked Stella a lot. She had enjoyed being in the glee club with her, but they had never become close because Stella was happy in her own little world, while Ruby wanted to expand hers. As Stella finished, everyone gave her a standing ovation. She smiled as she left the stage to join the rest of her classmates.

Principal Shaw took to the podium and thanked Stella and told her that she and her beautiful voice would be missed. "You can hit those high notes as clear as a bell." The principal then turned his attention to the crowd and began to say a few words in reminiscence of the year.

He recalled some of the highlights of football games and chess tournaments and closed with some funny moments that made the crowd chuckle but that also made the graduating class realize those fun times were coming to an end. Adulthood had arrived, and it was time to go out into the world. Principal Shaw then asked the Presbyterian Minister Blackwell to share some words of wisdom.

Ruby sat there as the minister talked about what the future may or may not hold. As he continued talking, Ruby daydreamed. She had dreamed of this day, and now it was here. Would she be able to go through with the next stage of her plan? People started clapping and she snapped out of her day-dream as the minister wrapped up his speech. She could not believe she had missed everything he had said. Then the valedictorian, Henry Gray, took the stage.

"Good afternoon," he began. "I promised my friends to keep it brief, and when I thought about this moment, I wondered, 'What am I supposed to say? What words of wisdom can I give when I am still learning?' Then I remembered what my grandpa—yes, you, Grandpa Ed—would always say to me, 'Son, life is a journey; you just have to live it.' So many times, I wondered what he was talking about, and now I think I finally understand. I look out at my classmates and realize we have been on a journey together through our school years that brought us all to this day—our 'journey of learning,' which has now led us to the beginning of our bright futures."

As Henry continued with his speech, he made people laugh and reminded the class that high school memories would always keep their friendships alive, no matter where life took them.

"We will no longer rely on our parents to make our way. It is up to us to figure out who we are and to go for our dreams. The days of only worrying, 'Who will win the football game?' are behind us. For some of us, there will be more tests to take; for others, the future means getting a job and starting our own families. Whatever the choices we have made and will make, may they be smart ones. May they be ones that keep us growing and willing to face challenges with strength and wisdom. May we keep up with politics and be sure to vote for the good of the town, our State of Oklahoma, and our great country, the USA. May we be remembered as the class that embraced the new world of change and prosperity, the class that set a good example for those that follow."

Henry paused, looked at the crowd, and, with a voice of inspiration, he closed by saying, "Let's be the class that makes the town proud, and, more importantly, let's make our parents proud. Congratulations, my friends—we did it. We are the class of 1923. We are ready to begin our new chapter in the journey of life!"

With that, everyone cheered. Henry took his

seat, and everyone continued clapping and cheering as the principal moved to the podium. It was time for the certificates to be passed out. The English teacher called out the names of the students in alphabetical order, and the principal shook their hands and gave each his or her diploma.

When Ruby's name was called, her entire family hooted and cheered, just like when her brothers got a touchdown, and Ruby walked across the stage filled with the confidence of a young woman destined for greatness. She shook the principal's hand and began to walk off the stage, smiling broadly. She then turned to her parents and gave them an even bigger smile. Her momma blew her a kiss.

I did it, and now my life is going to change. But, for the moment, Ruby would simply revel in her parents' approval of her accomplishments. She watched her classmates receive their diplomas and thought of the people she would miss and the ones who would not even care if she was around at all. She saw a few others receive their diplomas who, like her, wanted to explore the bigger world but were too afraid to venture out, while still others did not want to disappoint their parents by leaving and would continue the family business.

Ruby smiled and thought about her classmates and their lives. She let her mind wander for a moment and then rejoined reality as the last name was called out and the graduates were asked to stand and face their parents. The principal pronounced them official Oilton High School graduates of 1923. With that, parents exploded into applause, and brothers and sisters whistled and shouted as the rest of the crowd joined in. When the excitement died down, Reverend Cook closed with a prayer, and the graduates filed out. Everyone walked over to the refreshment tables on the other side of the courtyard.

The graduates enjoyed the celebration and shared stories with family, friends, and well-wishers. Music played while the juniors of the class served the food and punch as a way to show respect and for the town to recognize the up-and-coming seniors.

Arthur squirmed and turned red in the face as Mr. Dinsmore fished for what his true intentions were with Ruby. If Arthur had it his way, he would ask Ruby to marry him but wait for him while he went off to college. Nothing would please Arthur more than to ask Mr. Dinsmore for her hand in marriage, but instead, Arthur found himself answering Mr. Dinsmore's questions and then excusing himself from his dad and Mr. Dinsmore to go and speak to his friends.

Ruby had observed the exchange between Arthur and her father and was not looking forward to hearing the details of what had happened. She broke away from some of her classmates to join Arthur and her friends.

The two enjoyed laughing and speaking with their friends, and Ruby hoped she was sending signals to her daddy that all was well and that he should not get bent out of shape. As the family celebration came to an end, the graduates headed off to their party at the Hotel Royal in Oilton, where Ruby and Arthur had spent many an hour in the café mapping out their summer and Ruby's plan to earn money for college.

The hotel was all decorated with congratulatory signs and a special graduation cake made by the baker, which everyone oohed and aahed over. The ballroom had streamers and posters as well, and the tables were covered in white linen cloths and a floral centerpiece featuring the school colors. Ruby and Arthur made their way to a table to join Hank and Bessie.

Ruby could feel that the air was still not completely clear with Arthur. She knew it still gnawed at him that she had worn a revealing swimsuit and danced for strangers, and then her dad hinting about a marriage proposal had made it worse. They talked about graduation, but Ruby knew Arthur's mind was elsewhere. He told her he had been impressed with the money she had saved over the summer by winning the contests, tutoring, and even putting some time in on the family dairy farm. Arthur found her to be very resourceful, but where was all of this going to leave them if Ruby was still determined to go to college? He told Ruby that he was a little bothered that he did not know what her plan was, much less what college she was going to attend. Time and again, Ruby told him he was better off not knowing the entire plain. Arthur reluctantly agreed but hoped she would take to his idea that she would be better off attending university with him.

After dinner and before dessert was served, everyone wandered from table to table, mingling with their friends. Arthur listened half-heartedly to one friend after another talk about their plans and finally excused himself to join Ruby, who was busy chatting with her friends.

"Sorry to interrupt," he said as he gently took her elbow. "Can I steal you for just a moment?" He leaned down to whisper in her ear. "Can you come outside? We need to talk." He smiled at her friends.

Ruby excused herself and followed Arthur outside, anxious about what it could be. They went out to the courtyard at the back of the hotel, where it was lit up and set with small bistro tables and chairs for people to visit in smaller groups.

"Ruby, I was so proud of you at graduation. It was a special day for us to share. Now we need to make our plans. I think it is time you tell me the rest of your plan." He took her hand and drew her a bit roughly to sit down beside him.

It was much more authoritative than she was used to, and it gave Ruby the shivers. Plus, she did not like to be told what to do.

"Now Arthur, why do you want to go and spoil the night and talk so seriously? Please, we can have this talk later. Trust me." She gave him a peck. "Let me get a few more things lined up, and then I will tell you." She started to kiss him again, but he pulled back.

"Ruby, your kisses do not make the problem just disappear. I want to know."

Ruby was surprised at his response. In the past, she had been able to distract him with a kiss, but not tonight. She had to think of another approach.

"Darling, I do not want to spoil this night. Now come on. Let's enjoy our friends before we all go in different directions."

"Ruby, don't you beat all? OK, but we will finish this discussion tomorrow."

Ruby kissed him once more, knowing she had him wrapped around her finger . . . for now. "Of course, dear," she said.

Chapter 18

GUILT

RUBY WAS ALONE IN HER ROOM AND HAD JUST finished hiding her money away after double-checking how much she had saved when her sister Ida Jane came in.

"What are you up to, Ruby? You have a weird look on your face."

"No, I don't! You are silly sometimes."

"Whatever, I don't feel like arguing with you. I have something to tell you."

"Really? What?"

"Well, I heard Momma and Daddy talking about you and Arthur, and they are concerned Arthur is going to break your heart. I guess you have not mentioned to them that you already know he is going away to university."

"No, I have not. What else did they say?" Ruby said as she picked up a brush to straighten her hair.

Ida Jane bounced on her bed like a little schoolgirl excited about a secret. "Come, sit on the bed with me," she said and patted the bed.

Ruby hopped onto the bed. "OK, spill the beans."

Ida Jane leaned in and spoke in a hushed voice. "Well, they find it strange that you are happy to be at home and not even discuss what your plans are now that you are an adult and, at your age, should be getting married."

Ida Jane was so excited to tell Ruby the rest of the story that she bounced from a seated position onto her knees. She continued to whisper, "I also heard them say that they know your only prospect for a husband was Arthur, but you failed to seal the deal so . . . are you ready for this?"

"Not really. I am still upset over the 'seal the deal' reference," Ruby said.

Ida Jane tried to cover Ruby's mouth. "Shh, keep your voice down. They will hear you!"

Ruby caught Ida Jane's hand and pushed it away. "OK, then." She forced herself to whisper. "Go on." Ruby looked intently at her sister, scared to hear what Ida Jane was going to say next.

"Now get this!" Ida Jane happily continued. "Well, Momma said that Rilla needs help around the house with her expecting their second child. She told

Daddy that you should go live with them and help them out. There are more men to choose from in Seminole, and for sure you would find a man with all of Rilla's friends at church."

"Oh my gosh," Ruby responded. "This is dreadful. I have no desire to do that."

"I know! That is why I had to tell you so that you can figure out what to do." Ida Jane bounced up and down again. "So . . .?"

"So . . . what?" Ruby responded.

"What do you think you will do? Daddy is intent on you finding a man."

"Good grief! Thanks for telling me. When do you think they are going to spring this on me?"

"Well, I do not know, but it sounded like it will be soon. I think Momma will speak to Rilla about the idea first. That should buy you some time," Ida Jane said. "Ruby, I was a perfect spy for you, wasn't I?"

Ruby had been feeling pretty bad about all her secrets for a while, but now she could feel the guilt written all over her face. She thought about all the things she had done and the money she had saved.

As Ruby drifted off into another world, Ida Jane brought her back. "Ruby, Ruby, what is wrong with you, Ruby?"

Here was Ruby's chance to spill the beans and confide in her little sister, but could she trust her? It was always the question that kept Ruby from telling

Ida Jane. Would today be any different? *Today is different*, she thought. *I might be shipped off to Rilla's to be a nanny solely so that Rilla can help find a husband for me.* Should she tell her little sister? Was Ida Jane old enough to keep a secret this important? Ruby's mind was going a hundred miles a minute wondering what to do. She was so upset with her parents' thinking. They should know her better. They should have remembered that going to university was important to her, even though she had not brought it up since they had informed her that they would not pay for her to attend college. Ruby had so many thoughts running through her mind as she continued to think about how hurtful it was for her parents to even consider farming her out to her sister's place. She wondered why her parents did not want to pay for her to go to college like her older brothers. Surely they realized she did not fit the traditional mold of getting married and having babies right out of high school.

"Ruby, snap out of it. You look like you want to hit someone, and then, at the same time, you look like you want to cry. What are you thinking?"

"I am just so upset that Momma and Daddy still think I need a man. How can they not know me? Just because I have had fun with Arthur does not mean I have to marry him or any other man for that matter. I am just as smart as Will and Zach, and they let them go to university. I just figured they knew me better, is all."

Ida Jane gave Ruby a big hug. "Ruby, I am sure it will all work out. I wanted to tell you to give you time to figure things out. Just remember to act surprised when they tell you."

Ruby embraced Ida Jane again. In that moment, she decided it was in her sister's best interest to not know a thing. Ruby decided to keep her secret to herself, regardless of the guilt hidden deep inside, because now, more than ever, she needed her plan to work, and it seemed as if it needed to happen sooner rather than later. It was time to reveal all to Arthur.

Chapter 19

UPDATING ARTHUR

"THERE, DONE!" RUBY SAID AS SHE QUIETLY PLACED the phone back onto the stand. She started up the stairs to her room when she saw her reading spot in the alcove, and, just as if she were five years old again, Ruby grabbed a blanket and once more retreated as if it would make all her problems disappear.

She sat there gazing out the window and thinking of her parents' growing concern that she was not falling in line and marrying right after high school, as was the custom for young girls, if not sooner. Ruby thought she had successfully convinced her parents that she and Arthur would eventually marry. With the information Ida Jane had shared with her, she needed to think about what to do. She gazed out the window and let out a long, loud sigh. Tears began to roll down Ruby's face. She wondered how it had come to this. How could all her hard work and good grades not have proven that she was worthy for college? Why must she be forced to choose between her parents and following her dreams? Why couldn't she have dreams?

She wiped her tears. *Enough, Ruby. Get a grip!* She focused on her little, quiet space in the world—the one she was about to leave behind. It had been her favorite place ever since her family had moved to the big house. She found her little window seat even more precious the more she thought about saying goodbye to it, knowing it was right on this very spot that she had let herself hope and dream. It was the spot where her imagination had taken her on so many adventures. It was the place she retreated to when she was mad and needed to calm down and think. Now more than ever, she needed her thinking cap on, and she needed her hideaway to do its job to help her figure out how to move her plan ahead of schedule.

College classes did not start until August, and it was mid-July. Ruby drummed her fingers on the cover of the book in her lap. Then she smiled to herself, realizing this could be a good thing. Her smile grew even more as she thought about how this would give her time to get settled, find a place to live, and be all set for studying. Yes! *This is a good thing.* Ruby grinned, and a sense of calmness came over her. She was always able to think and get her head back on straight in her favorite spot. She sighed and gazed out the window, absorbing the sights of the front garden in full bloom. She inhaled the lovely smells wafting up the stairs from her momma's cooking.

She was going to miss her parents, her siblings, and her little alcove. A gentle breeze suddenly came up through the window, surprising Ruby, as the air was usually quite still in the alcove. She snapped back to reality and saw it as a sign from a higher power. A flush came over her face as she began to wonder how her parents were going to react when they found out she had been hiding her plan to go to university from them for almost two years.

Would they be able to trust her ever again? Would they even want her to come home to visit after deceiving them? She knew how much trust meant to her parents, and now they would realize she had led them on. How would her momma's friends treat her? After all, Zola had been the one to set the best example of how to control one's daughter amidst all the changes to the modern ways of life. Tears began to form once more, but Ruby fought them back as one tear managed to escape and trickle down her face. Ruby wiped away the tear and told herself she had to be tenacious and make her plan work, or she would be shipped off to her older sister's house, and that would be the worst possible outcome. *I know it is possible they will see how strong I am and be proud that I can stand on my own two feet!* she told herself. *Yes, that is how it will be. Now, enough of this worrying about what might be. Time to take care of things at hand.*

With that last thought, Ruby jumped up and went to her room to prepare for her date with Arthur.

Arthur arrived right on time at five o'clock to take Ruby out for a drive and a light dinner. He was always punctual, and tonight was no different. Arthur had known something was up when they had spoken on the phone, and he was eager to hear what Ruby had to say and to tell her what was on his mind too. They drove down Highway 99 for a while and then over to Drumright High School and the open field where they had spent many good times together. Arthur turned off the car, turned to look at Ruby, and leaned in for a kiss. Ruby put her hand on his chest and gently pushed him away.

"Why are we stopping here? I thought we were

going out for a quick bite and talk. I am not in the mood."

Arthur looked at her, a bit hurt. "Ruby, you know I have plans too. I had a lot to do today, but I still made it to your place on time. I'm tired of your silly games. It's time for you to tell me what is going on." He turned away and gripped the steering wheel. "I feel like you have been pulling away for some time. I do *not* feel like eating. I want to talk now. Right here, in our spot."

Ruby recognized the tone in Arthur's voice, and she knew that with all the support he had given her over the past several months, he deserved an explanation. She couldn't put it off any longer, and she needed the guilt in the pit of her stomach to go away. She didn't care what the consequences were.

"OK, if you insist." She pushed back to lean against the car door. She reached over to comb his hair back with her fingers and then stroked his face. Arthur grabbed her hand and kissed it.

"Ruby, just take a deep breath. You know I love you. You can tell me anything." He started to kiss her hand once more, but she pulled it away.

She took a deep breath as he had suggested. "OK, but it is not as easy as you think . . . Arthur, my parents know that we are not getting married, and they want to send me to live with Rilla and look for a husband."

"What! How do you know this?"

"Well, Ida Jane overheard them talking. They will most likely tell me as soon as they speak with Rilla and she agrees."

"Well, then you will tell them that you are going to university, like you planned. You tell your parents you worked hard and earned money to go and that they have no say," Arthur said in a firm voice.

Ruby shook her head. "Nothing is settled yet, so I need to put my plans into action sooner than I thought."

The words started to flow, and she spilled out her plan. Though she blushed more than once, and her stomach was in knots, she knew Arthur would understand and support her. As difficult as it was, she was speaking to a person she cared for, even loved, but not someone she was willing to settle down with forever.

There was so much more to discover in the world, and by God, she was going to do it. So, the words came out even faster as she spoke. "I cannot tell you where I am going for your own good, but one thing is for sure: it will not be in this state."

Arthur was so surprised to hear this news that he pulled away and sat up straighter. "When did you decide you are not going with me to the University of Oklahoma?"

"Arthur, you just assumed that is what I would do,

and that is what needs to be your answer. I am not telling you where I am going because I want you to be able to look my parents and brothers in the eye and tell them honestly that you had no idea what I was planning or where I am heading."

"But Ruby—," Arthur said.

"But nothing!" Ruby cut him off. "This is the way it has to be. We live in a small town, and your dad is a big deal in town. You do not want to make it hard on him by telling people you kept a big secret from my dad. You know I am right."

Arthur looked at her. He knew she had a valid point. "But Ruby, I assumed you felt the same as me and that one day we would marry and raise our family in Tulsa."

Ruby smiled and kissed him on the cheek. "Arthur, I do love you, and we are both about to go and explore a whole new world. There are so many more girls you will meet. You need to meet them. I know you love me, but you need to accept that I am not your 'forever' girl. We will stay in touch, but there is no way I will tie you down. If we are meant to be, then for sure we will be together, but for now, we have to live." With that, she leaned over and kissed him on the cheek again.

Arthur stared at Ruby, speechless for a moment. Finally, he spoke again. "Ruby, think about how often we have come to this spot. We have shared our ups and downs and, most importantly, discovered our passions." Arthur moved his hand from her knee and ran it a little farther up her leg and under her dress.

"Ruby, we have gone almost all the way. We are in love. Doesn't that mean anything to you?"

Ruby gently pushed his hand back to her knee. "Of course it does, but we also agreed we would work hard for our dreams. I love this spot and everything it represents, but now we are adults, and we have to think beyond our adolescent, backseat petting and think of the future. Do you understand?"

Arthur pulled his hand away and looked at her in amazement. He sighed. "I know you are right." He turned to face the steering wheel. "We both want to see the world beyond this small town. It is one of the reasons I love you; we are on the same page." He turned back to face her. "We both want to explore and learn from traveling, not just in surrounding towns but other states as well." He held up his hand to stop her from speaking. "Please, before you say anything, I need to finish. I had hoped this common ground meant we would venture out together after we both graduated from a school in Oklahoma. I'm not ready to move away. I'm still a bit old-fashioned and like the notion of a man protecting his woman."

"I'm sorry, Arthur. I guess as forward-thinking as you are, it is ingrained in you."

"I think you are right." He took her hand. "I like

the idea of returning here after university to live a simple life. It is the safety net I have counted on in case I don't like what I see in the city or don't fit in elsewhere. You are even stronger than I thought. You seem to have no problem striking out on your own." He pulled her hand to his lips and gently kissed it. "I can see you now for who you are . . . an independent woman. How could I have been so blind?"

"You were just hopeful, that's all," Ruby held his hand tightly.

"Yes, and blind." He chuckled. "I knew it when you hatched your plan and when I saw you dance, but I dismissed it because I love you so much. You sure are different from other girls; you are not afraid to speak your mind about politics, business, or even religion. Yet, you have a soft side to you, like an angel, the way you worked to make sure your tutoring students did well."

"That's so sweet of you to say, Arthur."

"Well, I am not happy about it, but I know I can't stop you, so I might as well help you."

Much to Ruby's surprise, he took her into his arms and gave her a long, passionate kiss that seemed to last a lifetime. She responded more out of relief that he seemed to understand than out of passion. When they finally parted, Arthur kissed her on the forehead, then cupped her chin in his hand, tapped her nose, and smiled.

"So, what is your plan, Ruby?"

Ruby hugged him. "Thank you, Arthur." She sighed loudly, then shared her plan.

He agreed to it, and they decided not to speak of it at dinner. Arthur started the engine, backed the car up, and sped off to the Robert's Hotel and Café in Drumright.

They had a quiet meal, occasionally smiling at one another, each feeling a little uncomfortable knowing what they knew. For the first time, Ruby had not enjoyed being in a car alone with Arthur. She had brought him up to date with her plans, but her feelings of relief had quickly turned to guilt, as if she had betrayed him. The drive to the café had felt like forever when it was just a few miles.

Throughout dinner, Arthur sometimes looked at her as if he would never see her again and at times seemed like he wanted to say something, but Ruby would give him a look, and he stopped. They had promised not to talk about "the plan." So, they both put on a brave face and talked about their friends' plans instead, as well as Arthur's plans for university, but they mostly ate in silence. A few folks who came into the café noticed them and greeted them as they made their way to their tables, but luckily none of their close friends happened along, as they would have known something was up.

Even Myrtle, the waitress who knew everyone

and their favorite meals, made a crack that they sure were quiet and hadn't even ordered their usual.

"What gives?" she asked.

Arthur saved the day by making a joke, and that seemed to make her happy. Arthur and Ruby looked at each other and smiled and quietly continued eating and making small talk.

After dinner, Arthur took Ruby home. He pulled into the driveway, got out of the car, walked around to Ruby's side, and opened the door for her.

"Good night, Ruby," he said. "I'm not going to walk you to the door because then I would have to speak to your parents, and I don't think I'll be able to look them in the eye."

She nodded, stood on her tiptoes, and kissed him on the cheek. She had a lump in her throat. Even though she was relieved that she had finally told him about her plan, it had still been a difficult night.

"I'll wait for your call," he said as she waved and walked up the steps and into the house.

Zola and James were surprised that Arthur had not come in, or even walked Ruby to the door. It was considered ungentlemanly to treat a girl in such a manner. Ruby only said goodnight and started up the stairs. She paused halfway to listen to her parents' conversation.

"Well, it is good we are going to Rilla's tomorrow for dinner," said Zola. "We can speak to her about our plan for Ruby. We certainly don't want Ruby to become an old maid. She will soon be eighteen. Can you imagine if she is not married by nineteen? What will people think?"

"Well, people are going to say what they want no matter what," James said. "The point is that we need to make sure our girl has a man. To think that I thought Arthur was a fine, upstanding young man. The young men today, they sure can fool you." He rustled his paper. "Poor Ruby. But we will take care of it, Zola. Don't you worry your pretty little head about it anymore tonight."

Ruby could imagine her father going back to reading his newspaper, ending the conversation, knowing Zola was going to fester and nothing he could say would stop her from the second-guessing.

Chapter 20

PLAN IN MOTION

THE NEXT DAY, SUNDAY, ARRIVED QUICKER THAN the blink of an eye, and Ruby wanted to spend time with her momma and daddy. Ruby decided to go with her dad to church, as it would be the last time for a while. She put on one of the pretty dresses her momma had made and a summer hat. Her dad always liked to show off his family to his friends at church.

After church, Ruby helped her momma prepare lunch. The family enjoyed the meal together and then, eventually, most of them scattered. Ruby asked if she could do the dishes. Her parents looked at her in surprise but did not argue She knew they just assumed her heart was breaking. When Ruby had finished in the kitchen, she started to head upstairs, but her momma asked her if she might help her with some canning. Ruby was not big on pickling watermelon rinds, but who knew when she would have this time with her momma again, so pickling it was. Zola was happy for the help. The year before, she had won the state fair for her pickle recipe, so now she was going to try her watermelon rinds.

"Ruby, it would be so great to win two years in a row! Just the thought of it makes me smile," Zola said.

"Oh, Momma, everyone loves your pickles," said Ruby. "I am sure the watermelon rinds will have the first-place ribbon as well." Ruby kissed her momma on the cheek.

Zola was very pleased, as she took excellent care of her gardens, which made her fruits and vegetables extra tasty. Most people grew some of the basic foods for their own use, as well as extras, known as "cash crops." Neighbors would sell the cash crops to provide additional income for their family.

Ruby and her friends were not as interested in growing their food. Her cohort was living and working more and more in the city and could afford to purchase fresh veggies and fruit from a local store. If they saw a person from their parents' generation selling their crops, they would buy from them while enjoying a little small talk that gave them a feeling of home.

The extra money would have come in handy in the Dinsmore household, but Ruby knew her momma always kept some hidden, as most wives did in those days. To the kids, the secret cash was known as "Momma's 'cookie jar,'" and it provided them with extra things. They would never dream of telling their dad, as it would spoil them getting special treats when Zola felt they were needed. Little did they all know that their dad knew about it but just pretended not to. He figured some things were not worth fighting over. Zola had her own need for independence.

Zola and Ruby were happy to be spending quality time together that afternoon. Each one held a secret. Ruby knew her momma's secret, thanks to Ida Jane, but she didn't think her momma knew hers, so her momma wouldn't be suspicious of Ruby's eagerness to help with the canning.

Ruby's secret was that she would be gone the next day and not see her momma for a long time. She did worry that her momma might never want to see her again because of Ruby's deceit, which made Ruby look at her momma and think about how she was the best momma ever. *If only Momma would let me go to college, it would make her the best momma for eternity.* Ruby sighed loudly.

"Is there something you want to tell me?" Zola asked.

"Oh, no, not really," Ruby said. "I was just thinking." Ruby quickly looked down and started cutting the rinds. Ruby thought about all the things her momma could do besides run a household. She remembered the day she had helped her momma deliver Gail's baby. She had been so proud of her that day.

"Well, on second thought, I do have a question," Ruby said.

"Oh?" Zola asked. "Is it about Arthur?"

"Oh, no, something totally different." Ruby wiped her hands on her apron. "Momma, did you ever dream of being a doctor? You are such a natural at knowing what to do."

"Why, Ruby, what makes you ask such a question?"

"Oh, I don't know. It just seems to me that you are very smart, and before you got married and had kids, you must have had dreams of being something other than a wife and mother." Ruby turned to face her momma.

Zola smiled. "Ruby, that was so long ago. Look how much the world has changed, from stage-coaches to motorcars, from most girls getting married at fourteen to now waiting until seventeen sometimes." She paused and rested the knife on the counter, taking a break from cutting rinds and turning her full attention to Ruby. "Sure, everyone dreams, but then life happens, and you cannot rely on what you dreamed of when you were young. You have to think about here and now, and your kids come before any of your dreams. That is why I have always told you to make smart choices. Dreams change and life changes based on what happens. And besides . . . a doctor? That is a man's job." Zola laughed. "Just thinking about the very idea of doing a man's job all day long . . ." She shook her head and turned back to chopping.

"Momma, every time you deliver a baby, you are doing what you call a 'man's job,' and you do it well."

Zola clucked her tongue but kept chopping. "Ruby, honey, the doctor taught me to assist him, not take his job. I do like medicine, and when I was young and just learning, I loved it, but I wanted to be a momma more."

"OK, so life happens. But before us kids came, did you ever dream of the future?"

"Well, I am not sure I dreamed about winning a ribbon at the state fair, though I could pickle by the time I was six." Zola screwed the lid onto another jar. "Oh, I really do not know. But I can tell you a dream my daddy told me my momma always wanted."

"Oh wow, you never really talk about your momma." Ruby plunked herself down on one of the kitchen chairs, ready for a story. "Please, tell me what she always wanted."

"OK, but bring me the box of new jars from the cabinet first." Zola smiled as Ruby jumped up to fetch them. She placed them on the counter next to her momma and sat back down.

Zola began her story. "My momma always wanted to see Galveston, and that is why my brother's middle name is Galveston. My parents were saving their money to move us there one day."

Ruby could see the sadness in her momma's eyes. "Wow, your life could have been so different."

"Yes, it could have," she agreed. "And if Momma had lived, you would not be here. But I still would not change a thing. Life happens, and choices have to be made. Now, enough with all this talk. We need to finish up here. Your sister has invited your daddy and me to supper today, and I need to get some other things done if we are to drive up to Seminole." Zola paused, then turned to Ruby. "But before we do, I have to ask. Is everything OK with you and Arthur?"

"Oh yes, it could not be better," Ruby said.

Zola smiled. "Good. I was a bit worried."

Ruby was glad her momma was satisfied with the answer, as she did not want to lead her momma on with things that could not be.

"Oh my, where has the time gone?" Zola glanced at her wristwatch. She was one of the lucky few who even had one in Oilton. "I need to start getting ready to go to your sister's for dinner. What a lovely Sunday, Ruby. Nothing could have been more perfect than spending it with you."

Her momma blew her a kiss as if she were a little girl. Ruby caught it, recalling the game they used to play, and put the kiss on her cheek.

"Aw, Momma, you remembered," Ruby said. "It was fun for me too." She untied her apron. "Well, I think I might take an afternoon nap. You have fun at Rilla's and tell them hello for me."

With that, Ruby made her way upstairs. Her younger siblings were down the street playing with friends and would not be returning home till her parents returned from Rilla's. It could not be any more perfect than if Ruby had planned it herself. She would be able to sneak out without being noticed.

She climbed into bed fully clothed, pulled the covers up to her chin, and strained her ears to hear her parents gathering their things to take to Rilla's. As soon as she heard the car start and then the tires crunching on the gravel as they headed down the laneway, she hopped out of bed and immediately began packing. She called Arthur, and they had a short conversation with their pre-planned code words in case the operator was listening in, as she always did.

"Well, I do hope you have a nice time visiting the university," Ruby said.

Arthur played along, knowing it was time to get to her place. They continued their conversation, and Ruby could hear the operator breathing lightly on the other end of the line.

"Ruby, dear, I do hope you will consider the question I asked you the other night," Arthur said, really giving the operator something to talk about.

Ruby stifled a giggle. "Oh, Arthur, I am considering it. But now I need to go, OK? Love you."

"Love you too," Arthur replied.

In a flash, Arthur was at Ruby's door. She let him in and grabbed the suitcase she had hidden under a blanket, along with a picnic basket. If someone saw them leaving the house together, they would just think they were going on a picnic. Ruby looked at the living room one more time. She wanted to remember this moment. She took a deep breath and turned around and walked out the door and to the car. Ruby and Arthur headed to the train station. Ruby's heart started pounding, and she demanded that Arthur pull the car over. Confused, Arthur kept driving, and Ruby screamed for him to pull over.

"OK, OK . . . What a temper!"

He waited for some horses to get out of the way and did as she wanted.

"Now, Ruby, what is it?"

"I don't know. I am scared all of a sudden. What am I doing?" She started digging in her purse. "Let's see. Do I have my money? I have clothes, toothbrush, walking shoes." She was shaking as she took mental note of everything she would need. "But I don't really know what I'll need." Her voice rose an octave. "I've never lived on my own before. Oh, please tell me I can do this. Don't let me back down." She reached for Arthur's hand.

"Ruby, nothing would please me more than for you to not go through with this, but I know you. You have to do this. You will regret it for the rest of your life if you don't. I love you too much for that. I have painted the perfect picture of us growing old together, but that is not you. You have to see what the big wide world has for you. I will be here for you if you change your mind." A nervous laugh snuck out of her as Arthur continued. "So, take a deep breath, and let's make sure you do not miss your train. You have worked too hard for this to turn back now."

"Right! Thank you. I just had a moment where I knew I was going to miss my momma. I will be fine. I will pretend I am in the middle of a novel and take life as it comes."

"OK, then let's go!"

Ruby looked at him with determination in her eyes, turned to face front, and sat up straight. She clung tightly to her purse with both hands and smiled.

"Yes, I have a train to catch!"

Arthur put the car in drive, pulled out onto the

road, and off they went, heading to the Drumright train station.

Ruby didn't let Arthur walk her inside, as she did not want people to see her with him. She also still refused to tell him where she was going. Ruby wanted him to be able to truthfully say that he had no clue where she was headed. They hugged in the car and said their goodbyes. Ruby promised to get in touch, but it would be a while; she would have to wait until people were tired of trying to see if Arthur had been in contact. Arthur drove off as planned, and Ruby purchased a one-way ticket to Tulsa. Ruby had set her plan in motion. She was college-bound.

Part Three

PLAN IN ACTION

Chapter 21

THE JOURNEY BEGINS

THE TRAIN COULD NOT PULL OUT OF DRUMRIGHT soon enough for Ruby. She was so worried that someone would see her on the train and tell her parents. As the train departed the station and gained speed, Ruby looked at the familiar surroundings whizzing by. Her stomach was in knots.

In the past, her few trips by train to Tulsa with her friends had seemed to go quickly, but in this case, it seemed to take forever. As the train came to a jerky halt, she stood up and grabbed her belongings and made her way to the ticket office. She had already done her homework months earlier to learn the train schedules and determine when and where she needed to be to make it to her destination the cheapest way. Ruby would need to go in the opposite direction to catch the longest train to her new life.

KMT was the next rail company she needed to take. Ruby had read about the Pullman and was excited to be taking the larger train on this particular line. The train would not leave for another hour. She purchased a ticket and made her way to the platform. In no time, the train was at the rail station, ready for passengers to board. Ruby showed her boarding pass to the porter and climbed onto the train. She quickly made her way to car six and found her seat. She put her luggage away and made herself comfortable. Ruby pulled out a magazine to hide her face from the window and anyone who was boarding the train in hopes of avoiding discovery. She kept taking long, deep breaths and slowly letting them out, hoping it would make the train leave sooner, but to no avail. The more Ruby anticipated taking off, the slower time seemed to go. With the last deep breath almost fifteen minutes later, the whistle blew, and the train finally started up. Ruby closed her eyes and gave thanks and a sigh of relief before she opened her eyes again.

The train started building speed as they moved out of the station. It was not till Ruby finally saw the wide open countryside that she was able to take a real breath and relax. A wide smile took over her face, as she was genuinely beginning her journey.

Then she remembered! Arthur had given her a small package and said to open it once she was settled on the train. She pulled out the sack it was in and opened it. Ruby grinned with satisfaction at Arthur's thoughtful gift— a book she had wanted to read for some time. Ruby saw a folded piece of paper, and she took it out and slowly opened it. Arthur had written her a short letter.

Dear Ruby,

If you are reading this, then for sure you are well on your way to your new life. I am think-ing I am a fool for letting you go. Then again, I know I really was not letting you do anything, as no one tells Ruby what to do. I think that is one of the qualities I cherish about you—your independence, your love of life and learning. You are my butterfly. You are beautiful, like no other, and you have wings of love for all the people you touch. You have a gift to be shared. I guess I always knew you would fly away, and eventually your strength will allow you to soar like an eagle. I believe in you. I got you a little gift to help the train ride go a little faster. I remembered you wanted to read this book, so I hope you will enjoy it and, every once in a while, glance up and look out the window

and think of me. I hope you discover what you
are looking for. You have my heart, and I will
always be there for you.

Love,
Arthur

Ruby stared at the letter, thinking how lucky she was to have given her heart for the first time to such a dear person. She folded the letter, looked out the window, and blew Arthur a kiss. Ruby kept staring out the window as if to watch her kiss catch a breeze that would take it to Arthur. As the train began traveling even faster, she took out her new book again and read the title, *The Enchanted April*, by Elizabeth von Arnim. She had been wanting to read it for some time but had not wanted to spend the money. *What a thoughtful gift. He knows me so well. This for sure will help calm my nerves*, she thought. But she soon discovered that no matter how much she tried to read, she could not concentrate. She read the same paragraph over and over and still did not know what she had read. Each time, she would glance up, take a deep breath, and let it out. There was no way she was going to get any reading done, so she tucked her book into her purse for later. Once more, she hid behind her magazine and pretended to be interested in what it had to offer.

Finally, they started slowing down, and Ruby prepared to exit the train, very much aware of her surroundings. Ruby felt pretty sure she would not be recognized by anyone. Even though she knew her dad had lots of friends in Tulsa, she prayed she wouldn't run into any of them. She stepped onto the platform and made her way to the powder room; and, of course, there was someone in there. She stood there tapping her foot in anticipation. Finally, the door opened, and Ruby squeezed inside, suitcase and all. The tiny room had a small mirror above the sink with barely any room to do the business at hand. She managed to pull a wig out of her purse and put it on. Ruby left the powder room with shoulder-length, straight blond hair and proceeded to the ticket office, where she purchased a ticket to Kansas City, Missouri.

Luckily, she did not have to give her name, but she was prepared if asked. The ticket master was so busy that he did not even look up. He just requested the destination, told her how much, handed her a ticket with the change, and asked the next person to step up. Ruby turned around and noticed several other people had joined the line. She looked down so as not to catch any of their eyes and headed to the platform to wait for her train.

Again, time seemed to pass in slow motion. Ruby watched as the smoke-colored train entered the station and people disembarked. Finally, the porter announced that the train was ready for boarding, so Ruby grabbed her things and climbed aboard. She prayed no one would be sitting next to her, but the chances seemed slim with so many people boarding. The Pullman had larger aisles compared to the other passenger trains she had ridden. The chandeliers were simple but elegant, and as for the seats, they were comfortable enough to make a long train ride bearable. Ruby located her seat on the right-hand side of the train, placed her luggage in the overhead compartment, and took out her magazine to hide behind and remain incognito. Much to her surprise, the train immediately pulled away from the station, bound for Missouri, with no one sitting next to her. She could not believe her luck. The train started chugging away, and she thought about how her dream was coming true. Her thoughts were going wild with anticipation of what was to come, and yet she wondered what her parents would do when they read her letter. She had tried to be as kind and loving as possible for a girl who was about to run away to go to college.

Her letter read:

Dear Momma and Daddy,

If you are reading this note, then I know you

have discovered that I am gone. I need to go away for a while. I did not tell you because I do not want you to look for me. I will not tell you what I am up to either. I have been planning this for some time. I will not contact you, as I have no desire for you to find me. Just know that I love you both so very much. You are the best parents any girl could ask for. I love my family, I really do, but I have this hunger to see the world. So, let me go. I will make you proud, I promise. I am sorry, Momma, to break your heart. I do not mean to, but just know that when I come home, you will be so proud of all my accomplishments. I just need you to let me go so that I may discover who I am meant to be. Please know that I love you both.

Love,
Ruby Pearl

Ruby's plan had worked. She was going to college. Mixed emotions coursed through her body—excitement about what was going to happen and guilt about how her parents would react to her leaving. Ruby knew she still had several hours before they would return home from Rilla's and find her letter. She didn't think she had been spotted by anyone she knew, so it would be a while before her dad and his friends tracked her down, as she knew they would eventually. Ruby felt split in half. On the one hand, she was living her dream, one she hoped her parents would see her way, but on the other hand, she felt a deep, gut-wrenching guilt that caused a massive knot in her stomach. With each new thought, the knot intensified. She wanted to throw up. She knew she had terrific parents and felt terrible that she had left without their knowledge. Trying desperately to rationalize it in her mind, Ruby just could not get over the fact that they felt the need to marry her off. Well, now she would focus now on making them proud.

The train was now going at full speed, and she looked up at the puffy clouds dotting the beautiful blue sky and saw what had to be a sign; there were angel wings painted in the clouds. She gave thanks, smiled, and began to relax and enjoy the ride, though not without a few twinges of guilt and anxiety along the way.

It was a constant mental battle. As each new person passed through the car or boarded the train at a new stop, she would just look at her magazine and let her long hair cover her face in hopes that no one would see her and be able to report back to her father once his "spies" started looking for her. With each lurch of the train, her mind would go back to her momma, who did not deserve Ruby leaving the way she had. She just hoped her momma could forgive her one day.

The five-hour trip seemed like a lifetime, but when Ruby had finally relaxed and dozed off, the train came to a shuddering halt, which woke her up. She opened her eyes and looked out at Kansas City, Missouri. It was the last stop, and all the commuters hustled and bustled, preparing to exit. Ruby grabbed her things and shuffled along with the crowd as everyone exited the train.

She was amazed at how much bigger the train station was there, but she knew the one thing that they all had in common was the schedules. Her research had shown that she would have to spend one night in Kansas City and then take two more trains to her final destination. She looked up the commuter train to a town called Cameron, and from there it would be another train to Chillicothe that left at ten o'clock in the morning. She purchased her ticket for the next day and caught the streetcar to Raphael Hotel, where she would stay the night.

Ruby checked in and made her way to her room. Once she was in her room, she opened the window for fresh air and a little breeze. Ruby hit the bed and fell asleep with her clothes on. She had no idea how tired she had been until the sun woke her the next day. Ruby slowly got out of bed and made her way to the bathroom, splashed her face with some cold water to wake herself up, and began to towel off. She had time to relax before she needed to head out but found it hard to sit still. She pulled out a banana that she had packed and ate it while she sat there thinking about how it was all going to work out. Her wig had moved around while she was sleeping, so she straightened it and made herself presentable for the last leg of her journey. She waited in her room till it was time to check out, and then, once more, she made her way to the train depot to wait for her train.

By now, the word would be out, and people would know she was missing, which made her nervous and self-conscious when anyone looked at her. She buried her face in her magazine and prayed that there would be no members of her dad's Mason network around. They were a tight-knit group, and word could travel quite rapidly from town to town. It was the one time Ruby wasn't happy about all the time she had spent with her father, listening to him as he conducted business. She had always felt unseen, but now she was unsure.

She boarded the small commuter train and headed for Cameron. As the train was pulling into the junction, Ruby saw how beautiful the train station was; it was painted red with green trim and had a sign that read "Welcome to Cameron." *One more stop to go*, she thought as she purchased her final ticket to Chillicothe. She had a one-hour wait and reached into her bag for an orange, thinking how she may never eat another orange again. She longed for one of her momma's breakfasts, but that is the price you pay when you strike out on your own.

The hour crawled by, but eventually the train pulled up and Ruby boarded. Before she knew it, she was stepping off the train at her final destination; Chillicothe, Missouri. She had done it! She was standing there in the town she had dreamed about, the town where she would start her new life! She stood in wonder. She could not believe she had arrived.

After taking it all in and hearing the sound of the next train blowing its whistle, she turned her focus to getting a place to stay. Ruby looked for the newsstand. She would pick up the local paper to have in her room to comb through the want ads. Ruby planned to stay at the Leeper Hotel for a few nights, thanks to her friends who had surprised her with money to pay for three nights at a hotel. She hoped this would give her enough time to find a job as well as room and board.

She made her way to the street and got directions to the hotel. The gentleman working at the newsstand told her which streetcar to take and where to get off. She adjusted her wig. He was the one person she had been in contact with for an extended conversation, so she hoped that if anyone asked, he would recall the girl with long blond hair, and nothing else.

She got off the streetcar half a block from the hotel and walked in, trying to look "worldly" while her heart practically pounded out of her chest. Much to her surprise, the desk clerk didn't seem at all suspicious of a single girl checking into a hotel, which clearly would not have been the case if it had happened in her hometown.

Ruby thanked the desk clerk, took her key, and walked down the freshly carpeted hallway. She stopped at her door and turned the key in the lock, then closed the door behind her and leaned her back against the door. She perused her surroundings, soaking it all in. She wanted to remember every little detail to tell Ida Jane the next time she saw her, whenever that would be.

She flopped enthusiastically onto the bed, looked up at the ceiling, and took a deep breath. "Oh my goodness, I am here," she said out loud.

She spent the rest of the evening eating crackers that she had purchased at the newsstand and drinking water from the faucet. She marked up her newspaper, circling possible jobs and places to stay close to the college. She was a few weeks early for school, and she realized that would work to her advantage. It would give her time to get settled into a job before she added her studies to her schedule. The next chapter in her life was indeed beginning.

Chapter 22

ROOM AND BOARD

THE MORNING SUN CAME SHINING THROUGH THE lace curtains and woke Ruby to a beautiful new day. She popped out of bed, washed her face, and dressed with confidence that the world was there for her taking. She grabbed the newspaper with the want ads she had marked the night before, as well as the possible places to live. She was on the second floor of the four-story hotel, and as much as she wanted to take the stairs, she decided she would be less conspicuous if she took the elevator. The gentlemen working the elevator went by the name of Mr. Jeb. He was very friendly, as she had assumed he would be considering the job he was doing. He asked where she was heading, and they exchanged a few pleasantries. He suggested that if she was looking for something to eat, he would highly recommend the restaurant in the hotel, but if she wanted to dine outside, he was partial to the nearby Schneider's Star Café. Ruby had seen an ad for the café and was happy to hear that it was one of his favorites and was close by. She walked off the elevator with a spring in her step, ready to take on the world. But first things first. Today, she was actually going to enjoy a hot breakfast . . . her first real meal since she had left home.

It was a warm summer day with a clear blue sky. There were stores on both sides of the street surrounding the hotel, and people were already up and bustling around with their daily activities. As Ruby was taking it all in, a gentleman walked by and tipped his hat at her and wished her good day. She smiled and returned his greeting. Ruby thought, *How strange to be greeted like a grown-up, just like Momma would have been.* Then it dawned on her—she was officially a grown-up! *Silly girl.* She had made her own decision and run away to college because she was an adult now. And now she had gotten her first tip of the hat without her mom being around. She giggled and then recalled some of her firsts . . . her first brassiere, her first double-digit birthday, her first updo, and her first kiss. Firsts were important in Ruby's mind, as she saw them as milestones. So, with those memories noted,

Ruby looked at the stores surrounding her hotel to remember a few landmarks so that she would be able to find her way back.

Feeling very grown up, she strutted down the street, following Mr. Jeb's directions, smiling and greeting everyone she saw. Before she knew it, she was standing in front of the café. Mr. Jeb's directions were flawless. As she walked in, she read a sign that said, "Make yourself at home and find a seat." She spotted a corner table away from the window and made her way there. Her stomach seemed to jump for joy with the aroma of so many breakfast foods being cooked. She sat down and put her purse on the seat next to her. Ruby ordered two over-medium fried eggs, bacon, hash browns, toast, and a cup of coffee with cream. As she waited for her food, she pulled her paper out of her bag and began reading it. She didn't want to talk to anyone just yet. She knew her dad's Freemason brothers would eventually be looking for her, but for now, the less people noticed her, the better. Once she got settled, it wouldn't matter as much. She relaxed and started reading the local news and learning about her new town.

The waitress brought Ruby her coffee and, as all good waitresses do, started asking questions as she poured.

"So, you're new around here." It was more of a statement than a question.

"Why, yes, I am," Ruby responded.

"So, what brings you here?"

"I am registered to attend college. I am very excited."

"Oh, I should have guessed. You look really smart." She smiled. "Enjoy your coffee. I'll have your breakfast out shortly."

Ruby laughed. *This day just gets better and better,* she thought. *Yup, this is going to be a good town to live in.*

Ruby continued to read the paper until her breakfast was served. Her stomach did somersaults, knowing the food on the table in front of her was about to be devoured.

"Enjoy your food, and, by the way, my name is Lizzy," the waitress said. "What's yours?"

"I am Pearl," Ruby said. She had been practicing her answer to that very question on the train ride and felt it had come out very convincingly. After all, it was part of her name.

"Nice to meet you, Pearl." Lizzy shook her hand. "If you need anything else, you just holler."

Ruby smiled and said thank you, then turned to butter her toast and smother it with fresh grape jelly. There was nothing like a piece of hot toast with melted butter and grape jelly. It was a heavenly feeling, especially when you had not had a proper meal in a few days. Ruby chewed slowly, enjoying each bite as if it were her last. She almost hated to see her plate emptied of food, as she did not want her meal to end. So, she ordered a third cup of coffee, as refills were free.

Finally, she couldn't stretch breakfast out any longer. The time came to pay up and hit the road. Ruby did not dare ask for directions; instead, she decided to first walk the main street and see if any of the businesses had a job posted in the window. Walking the main road also allowed Ruby to learn how the town was mapped out and get a feel for the different street names without drawing attention to herself. The town was much bigger than Oilton, and even Drumright, for that matter. There were no buildings made out of wood. They were all made out of brick instead. The storefronts had large windows to attract buyers. You could practically see the entire store without even walking in. The stores were at ground level with sidewalks in front. Women who were still wearing floor-length dresses were no longer getting their hems dirty as they didn't have to walk on the dusty roads. Girls of Ruby's age were wearing more revealing clothes that actually showed their legs, which often brought a disapproving eyebrow raise from some of the more prudish women. But as Ruby saw it, she was a modern woman now, a woman who could make up her own mind about what she wanted out of life, including how she was going to dress. So Ruby thought, *Let the eyebrows be raised.*

She knew she was a good Christian girl with strong morals. Ruby was raised properly, taught to study, work hard, and help others. So even if her legs were showing, it was just a sign of the times. It was time for a woman to break away from old habits, to be brave and bold, and to take a stand for women to be educated and do things beyond running a household. Of course, this was where she and her parents had a difference of opinion. Ruby only hoped that one day they would be proud of her.

She stopped to read a sign in one of the shop windows: "Wanted—Store Clerk."

"This is it." Ruby threw back her shoulders and walked in, so excited to see the job opening that she did not even realize that she had walked into a hardware store, which was basically a man's store. As Ruby looked around and saw all the tools and paints, it made her think of Arthur. She spun quickly around and left the store. Once outside, she could not help but giggle. Of all the stores to have a job opening, it had to be one more suited to Arthur. One day, she would write to him and tell him. He too would think it was funny. So off she went to continue her search. She got to the end of the road and crossed to the other side, where she saw a bench for customers in front of a store. She took a seat and got out her paper to scan the want ads again.

There were only three job openings, and she thought she might have better luck if she went in person. She looked at the addresses and now knew exactly where the streets were, as she had passed them earlier. It turned out that she was on the right side of the road. So, off she went to see if her luck would change. The first ad was for a butcher. That was not going to work. Even if she wanted to, she could not stand a chicken with its head cut off, so she certainly could not stand seeing a cow hanging from a hook. The WW Smith Produce store was looking for a bookkeeper, but even though she was at the store early, they had filled the position the day before. It turned out they wanted someone with experience, so she was not qualified anyway. Ruby hated having to go to so many places. It felt as though, with each stop, she was leaving bread-crumbs for her dad to locate her, but she had no choice but to continue looking. She needed a job.

The third job opening was at the general store. As Ruby walked there, she hoped this would be the one, but someone had beaten her to that job too. She was feeling down at that point and a little nervous. She only had enough money for two more nights, and a job would be essential to pay rent, unless she found a boarding house where she could work for her rent. As Ruby continued down Main Street, she didn't see any more "help wanted" signs, so she decided to check down the next street, hoping for better luck. As she turned right, she heard laughter from a distance, so Ruby thought she would head toward it and see what she could see just to get her mind off her current dilemma.

She rounded a corner and she saw where the laughter was coming from. There was a small park where moms were letting their young children play. Ruby walked over to an empty park bench a short distance away from the moms, hoping none of them would speak to her. She pulled out her paper and started looking for any houses that were advertising room and board. Ruby looked at her watch and saw it was almost eleven o'clock, but maybe she could see one house before lunchtime. She checked the address of one she thought was close by and went to find it.

It was difficult not having a map and not really knowing where she was or how the street names could change midway. Ruby walked and walked and never saw the street she was looking for, so she headed back to the hotel because she knew it would be impolite to call on someone during the noon hour.

Once in her room, she flopped onto the bed, a little worried about how the day would end. She wanted to keep positive, but negative thoughts kept popping into her head. In frustration, she grabbed a pillow and covered her head, hoping to quiet her mind and think happy thoughts. Under the pillow, she took a deep breath and prayed that the angels would watch over her. She decided to take an afternoon nap.

It was three o'clock in the afternoon when Ruby woke up. Realizing she had slept longer than she had meant to, she quickly freshened up and headed back out. Ruby walked and walked and finally found one of the houses that had advertised room and board. She knocked on the door and asked if there was still a room available, as she did not see the sign in the window. The lady explained that she had rented out the last room about five minutes before. Ruby thanked her and asked if she knew where the next street on her list was. With new directions, she walked briskly in hopes that she was ahead of the next person looking for a place. The house was about three blocks away, and once she had found it, she thought it seemed perfectly warm and inviting, with flower boxes on the steps and pretty white shutters on the windows. Ruby knocked on the door and inquired about the ad in the paper. The woman repeated what the previous landlady had said. She had rented out her last room earlier in the day. The woman was very kind and told Ruby about another neighbor who was looking for a young lady boarder. So, Ruby took down the information and headed that way, only to find out that it had been rented too. It was now five o'clock, and there would be no more looking for jobs or houses to rent that day. Ruby headed to the grocery store to pick up a few items to eat and drink in her room, as well as the afternoon edition of the *Chillicothe Constitution-Tribune* for more leads. She would need to spend the evening scouring it to plan her hunt for the next day.

Morning came, and off Ruby went to the café to have breakfast. Lizzy was working, and Ruby had decided that she would make a good ally. She would make sure to tip Lizzy and maybe take her into her confidence. Hopefully, Lizzy would keep Ruby's secret when people came looking for her.

Ruby took the same table in the back and began scanning the newspaper, hoping to see something she might have missed, and, sure enough, she did. Lizzy was happy to see Ruby return, and she made sure Ruby had plenty of coffee and, of course, peppered her with questions that Ruby tried to answer with as little information as possible. A new customer walked in, so off Lizzy went to greet them.

"Bacon, eggs, hash browns, butter, and toast . . . yum . . . but what I would give to have one of Momma's fresh biscuits with gravy," Ruby mumbled under her breath. She had seen biscuits with gravy and grits on the menu but was not ready to taste anyone else's recipes, as it would be like letting a piece of her momma go. Her momma took so much pride in her biscuits and gravy, and Ruby was afraid that she would take one bite and it would make her cry. She was missing her momma more than she could have ever imagined she would. Ruby had to work hard to put those feelings out of her mind so that she could stay focused on the goal for the day. Positivity was what she needed. Ruby took her last sip of coffee, left Lizzy a tip, and left to job hunt.

On Ruby's way out, Lizzy called to her. "Good luck with your hunt, Pearl."

"Thanks, Lizzy," Ruby called back over her shoulder as she walked out the door.

The day's job hunting took her to places closer to the train station. Thanks to Lizzy, Ruby had been able to get directions. Ruby had to trust someone, and she decided it might as well be the person who seemed to want to know everything about her. It was a good walk, but Ruby had brought flats and would change into heels once she arrived at the job sites.

Each job opening only brought disappointment.

Ruby was determined not to give up, so she walked back to the park and looked at her paper, deciding she would switch and look for room and board. She could not waste time. She was very much aware that her money was running out, and there was no way she going to give up and call home.

Ruby was very industrious. She mapped out the street names as she went so that she would recognize them in the future. It proved to be very helpful, as she found a few homes quickly, but other students had beat her to them. A job and a room were nowhere to be found. The day came and went, and Ruby returned to her hotel, discouraged. She saw Mr. Jeb, who gave her a lift to her floor. He was in a chipper mood, which always made Ruby smile. She thought about how her parents would like him, a hard worker who knew the people and history of the town. He was very proud to say that he had been born and raised in Chillicothe. Ruby did not let on that she was worried about her job search; she left him with a smile and walked to her room.

Once inside, she opened her window, hoping for a cool breeze, and plopped onto her bed, wondering what she would do. She tried reading to keep her mind off her problems. She was using the letter Arthur had given her as a bookmark, and before she knew it, she was reading the letter once more. With each sentence, she wondered if she had made a mistake. Maybe she was not meant to be here; maybe her life was supposed to be with Arthur. After all, he understood her more than anyone. Perhaps she would end up going to school after he finished his education. Maybe her sister was right. Was she supposed to stay home, marry, and have babies? Maybe Bessie was right, and they were supposed to have kids at the same time so that their children could be best friends, just like them.

The second-guessing flooded Ruby's mind till it drove her crazy. She had to go to the window and inhale some fresh air to see if she could jar her thoughts and clear her mind. She looked out at the big blue sky filled with puffy white clouds and then glanced down at the street where people were carrying on with their daily lives, oblivious to her turmoil. Ruby took a few more deep breaths and closed her eyes. She imagined that everything was settled, and her parents knew where she was, and everyone was happy. Finally, she came out of her trance as her stomach started to growl, so Ruby decided to eat some butter and rolls she had saved for dinner. She glanced at the paper and felt that she had looked at it enough. She would retire early. Tomorrow would be a better day.

Morning came, and Ruby went downstairs, picked up a newspaper at the desk, and brought it back to read in her room. She looked at the ads for jobs, but there were no new ones for which she was qualified. Ruby looked for the accommodation ads, saw a few new ones listed, and circled them. Around nine o'clock, she left the hotel and started walking to the homes listed in the ads. It was an unusually chilly morning for that time of year, but Ruby was grateful since she was on foot and the walking would warm her up. Three houses later, she had no good news, and it was getting on to lunchtime. Ruby decided to head to the café and eat her frustrations away. As she entered, Lizzy was so excited to see her.

"Well, speak of the devil, look who just walked in," Lizzy said to the customer she was serving.

Ruby smiled and waved. Lizzy waved back and motioned for her to come over.

"Pearl, this is Mrs. Bocook," Lizzy said. "I was just telling her all about you. She's all by herself, and she'd love for you to join her for lunch."

Mrs. Bocook wouldn't take no for an answer, so before Ruby knew it, she was having lunch with her.

Mrs. Bocook peppered Ruby with all sorts of questions, and, in the end, she learned that Ruby was looking for room and board while she attended school. Mrs. Bocook told her that she had just filled her room but thought her friend still had a place open.

"Pearl, how would you like me to call my friend and see if she will interview you today if she still has a place open?"

Before Ruby could answer, Mrs. Bocook excused herself to make the call. She returned to the table soon after with good news. "Come on, Pearl, you will not believe this. She wants to meet you now. I told her how you passed my interview, and she's eager to meet you. Let's pay our bill and go."

"Oh, my! Thank you so much!" Ruby did not even ask for the check, as she already knew how much to leave and placed the money with a little tip on the table.

"Thanks, Lizzy. I left my money on the table, and so did Mrs. Bocook," Ruby said as they rushed toward the door.

"Yes, I am paid up too. Thanks, Lizzy. See you soon," Mrs. Bocook said as she followed Pearl out the door.

"Thank you so much, Mrs. Bocook," Ruby gushed.

"Don't thank me yet; you don't have the room," she said with a smile and a wink. "And she'll expect you to do some housecleaning if you're living there." The older lady bustled along. "Follow me, Pearl. She lives just around the corner. Oh, and her name is Phoebe MacAfee."

Ruby had a good feeling about this house as they approached the front door. It reminded her of home, except it was much smaller and the porch walls were made of stone. Ruby thought it would be easy to clean a house that size and go to school as well. She saw a woman peek out the white lace curtains, and then the door opened. The woman greeted them and escorted them into the parlor, where tea was waiting.

"Phoebe, this is Pearl, the young lady I told you about," said Mrs. Bocook.

"Thank you for seeing us on such short notice, Mrs. MacAfee," Ruby said.

Mrs. MacAfee smiled. "Well, you have my friend to thank for that. It's nice to meet you, Pearl. Please, come in and sit."

Ruby was starting to get used to being called Pearl. She learned that Mrs. MacAfee was a widow, even though she was only fifty. She was happy to have a young girl who wanted to be educated, clean her home, and keep her company. Mrs. MacAfee shared what she expected from a young lady in return for her room and board. Ruby was taking in her surroundings as Mrs. MacAfee spoke. *This should be a piece of cake.*

Mrs. MacAfee finished with her spiel but then caught Ruby off guard when she asked, "So tell me young lady, why the wig?"

Ruby looked startled and said, "Oh, you can tell?"

Both women chuckled. "Of course we can," said Mrs. Bocook.

"Well," Ruby stammered. "Oh dear . . . OK, look. I will be frank. I need a place to live, and I will work very hard to make you happy. I saved all my money so that I could attend school and live in a big town. I did not want to get married and just can pickles." Ruby gasped, seeing the ladies' eyebrows raise. "I mean, I hope I—"

She was cut off by Mrs. MacAfee. "You mean you don't want to be old maids, like us?" she asked, pretending to be offended.

"No, I didn't mean that. I just meant that a girl can do lots more, just like a boy."

The ladies asked more detailed questions, wanting "Pearl" to clarify what she meant. Ruby was getting a little nervous, but this time she chose her words more carefully so as not to offend the women.

Finally, Mrs. Bocook laughed out loud. "OK, Phoebe, quit teasing her. She has had enough."

Ruby looked puzzled but did not say a word.

"All right," Mrs. MacAfee said. "Pearl, I was just putting you on. I am a firm believer that women should be able to vote, and now we do, and we certainly can work a cash register as well as any man. You are what I am looking for. I just have two more questions." She paused as Ruby squirmed. "Is the law looking for you, and what is your natural hair color?"

They all laughed, and Ruby relaxed, feeling she could trust both of these women, who were motherly yet obviously open-minded. She informed them that the law was not looking for her, but her dad, who was a thirty-two-degree Mason, would most certainly have people looking for her, hence the disguise.

"My name is Ruby Pearl, but I usually go by just Ruby. I decided to go by my middle name so that if anyone from out of town asked about me, the locals would only know me as Pearl and the name Ruby would not be familiar to them."

The women just listened till Ruby removed her wig and her beautiful auburn hair fell down to her shoulders.

"Lord have mercy!" Mrs. Bocook said. "Isn't she a looker!"

"She sure is!" agreed Mrs. MacAfee. "Now Pearl, as beautiful as that hair is, you must keep it up in a bun, no makeup, and there are no boys allowed in the house. We will work on a chore schedule once you get your school schedule. You will have free room and board, and if you do a good job, I will give you a little spending money each week. How does that sound?"

"That sounds just perfect," Ruby said. "Oh, thank you kindly. You both will not be disappointed."

"I better not be," said Mrs. MacAfee in a voice that reminded Ruby that she was her boss, not her mom. "Now, I have one more question. Do you still wish to be called Pearl?"

"Yes, please, as it will help to delay my dad finding me. I will eventually tell my parents, but I want to prove to them that I can make good grades and stand on my own. I want them to be proud of me," Ruby explained.

"Fine. Then Pearl it is," said Mrs. MacAfee. "It is exhilarating to be part of a young girl's plan to better herself in the world. Your secret is safe with both of us."

Mrs. Bocook nodded in agreement, and they all exchanged pleasantries as they finished their tea.

Mrs. Bocook made her way home, which was just around the block, while Mrs. MacAfee showed Ruby around the house—where her room would be, where all the cleaning supplies were stored. She then explained in more detail how she expected the house to be kept tidy.

"How soon can you move in?" Mrs. McAfee asked.

"I can move in tomorrow," said Ruby. "I am all paid up at the hotel but can check out first thing in the morning, unless you want me tonight."

"Tomorrow morning will be fine. Let's say after eleven o'clock. I have a meeting early in the morning."

"Perfect," Ruby said. "Oh, thank you so much. You will not regret it."

"I hope not." Mrs. MacAfee stood with her hands on her hips and then winked.

Ruby smiled. Mrs. MacAfee was a warm, gentle woman, whom she thought her momma would for sure like.

"Well, I will excuse myself and see you in the morning," said Ruby. "Unless I can help you with anything before I leave?"

"Thank you. I am fine. Let me see you to the door."

As Ruby turned around to wave goodbye from the street, she saw Mrs. MacAfee take the "room available" sign out of the window and wave back. Ruby smiled and walked back to the hotel. That night, she had the best sleep that she had had since leaving Oilton. She had finally found her new home.

Chapter 23

COLLEGE DAYS

RUBY WOKE UP WITH A MASSIVE WEIGHT OFF HER shoulders; she had room and board. That morning, she had breakfast in the hotel and enjoyed every bite along with her cup of coffee. Ruby took extra time for a leisurely scan of the local paper, minus the want ads, which was a fabulous feeling. As she read, she learned more about her new community.

Ruby had already learned in the few days since she had arrived that, like Drumright, fires had claimed many of the original oak and walnut wood frame buildings in Chillicothe. Now the town had beautiful, tall two- and three-story brick buildings. She learned that Chillicothe had begun to grow and prosper even more with the railway station. City lights were even run by electricity. Ruby thought about how many towns still did not have electricity, but she was happy to have the conveniences that she had had in Oilton in her new home of Chillicothe. A small, satisfied grin grew wider on Ruby's face with each turn of the newspaper's pages, but it all came to a crashing halt as she read an announcement about the unexpected death of a baby girl in town named Lilly. For a moment, Ruby's kind heart and gentle ways overshadowed the determined young woman who was ready to change the world, and she wept for the family who had lost their baby.

Ruby recalled helping her momma with the delivery of Gail's baby and the sadness she had felt about the young father never knowing he was a dad. Once more, Ruby thought of her momma and the heartache she must have felt when reading the letter Ruby had left behind.

With that thought, Ruby took a deep breath and sighed as she folded the newspaper, took her last sip of coffee, and went upstairs to pack. She couldn't help thinking about her momma and wondering what she was doing. Ruby missed her more than words could express. She had never dreamed that she could miss home as much as she did. She looked in the mirror and saw the blond Pearl looking back at her. She told herself to snap out of it. She had to regain her determination. She would be successful and reach her goals. She reminded herself that she was meant to go to college, and, with that last thought, Ruby left the room, once again ready to tackle the world.

Ruby thanked everyone at the desk for their warm hospitality, including Mr. Jeb. He did not ask what she would be doing next, since Ruby had told him she would be seeing him around town. She smiled, waved goodbye, and walked out of the hotel with a bounce in her step, then proceeded to make her way to her new home.

As Ruby walked, she began thinking about her next steps. She paid no attention to the people she passed, until one gentleman tipped his hat and said, "Hello." Without thinking, she responded with an enthusiastic "Hi!" and a smile but then turned away quickly, realizing she was not being very smart. Ruby realized that if and when her dad's spies made their way to Chillicothe, she would become a "person of interest," so her response to kind people passing on the street would have to be more subdued for the time being.

Ruby picked up her pace, which was hard to do with her luggage in hand, but a few turns and a couple of blocks later, she was finally standing in front of Mrs. MacAfee's house. Ruby stood there for a moment, just looking at the house and thanking God for her good fortune. She walked up to the door and rang the doorbell. Mrs. MacAfee must have been ready and waiting at the door, as it promptly opened.

"Welcome home, Pearl." Mrs. MacAfee waved her arm grandly and stepped aside to let Ruby in.

She escorted Ruby to her room, where she settled in and changed into cleaning clothes. She then headed to the kitchen and began with the morning dishes. Ruby looked over the kitchen supplies, food, and canned goods for the winter days. She made a list of items they needed as well as things her momma would want to see in the cupboard for the winter.

Over the following weeks, Ruby and Mrs. MacAfee warmed up to each other to the point that they went shopping together for groceries, and Ruby began cooking dinner for the both of them.

Mrs. MacAfee was enjoying her company very much, and the feeling was mutual. Sometimes Mrs. MacAfee would have Ruby take a break, and they would share a cup of tea. Ruby would listen to Mrs. MacAfee's stories, which would send Ruby's mind wandering while she was exchanging pleasantries with her new friend. Ruby thought about how it would be nice to share moments like this with her momma.

She felt guilty for deceiving her parents but reminded herself that she had really had no other choice. She knew she could trust Mrs. MacAfee to keep her secret, as she was already helping Ruby become accustomed to being called Pearl.

Mrs. MacAfee had agreed that "Pearl" should continue to wear a wig but needed a better one. It just so happened that Mrs. MacAfee had a sister who had passed away, and her sister had been a hairdresser who had acquired several wigs over the years. Mrs. MacAfee had the wigs in her possession and thought of a golden wheat blond one that would suit Pearl's skin tone.

Ruby tried it on, and, sure enough, the wig—which was made from real hair—framed her face and flowed perfectly down to her shoulders.

"Oh my, it's perfect," said Ruby. "Thank you so much." Ruby hugged Mrs. MacAfee.

"It is my pleasure," said Mrs. MacAfee. "It warms my heart to play a part in helping you go to college." She sipped her tea. "It's also fun to be playing a role in your adventure. I will live vicariously through you."

Ruby Pearl would now have wavy, wheat-colored hair, which would throw anyone off who was looking for her. Mrs. MacAfee told Ruby that she was looking forward to her beginning school, as it made her feel like a part of her was going to college as well. Mrs. Bocook was in on the adventure as well. She promised that she would never let on to anyone about the grand secret the three shared, not even her husband.

Ruby was already learning to love her new town and her new school. Chillicothe Business College—better known as CBC— had opened in 1891 and welcomed women to the school. Chillicothe was a town that seemed to be embracing the new world, and CBC was known as one of the best schools in the West. What convinced Ruby that this was the school for her was the school motto, "We see you through." Ruby felt the school would prepare her well for jobs that needed workers skilled at using the new technology. Ruby was beyond excited when she discovered that, as part of her bookkeeping classes, she would be taking telegraphy, stenography, and general accounting.

Ruby registered under an assumed name, Pearl R. Terrill. She was relieved when the school officials did not ask for identification. Ruby just filled out the paperwork, paid the fees, and attended an orientation session, where she was told to be ready to start classes at nine o'clock the following morning.

Hardly able to sleep, Ruby woke up at five and did most of her chores. She made breakfast, cleaned up the kitchen, and prepared a light lunch for Mrs. MacAfee, as well as a few nibbles to snack on till Ruby returned from school. Ruby's mom had taught her how to manage a kitchen, so she had dinner veggies all chopped up, and Mrs. MacAfee was very impressed. She said she hadn't realized that she had an accomplished cook on her hands.

Ruby knew that it was an extra duty but figured she had to cook for herself anyway, so she might as well make the most of it and win Mrs. MacAfee over. Ruby thought about how her momma would get a kick out of hearing someone refer to her as "an accomplished cook," and this thought made her tear up. She knew her mother and father must be so worried. Ruby shook her head to defeat such thoughts, gathered her things, and headed out to class.

"Good luck, Pearl." Mrs. MacAfee sighed. "I wish that I was young again and could go to school."

Ruby looked back, smiled, blew her a kiss, and waved goodbye.

Ruby walked up to her new school with its red brick and white mortar. She stood there for a moment, just looking at the walkway to the entrance of her building, Minerva Hall. She looked around at the tall trees and thought about how far away from home she was. It was such a feeling of mixed emotions—scary and exhilarating all at the same time. She reminded herself to walk tall and not be afraid; it would not be scary once she opened "the door." Ruby took a deep breath, as she had done so many times before, and walked up the steps, through the door, and down the hallway.

She opened the classroom door to find that most of the seats were full. Ruby was surprised, as she thought she had come early enough, remembering the old saying, "The early bird catches the worm." Well, in this case, she was not the early one. It then dawned on her that most of the students were men! *Good grief . . . I thought this was a class for women to begin preparing for the workforce.* But there they were, as always, men being dominant, preparing for their management jobs. Ruby shook herself and finally noticed an empty chair next to a few girls in the middle of the room. She quickly made her way over to claim the seat. The three girls introduced themselves to Ruby. They were Edna, Clara, and Ruth. She told them her name was Pearl. They quickly agreed to meet after class. Ruby gave a small smile to herself. *It is all going to be OK.* She snapped out of it when the teacher began class. She opened her basic math textbook and turned her attention to the teacher.

He did not waste any time diving into the subject matter. Unlike high school, there was no introducing yourself to other students. Teachers left the socialization to be done outside the classroom. He did welcome the students to the class before telling them that only the strong would survive, and if they had a question, to make sure it was not one that wasted his time. They were to work hard, and if they understood the math and how it applied in the workforce, then, with any luck, they would pass the class. This last phrase seemed to be directed at the female students in the room. Ruby decided then and there that all the girls were going to excel, and this teacher would discover the intelligence and power of a girl—or rather, a woman. At the end of class, Ruby walked out with her female classmates. She noticed they all seemed to know each other well.

"Well, Pearl, what class do you have next?" Edna asked.

"English," Ruby replied.

"OK, we have a different class, but how about we all meet up for lunch at noon?" Edna suggested. All the girls agreed.

Ruby's English class concentrated on writing for businesses. She was looking forward to it, as she had already excelled in her writing courses back home, and her debating skills added extra strength to her writing ability.

Chillicothe Business College was unique in the degree program it offered, as it did not have the standard university requirements. Its philosophy was to prepare students for the workforce and, in this case, a job in business management. Ruby felt the English class would give her a breather, and she could concentrate on her math. That class was going to be tougher for her.

She had spent too much time talking to her new friends and walked into English class a bit late. She had to take a seat in the back behind a very tall guy who blocked her view of the chalkboard. She found it quite frustrating, to say the least, but there she sat, eager to learn.

This teacher had a much different approach to welcoming the class. He introduced himself but then discussed his way of teaching. It was more of a workgroup approach, as if the students were in business already. The first thing he did was have them draw numbers between one and three and gather in a group with the other students who shared the same number. The commotion broke down the heaviness in the air, and, just for a moment, Ruby felt like she belonged, just like in high school, as if she already knew everyone. The teacher then had one student from each group draw from another hat. This time it was a company name. Ruby's team drew Westinghouse Electric & Manufacturing Company. The team then read the highlights of their company, which the teacher had provided; the company's corporate office was located in East Pittsburgh, Pennsylvania, and it was known for making electrical appliances for the home. Ruby's team also learned that the company was moving into the radio broadcast industry and had many prominent business and community leaders on its leadership team and board of directors. Westinghouse was one of the first companies to expand their market into the general public, making their radio receiver widely available. Another team drew the American Telephone and Telegraph Company, and the last group drew the Radio Corporation of America (RCA).

Once everyone had their company names, the teacher had the students move their desks to form circles that would represent each company's building. The students were excited to see how the lesson was going to progress, but, for the moment, Ruby was just thrilled she could see the board. Ruby had never had a class that worked in groups like this, and she was curious to see how it would all pan out.

By the end of the class, Ruby knew this would be her favorite course. The teacher was very progressive in his thinking and was always having them look beyond the four walls. They were tasked with coming up with ideas for the company they were working for—how they could improve the bookkeeping, and what role they would play in the overall improvement of the company. The class was over in a heartbeat. Everyone was enjoying it so much that when the bell rang, someone asked, "The bell? Already?"

Their first assignment was to learn about their

company and the job they each drew within the company. They needed to have enough knowledge about their situation so that they could tackle the next day's assignment.

Ruby left the room, all smiles and excited to make her way to the dining hall, all the while thinking that her first day of college was off to a great start. She found the three girls, and they went through the lunch line and found a quiet table where they could eat and become acquainted. It turned out that Edna and Ruth were from Butler, Missouri, and they knew Clara because she was from a town close by called Nevada, and the schools sometimes competed in sports. The girls immediately clicked because they had two things in common: one, they were all from small towns, and two, they all wanted to learn and discover life outside of their towns. The girls were all getting business degrees and hoped to become part of management one day and maybe open the doors for women to become presidents and CEOs. Ruby found it refreshing to meet girls who had some of the same aspirations as her.

The girls also discussed their classes and peppered Ruby with lots of questions since she was the new girl on the block. Ruby found herself having to live a lie, as she had for so long back home. In her various books, Ruby had read about kids running away from home and from bad parents, and now she found that she had run away from home—not because her parents were terrible, but because she just wanted to keep learning and become an educated woman. Ruby was one of what the older generation called "those progressive girls." Now, she was surrounded by three like-minded women of her age, and it was a first for her. It was refreshing, to say the least, but for now, till she got to know them, Ruby had no intention of telling them who she really was or anything else about her past. Ruby led them to believe that she was from Arkansas, as she knew enough about the town her dad's parents had been from to pull it off. For the first time, she was grateful for all her dad's family stories. Ruby and the girls enjoyed lunch and then made their way to the library to complete their assignments of the day.

Weeks passed, and Ruby fell into a rhythm of school, work, study, sleep, school, work, study, sleep. The weather was much colder, and the snow would be coming soon, according to Mrs. MacAfee, so Ruby had to make sure there were plenty of staples in the cupboards in case they were snowed in. Ruby enjoyed working and living with Mrs. MacAfee. She felt like a guardian angel must be watching over her for things to have gone so smoothly. Mrs. MacAfee grew to enjoy Ruby's company even more as the days went by, and they would have chamomile tea at the end of the day so that Ruby could share the day's events with her. Then, after dinner, off to bed they each would go.

One day, Ruby was in the library, just staring into space, thinking about home.

"Pearl, are you OK? You look lost." Clara joined her at her little corner table by the window.

"I am fine, just missing home a little," she said.

"Well, I know how that is." Clara patted her hand. "So, what are you working on?"

"Nothing really. I already finished my work for the day. I thought maybe I would check out some fun fiction to read. I have always enjoyed reading. What are you up to?"

"Oh, I am about to work on an English paper." Clara started sorting her papers and pulled out a pen. "Say, Pearl, I was wondering . . . Well, I don't know how to say it, but I want to ask you something."

"OK . . ." Ruby knew what was coming.

"It is not my business, but I just have this feeling you are hiding something." Clara leaned in and dropped her voice to a whisper. "I want you to know you can trust me."

"Oh? What makes you think I am hiding something?"

"Well, it does not take a smart person to figure it

out." Clara leaned back and counted on her fingers. "First, sometimes you do not seem to respond to your name; and second, your hair is a wheat blond, but your eyebrows are auburn." She shrugged. "So, it seems to me, you have a secret."

Ruby looked at her, almost relieved that she had figured it out. She so wanted someone her age with whom to share her secret.

"Nonsense, Clara. You have a vivid imagination. Yes, my hair is dyed, but lots of girls are playing with their hair color. Now, you are right about the name. I just decided I did not want to go by my first name anymore. I wanted a fresh start. I like my first name, Ida, but just wanted a change. There . . . satisfied?"

"Well, maybe it makes sense, but it does not sound true. I think you are not telling me everything because you are worried about trusting me. Well, you can. I promise," Clara said and crossed her heart.

Ruby stared at her and thought once more about how she really wanted to tell. She looked out the window, then back at Clara.

"Clara, how do I know I really can trust you?" Ruby asked. "I have only just met you, really." She grinned. "Can't you just have faith that I am telling you the truth?" She started smiling wider. She knew she was so busted for even asking the question. The two girls just stared at each other, and, finally, Ruby decided to give in. "Well, Clara, if I tell you what is going on, you have to promise me you will not tell a soul, especially Edna. I heard her say her dad is a Freemason."

"Oh, I promise." She crossed her heart again and raised her hand. "So, do tell!"

"OK, let's go outside."

The girls packed up and left the library. It was a little chilly outside, so they huddled close together. They sat on the steps so that they could watch who was coming and going.

"You really promise?" Ruby asked again.

"Yes! Now, spill the beans."

"OK . . . you are right. My real name is Ruby Pearl; my dad's family is from Arkansas, but I am really from Oklahoma. Oh, and I do have auburn hair. Pretty smart of you to notice the eyebrows. I tried to lighten them; I guess I needed to do it more."

"Thank you. I like to think I pay close attention to details. Tell me, why the pretense?"

"It is a long story, but the short of it all is, I wanted to go to college, and my parents wanted me to marry. I saved money, and now I am here. I changed my identity so my dad, who is a Freemason, could not find me right away. So, there you have it in a nutshell. Will you keep my secret still?"

"Of course. I love secrets. I'm just glad I was right! I would make a good detective!" said Clara.

"That is for sure." Ruby laughed and bumped her

on the shoulder. "Oh, Clara. You would not believe how relieved I am that I have a friend to talk to. Thank you so much," Ruby said as she hugged her. With that, the girls went back into the library, knowing they were becoming friends for life.

Over the weekend, Clara talked Ruby into ditching the wig. Clara bleached Ruby's hair blond and her eyebrows a light brown. It was a good look for Ruby and one she welcomed. Her new friends gave her compliments and wished they were brave enough to do the same. Mrs. MacAfee and Mrs. Bocook were happy she was wig-free. Ruby could tell they both wished they were young again, like Ruby and her friends, as their lives seemed so exciting.

A few weeks went by, and Ruby was grateful that her parents had not found her yet. It was the weekend, and Ruby was busy cleaning the dusty shutters. She knew they would be used a lot with the cold weather approaching. The doorbell rang, and Mrs. MacAfee was out back, so Ruby went to see who it was. She opened the door, and much to her surprise, it was Clara.

"Oh, hello, Clara." Ruby smiled. "What brings you here this afternoon?"

"Ruby, there is a young man in town. He was in the

café asking if anyone had seen a pretty young girl by the name of Ruby in town." She hung up her coat as Ruby invited her in. "Lucky for you, everyone knows you as Pearl. It is a good thing we bleached your hair."

"Oh, I bet you anything it is my brother," said Ruby. "Where was he last seen?"

"I actually saw him go into the Masonic Lodge." Clara looked over her shoulder. "Apparently, some friends back home figured out that you had gone to Tulsa, and they have been checking out various cities based on the train schedule."

"Oh dear. Thanks for the warning. I am glad it is a young guy and not my dad." She let out a sigh. "If it is my brother, I can handle him," she said.

"You're so brave." Clara hugged Ruby. "I'm honored to be trusted with your secret. It's all so mysterious."

The girls giggled. Mrs. MacAfee walked into the parlor, folding her gardening gloves. She had been checking on her winter cabbage.

"Oh, hello. Who's your friend, Pearl?" she asked as she nodded her head, acknowledging Clara.

"Oh, Mrs. MacAfee, this is Clara, whom I told you about. She is the one who helped dye my hair. Clara, this is Mrs. MacAfee, the sweetest lady in town," Ruby said with a smile.

"Good afternoon, Mrs. MacAfee. It is a pleasure to meet you."

"Likewise, young lady. You did a great job with Pearl's hair. Now, it appears to me, by the look on your faces, that something is up." She took a seat across from the girls, who were sitting on the sofa. "OK, fill me in."

Clara looked at Ruby and then at Mrs. MacAfee in her favorite blue wingback chair. Clara knew Mrs. MacAfee was in on the secret, so she immediately launched into the story about the visitor in town looking for Ruby.

"Well, if he comes knocking on my door, I will send him on his way," said Mrs. MacAfee. "So, don't worry one little bit." She stood with her hands on her hips. "Now be dears, you two, and go make us some tea while I finish watering the flowers in the living room."

They nodded, and Clara followed Ruby to the kitchen. They continued to chatter about all the new developments as they prepared the tea.

The girls returned to the living room with the tea and some cookies. Mrs. MacAfee told them to take a seat, relax, and not worry their pretty little heads about anything.

"Let's just enjoy our tea. Tea has a way of calming one's nerves."

Mrs. MacAfee asked Clara about herself and her family. She was enjoying the company and shared how she wished she were young again to have all the opportunities that girls "these days" had compared to her day.

While Clara and Mrs. MacAfee got to know each other, Ruby stood by the living room window to peek out and see if the street was clear. Clara was busy describing what she hoped to do when Ruby gasped.

"Oh, no!" She spun away from the window with her back to the wall and hissed, "It's my brother Zach. He's coming down the street." She could not believe he had found her already.

Mrs. MacAfee put a finger to her lips. "Shush now. I'll go to the front porch and pretend I'm checking on my plants. You girls move away from the window and go into the parlor where he can't look in and see you."

Ruby and Clara scooted into the parlor and heard Zach address Mrs. MacAfee.

"Good afternoon, ma'am. Sorry to disturb you," he said. "I am looking for my sister. Here is a picture of her. I was wondering if you might have seen her."

"Oh?" Mrs. MacAfee replied. "Is she missing?"

"Well, it is a long story. I just need to find her to be sure she is OK," he said. "You have not seen a girl with auburn hair who goes by the name of Ruby, have you?"

"No, I can't say I have. Would you like to come in and tell me more? You look a little tired."

Ruby and Clara looked at each other, shocked, as

they mouthed "What?" at the same time and then almost giggled, but Ruby held her finger to her lips.

"Well, thank you for asking, ma'am, but I need to keep looking. It was mighty kind of you to offer."

Zach tipped his hat and continued on his way down the street. She waved at him and waited until he was down the road before she went inside.

The girls ran toward her, almost tripping over each other. "We thought you were going to bring him in." Ruby fell onto the couch.

"Oh no, my dear," Mrs. MacAfee said. "I knew he was on a mission and would be on his way. And I really do not feel like I was lying . . . just stretching the truth." She smiled and gracefully lowered herself onto her chair.

"Thanks for keeping my secret, Mrs. MacAfee," Ruby said. "I don't know what I would do without you."

"Now, listen here, you two. I do not want you to think it's OK to lie, as it is not! You should never lie. The truth is, I did answer his questions honestly. He asked if I had seen a girl named Ruby with auburn hair. Well, you are Pearl to me, and you have blond hair. Now, do we understand each other? I do not want to let people in the community think that I was going around telling little lies. Do you hear me?" They both nodded yes. "Now Pearl, I have grown fond of you, and I am not about to let your brother, or anyone else, drag you away . . .

unless that's what you want. Clara, I think I like you as well, so you are welcome to come over anytime you like. In fact, I think you should stay for dinner. If you leave now, he might see you coming from the house, and he could question you. I do not want you in that situation."

"Yes, ma'am, that sounds like a smart idea."

Ruby went to the window and peeked out. She wanted to make double sure that Zach had really gone. They spent the rest of the afternoon preparing dinner and working around the house. Clara did not mind helping Ruby at all. They even managed to do some of their homework together. Before they knew it, the sun was going down.

Ruby and Clara set the dinner table. They had made ratatouille for dinner, following Mrs. MacAfee's recipe, with some warm bread that Ruby had made from dough she had started the night before. After saying grace, Mrs. MacAfee chuckled.

"I bet you were scared when you heard me invite Zach into the house, weren't you? I could just picture the two of you with your wide eyes, thinking, 'Has she lost her mind?' I got a kick out of just imagining what you were thinking. You know this is not my first secret to keep; I mean, I have lived for a while," she said with a soft chuckle.

"Oh yes, ma'am, you are right," said Clara. "We did wonder . . . but, I must say, it was a great cover.

You were so cool and collected. I hope I can be like you if I find myself in the same situation."

"Well, like I said, my dear, it comes with having lived. You will understand one day."

They continued eating in a comfortable silence for a few minutes. Ruby moved her vegetables from one side of her plate to the other, then she finally broke the silence.

"I honestly cannot believe that my dad didn't come." She was a little hurt and relieved at the same time. "The good thing is that if I do wind up confronting Zach, it will be a lot easier to tell *him* what to do—namely, to leave me be!"

After a day or two, Ruby started to relax. It seemed her brother had left town, as she had not seen him for a while. One evening, Ruby was drawing the curtains for the night, and she saw him across the street. She quickly jumped back and closed the curtains. Ruby could not believe it. He had been hiding out. She hoped to God that he had not spotted her. She quickly ran upstairs and peeked out the upstairs window.

Chapter 24

MYSTERY SOLVED

MUCH HAD HAPPENED SINCE ZACH HAD COME TO town. As a new member of the Freemasons, he had been welcomed by the chapter in town. The men had told him there were many eligible young ladies in town, especially at the college. He had made friends with a few men in the chapter and one in particular named Tom. One day, they were sitting around sharing chapter stories, and Zach asked about the college. He mentioned seeing a blond girl in a boarding house window and wondered if she went to school there. When Zach had seen her, he had kept walking. The more he thought about it, the more he believed it could be Ruby, but he was playing it cool. Zach had been about to leave town but now had a reason to stick around. He could not be sure the person in the window was his sister, but he was going to find out.

"My daughter, Edna, actually goes to school there," Tom said. "If you're looking for someone in particular who's new in town, I can do some digging around. We moved here from Butler when Edna decided to go to school here, but I've gotten to know folks quite well, thanks to my Freemason brothers."

"That would be great," Zach said. "I also met a girl named Clara who said she goes to the college too."

"Yes, that would be one of Edna's friends," said Tom. "She can probably help you out too."

The following day, Tom informed Zach that the girls had a new friend named Pearl. Once Zach heard the name Pearl, he knew that it was most likely his sister. He thanked the man and headed toward the hotel, then decided he needed to take a walk to figure out what to do next. When he had met up with Clara the night before, she had played right into Zach's hands as he casually struck up a conversation with her outside the café and then invited her to join him for dinner. Zach was attracted to her, so he figured he might as well have a little fun. . . . After all, he was a Dinsmore boy! She was attentive, kind of flirtatious, and easy to talk to. He had been careful not to ask too many questions about Ruby Pearl. He did not want to spook her. Once she was comfortable with him, he would catch her off guard.

She had become very comfortable rather quickly. He replayed the evening's events in his mind as he strolled.

"Will you be staying long?" Clara had asked.

"I wish I could." He had reached for her hand and held it as he said, "I've got to go. I still need to find my sister." He then released her hand and took a sip of his soda. "I have a few leads, and if they don't pan out, I will return home."

"Well, I am sure she is OK, wherever she is."

"What makes you so sure?"

"Well, if something had happened to her, it would be in the news, right?"

"Oh, good point."

"Well, I am sorry you have to worry about her," Clara fussed with her purse. "I understand you need to go, but I was kind of hoping you would like it here," she said with a flirtatious smile.

"Well, I do like you, and who knows, maybe I will come back this way and look you up." He flirted right back, reached for her hand, and kissed the back of it the way he had seen it done in the movies.

"Oh, Zach, I would really like that." Clara looked down at her lap. He knew she was pretending to be shy.

"Well, Clara, I have an early morning, so I better get you home." He paid the bill and left a generous tip. Clara smiled at him as they went outside. It had become chilly, so Zach gave her his coat, and they quietly walked home with only a few streetlights illuminating the way.

He was enjoying her company more than he had expected to. He thought she was enjoying his too. Clara had sent some strong signals that she wanted to kiss him. She was obviously a modern girl of the twenties. She had let him hold her hand, and when he pulled her close to keep her warm, she did not pull away. Zach walked her up the steps to her door, and when he went to take his coat back, they found themselves in a passionate kiss. When they came up for air, Clara's big brown eyes wooed him even more. She leaned in, and he kissed her again.

"Well, you are a good kisser, Ms. Clara," he told her. "Now I will for sure have to see you again."

"Sounds good to me. Now, you better go before my landlady comes to shoo you away." She glanced over at the living room window. "Will I see you tomorrow?"

"Well, I am not sure. What are you doing in the morning?" Zach knew she had school but he wanted to see what she would say.

"Oh, in the morning, well, I am busy, but maybe in the evening."

"I might be gone by then. Tell you what, how about if I have to leave then I will drop a note off to you. How does that sound?"

"Fine. You can just leave it with my landlady. She will make sure I get it. But I do hope you will still be here."

"Night, Clara. I am sure we will be seeing each other."

Zach left, a grin lingering on his face all the way down the street. He had enjoyed her company, but he was going to enjoy Clara's face even more when she found out who he was. The next day would be a big one for Zach, as it would be the day that he would confront his sister. Zach decided he would let Ruby go to class and then meet up with her on her way home.

The next morning, he went up to the school and watched the students arrive. There were so many of them. His only hope to spot Ruby was by watching for Clara. He figured the few girls who were in school would stick together. Sure enough, Zach was right. He spotted Clara, and before long, two other girls joined her. Zach did not recognize one of the girls, but the other looked familiar. He took a second hard look at the girl with blond hair.

"Well, what do you know?" he whispered under his breath. "That sneaky girl, becoming a blond. No wonder no one has seen a red-haired girl."

He knew he would have plenty of time for breakfast while they were in class, so he went down the street to the diner. After devouring a huge plate of bacon and eggs and a couple cups of coffee, he headed back to the school to wait. Finally, he saw Ruby walking on her own, and he caught up with her.

"Hello, Sis." He grabbed her arm and swung her around to face him.

"Let go of me!" Ruby pulled away from his grasp.

"Look here, Dad sent me to bring you home, and I have been looking for you for weeks. I'm tired, and I want to go home, so come on." He reached for her again.

"Too bad. I am not going." Ruby avoided Zach's hand. "How did you find me anyway?"

"Well, I have to admit, it was not easy. The way you changed your name and never told your friends back home, even your boyfriend, what you were up to. Besides, where do you get off leaving Momma and Dad the way you did! Momma has been worried sick. Arthur had to come over and comfort her. I must say he has a way with her. If it makes you feel any better, once he explained how you saved and dreamed of going to school, she seemed a little proud of you, when Dad was not around that is— not that I should be helping you feel better," said Zach. "You know, you left me behind too." His hands dropped to his sides and his shoulders drooped.

The two siblings had a special bond. They had always helped each other out of tight places and genuinely liked each other.

"Oh, Zach, I am sorry to have done this to Mom and Father, but you can just go home and tell them that I am grown up now and can make my own decisions," she said. "You can also tell them that I am in school, and I plan on getting a degree. Furthermore, you can tell Father, especially, that I have a job and a place to live, and I am not going anywhere, and that is final."

"Fine. I thought you'd say that." Zach sighed. "But do not come running home when things don't work out. All the girls back home are already saying you think you are better than them, running away to have a city life instead of getting married and letting a man take care of you."

"Fine! That just makes me realize even more that I'm doing the right thing." She crossed her arms over her chest. "Do you really think I care what the girls in town think?" She straightened her sweater and stood proudly. "I am never going back there except to see Mom and Father and the family. So, you and all your Freemason friends can stop harassing me. I am doing just fine on my own," she said as her voice caught in her throat. "Oh but do tell Mom and Da—I mean, Father, that I love them. And give Mom a kiss for me. I do miss her so."

"OK, Sis, but if it makes you any happier, I knew you wouldn't give in . . . and, for what it's worth, I am really proud of you." He gave her a hug. "Oh, by the way, when you do see them, they will not be happy with you calling them 'Mom' and 'Father.'" Ruby just eyed him. "What?" Zach shrugged. "I am just saying, you know the town rules. The moms want to be called 'Momma.'"

"OK, I will remember, but you remember to tell Momma I love her, as it will mean the world to me. Really, it does. Oh, and can you tell Momma something that will make her laugh?"

"Sure, if that is even possible."

"Tell Momma that the lady I clean house for in exchange for room and board calls me a great cook!"

"Seriously? That is the funniest thing I ever heard. You hate cooking." Zach shook his head. "Well, you're right. That is really going to make Momma smile. Why, she might even laugh!"

"Well, it is not that funny. Momma did teach me a thing or two in the kitchen."

"I know, but who would have ever thought?" Zach put his arm around Ruby's shoulder and gave it a squeeze. "OK, I might as well catch the next train out of here and get back to the store. I will report to everyone that you are fine," he said.

With that, he pulled her in for a big brother bear hug.

"Say, Ruby, can you do me a favor and deliver a message to one of your friends for me?"

Ruby looked at him with a frown. "What friend? How would you know one of my friends?"

"I met Clara. And you can tell her thanks for helping me find you. Too bad I have to go. I kind of like her."

Ruby stood speechless. He tipped his hat and said, "Mystery solved. Now to report back to Dad. See you around, Sis."

He neglected to share with her that he had suspected it was her he had seen in Mrs. MacAfee's window. *Let her figure that out*, he thought. *For once, I'm the smart one.*

Chapter 25

DAD'S TURN

A WEEK HAD GONE BY WITHOUT ANY DRAMA—well, except for the fact that all the girls now knew Ruby's secret. Edna's dad had also told his friends what was going on, and word spread. Now, all of Ruby's friends and even the teachers at school knew Ruby's story. Some of her teachers were impressed with her story, while one teacher found it ridiculous.

One morning, when Ruby came to class, her teacher said, "Welcome to class, Pearl—oh wait, shall I call you Ruby now?"

Many in the class giggled, while her friends looked at her sympathetically. Ruby was embarrassed and said, "Either name will do, sir. My name is Ruby Pearl." Then she took her seat, wondering what everyone was thinking. Lucky for her, the girls found her story so exciting that they were not the least bit upset about not being in on the secret. Ruby was a bit sore with Clara for the part she played, but she was more relieved to have everything out in the open now.

The school administrators were not too happy, but her guardian angel must have been watching over her, as a lady working in the admin office took a liking to Ruby and her story and quietly changed her file name without giving Ruby a hard time. She just winked at her and said, "Attaway, girl." Ruby thanked her and walked out thinking, *Once more, things are on track.* She was back to being Ruby. What more could she want?

The weekend came, and Ruby heard about a new face in town. When she heard a knock at the door, she knew it was going to be her dad. Sure enough, when Mrs. MacAfee answered the door, Ruby heard her dad's voice.

"Good morning, ma'am, I am James Dinsmore," he said as he tipped his hat. "I understand you have a blond girl living with you by the name of Pearl."

"What if I do?" she asked. "What business is it of yours?"

"Well, ma'am, I have every reason to believe it is my daughter. My son told me he saw her come into your home and that she is most likely working for you for room and board while she attends school. Now, I do not want any trouble; I just want a word with my daughter." James kept his manners while speaking to her, as he liked to think of himself as a gentleman, and he had also learned that Ruby's landlady had recently become a widow.

Ruby appeared behind her and said, "That is OK, Mrs. MacAfee. You can let my dad in."

"Very well, you may come into the parlor," she said. "And I will leave you two to sort out your business." She showed him in and quietly turned around and went into the kitchen.

"Hello, Father."

"Since when do you greet me as 'Father'?"

"Since I am a college girl now and all grown up." Ruby squirmed just a bit. She had never spoken to her father like that.

"Ruby, now you listen to me. The way you left town is not being a grown-up. You had no right to scare your momma and me like that. Do you know how many strings I had to pull to find you? Why, I had my Freemason brothers looking everywhere for you. I must say, you didn't make it easy."

"Really?" Ruby stifled a smile. "I mean, that was my plan." She tried to regain her composure, but she was so excited that he had admitted it had been hard to figure out her whereabouts. That was an accomplishment all by itself, and her dad knew it. It was his way of saying "excellent job" without losing face.

"Now, Ruby, don't be too proud of yourself. I just do not understand. You had a good beau. Your momma and I figured things were going well and you would marry him. Then we learned he was going to university, so we thought you might marry him once he finished his studies. When we learned that was not going to happen, we figured out a way for you to meet other suitors. Why did you mislead us?"

"Father, I did not mislead you. You and Mom had figured out what my life was going to be like without even asking me. So, I just let you think what you wanted."

"Asking you? We are your parents. We do not have to ask you. You are a young lady. Why can't you be like your older sister and do what girls are supposed to do? She is happy, and you would be too if you found a good man and settled down to raise a family. A man is supposed to take care of a woman. Your momma tried to tell you that, and I know I have. Young people these days have too many crazy notions in their heads." He sighed loudly and shook his head. "Oh, and I heard how you earned part of your money. Dancing! Dancing the Charleston of all things! My Ruby, sneaking out of the house to the red-light district and dancing for money. If you do not beat all. You should have seen your momma's face when I told her. Did you ever stop to think about how this would affect her and how she was going to face her friends, much less the town?" He didn't wait for Ruby to reply. "Her quilting circle really let her have it. You know how they have always looked up to her, and now they see her as a momma who could not handle her own daughter. Do you know how that made her feel? I will tell you! Shameful! She was upset for weeks."

Ruby let her father rant until he ran out of town gossip about her.

"Oh, Daddy," Ruby softened her voice and tried a different strategy. "I truly didn't mean to scare you and Momma, but you never really listened to me. Think about it. All the times I went to the city with you and learned about business. Did you not think all the questions I asked showed that I was going to be a good businesswoman one day?"

"No, it showed me that you would be supportive of your husband when he came home from work; that is why I let you come," he said.

Ruby raised her eyebrows at him and shook her head. "Oh, fine, I should have realized you would be thinking like that. Just tell me one thing." She looked him straight in the eye as he waited. Ruby pouted as she had done with him when she was a little girl. "Daddy, why do you not love me as much as the boys?" Her chin quivered, and her eyes began to well up, but she fought back the tears.

"Of course I love you as much as your brothers. Why would you ask such a question?"

"Daddy, if you really loved me, you would have let me go to college, just like the boys. I am just as smart as they are." She started gaining her confidence back.

"Ruby, if you do not beat all. I wish some of your brothers had half the fire in their gut as you have! OK, this is how it is going to be. Mrs. MacAfee, can you join us please?" he called, and she came from just around the corner. Ruby and her father laughed, and Mrs. MacAfee blushed just a bit. They all knew she had heard the whole thing.

"Mrs. MacAfee, Ruby and I have come to an agreement. I am going to pay for Ruby to remain in school, and I would like for her to continue to live with you, but on two conditions," he said.

Ruby was watching with wide eyes. She had won her dad over and wondered what was next.

"Yes, and what would those be, Mr. Dinsmore?" she asked.

"Well, now you seem like a mighty fine woman, just like Ruby's momma, and what '
do is pay for her room and board a
more to help pay for the cost of a cle
would that be?"

"Well, I don't know. Pearl does a mighty fine job, and she cooks for me too."

"Cooks? I heard that, but I thought her brother was pulling our leg. Why, Ruby, your momma would be impressed! Well, Mrs. MacAfee, I am sure you and Ruby can work something out." He turned to his daughter. "Ruby, how does all this sound?"

"Oh, Daddy—I mean, Father—this is grand! What is the other condition?" she asked.

"Yes, Mrs. MacAfee, please refer to my daughter as Ruby, not Pearl. She is our Pearl, but we prefer to call her Ruby."

"Ruby, of course! I will be happy to."

"I love my name! I get to be Ruby again!" She hugged, kissed, and thanked her dad.

Mrs. MacAfee looked on as Ruby worked her magic with her dad. Ruby's dad tried to contain himself and be stern, but he pulled her in for a big hug, and then held her at arm's length.

"Ruby, I admire you for the guts it took to pull off something you were willing to fight for." He hugged her again. "Very good, Ruby. Now back to business. There is more." He motioned for her to sit again. "Now, I had planned on bringing you home, but I see just how much you have accomplished and how adamant you are about staying. Your momma will not be pleased that you are not with me when she mes to meet me at the train station. I will have to deal with that. So, you listen carefully, young lady. I expect good grades and for you to call once a week and tell us how you are," he said.

Ruby sat straight up and listened intently to her father as her mind was racing. It was surprising that she even heard him at all; her mind was overwhelmed with happy screams of joy.

As he continued speaking, she watched his lips say, "I will be sending you spending money once a month to live on. I expect a report and a letter to your momma once a week. I expect you to come home when you graduate and find a job close to home. We do have big cities in Oklahoma, you know."

Ruby knew his "stern father" voice and knew to just be grateful. There was no way she was going to argue about the future. One step at a time, she told herself.

"Oh, Daddy, I will make you and Momma so proud that you will be busting at the seams when you talk about me back home."

"Ruby, I have been proud of you since the day you were born. You are our little jewel. Never think that I do not love you as much as your brothers. You hear me?"

"Yes, sir!" she replied.

"Now, how about you two come and join me for dinner tonight? I want to celebrate Ruby going to college." He smiled.

They both agreed, and later that evening, they had an early dinner at the Leeper Hotel, where Ruby's dad was staying for the night. He used dinner as a way to learn more about Mrs. MacAfee, and Ruby knew he would report back to her momma. Hopefully, it would settle her ruffled feathers. If not, Ruby would be on the next train back to Oilton.

Ruby also learned more about Mrs. MacAfee, like that she was actually from Arkansas but had married and moved to Missouri with her husband when she was young. Her husband had died several months before, and so Mrs. MacAfee took in boarders. She found that having boarders kept her in touch with what was going on with the world and young people. It also filled her lonely nights. She did have friends, but when holidays came, they seemed to disappear, and she could not just pack up and go to Arkansas every time she wanted. It turned out that she had grown up not too far from James Dinsmore in a small town, Etta, outside of Hot Springs, while the Dinsmores had been just down the road in Mason. She had actually heard of the Dinsmore family, as her parents had run into them every once in a while, during the peak of the cash crop days.

This information brought a smile to the faces of both Ruby and her dad. "Well, Mrs. MacAfee, you have given me the golden words to calm Ruby's momma down," James said. "She will be happy to know you grew up not too far from my family. I think I will not be in the doghouse, or at least, not for long." They all laughed.

He asked the waiter to bring him some paper. "Now, let's make this official." James pulled out his pen and drew up an agreement. Mrs. MacAfee read through and agreed to it. They both signed it, and he gave Ruby some spending money as well as two months' rent and the cost of a part-time clean-ing lady.

He walked the two ladies home and thanked Mrs. MacAfee one more time. Mrs. MacAfee went into the house and gave Ruby and her dad some time alone to say goodbye.

Her dad pulled her in for a big hug.

"Now, remember, Ruby," he said. "The local lodge in town knows who you are, and if you are ever in trouble, you are to go to them."

Ruby smiled. "Oh, Daddy, I never doubted that one day they would know who I really was."

James was trying to look strong and stern but was all choked up. "I cannot believe you are so grown up," he said. "Just for a moment, I wish you were my baby girl again." He gave her another hug. "Ruby, I am very, very proud of you—not happy about how you went about it, but I am proud of you." He tightened his hug. "Yes, no matter how grown up you get, you will always be Ruby Pearl Dinsmore, daughter of James and Zola Dinsmore."

"Yes, I will," Ruby agreed. "And I will not call you 'Father' anymore now that I know you don't like it. You will always be my dad."

They had one last goodbye hug and kiss. Ruby Pearl Dinsmore had her family's blessing to be in college. She went to bed with her mind at rest. Finally, she was no longer battling the guilt over what she had done and trying to remember what fibs she had told. The truth was out, her dad had agreed to her being in college, and she had the best night's sleep she had had in a long time.

Chapter 26

CHRISTMAS

TIME SEEMED TO BE FLYING BY AT SCHOOL AS Christmas break loomed. Ruby couldn't believe how much she had learned, but she also discovered that her little town of Oilton had actually done a great job of preparing her for college. Ruby thought for sure she would have to catch up to some of the students in her class who were from big cities. Instead, it was the other way around. Once more, Ruby had to admit that her momma had been right. She could almost hear her mother's voice whenever Ruby had complained to her about living in a small town and how the schools might not be as good. Her momma would remind her that Oilton was all about oil, and the people out east made sure the oil towns had quality schools to encourage people to move south.

Ruby had just thought her momma was making that up, but the fact was, she was right.

Ruby was coming to realize that her momma was full of wisdom, and it warmed her heart to think of her. She only hoped her mom would be proud of her decision to attend college. Ruby was still feeling a little guilty for leaving her the way she had. Ruby kept her promise to her dad and made sure she wrote her parents every week. Her mom wrote back but still had not mentioned whether she was proud of her or not. Ruby longed for her approval.

So much had changed since that day so long ago, driving home with her dad, when Ruby had first decided she would study math. Wilson had been president when politics had started to catch her attention, and with the sudden death of President Harding, there had been three more presidents, including President Coolidge, each of whom had made an impact on everyday life. Newspapers around the country were talking about the big Christmas event at the White House. The very first national Christmas tree would be located on the White House lawn. It was a tree for all the visitors to see, and it was especially exciting because it would be the first tree with electric lights, which President Coolidge would do the honors of turning on. This was just one more example of the faster pace of life in the new, modern world.

The talk of the national tree around town and the exams she had to study for helped to keep Ruby's mind off the fact that she would not be going home for Christmas break as her parents wanted. The weather in Missouri was extremely cold, and she worried about snow. She did not want to take the chance that she would not be able to return due to the weather. If the weather turned wet and snowy, there was no way the roads would be safe to drive on, and sometimes the trains did not run on time.

Ruby came to understand that Oklahoma was not the only state building its infrastructure. She came to appreciate more of what her dad did in paying attention to where roads should be laid and what that meant for the community. In her business classes, she learned all about the importance of moving products and the cash flow in and out that was so reliant on a solid transportation structure.

Roads needed ongoing maintenance, and in 1921, Missouri set up its state highway department. The streets in those days were not very wide, usually around eighteen feet, with a tiny shoulder. This led to many accidents, as new drivers would lose control of their automobiles and end up in oncoming traffic. There were still horses and buggies on the shoulders, and that only made it more dangerous. It was common to read about head-on collisions in the newspaper with more and more people buying automobiles. Some windy roads were referred to as "bloody roads" due to the number of accidents. Ruby had heard a similar phrase back home with the "Deadly Collins Curve." She knew why the roads in Oilton were designed with plenty of curves. It was because the workers were paid by the hour, and a windy road took longer to build, which meant more money in a builder's and a surveyor's pockets. But now that Ruby was older and paying attention to infrastructure, she knew the grid layout system was transforming the roads and highways around the county. But for now, lousy weather could mean being snowed in. She was staying put.

It would be Ruby's first Christmas away from her family, and she was going to miss them. But if she could not be at home, she was happy to spend Christmas with Mrs. MacAfee, who would need Ruby and her friends. It was a sad time for Mrs. MacAfee. She had a daughter named Ada who had died from influenza when she was just four years old. Mrs. MacAfee never had any more children, and it was going to be her first Christmas without her husband. So, Ruby and her friends decided they were going to make Christmas special for her.

Ruby helped Mrs. MacAfee decorate the house, and they baked Christmas cookies together. Ruby shared some of the family traditions from back home, and one tradition Mrs. MacAfee really liked was having a cookie decorating party. She loved the idea so much that she decided to host one herself. She asked Ruby if she and her friends would help out, since the school semester was over. It was a unanimous yes!

The girls got busy making several copies of the recipes onto cards to share. The dough was ready to be rolled, and they had plenty of Christmas cookie cutters. Ruby put on a Christmas record for background music, while Mrs. MacAfee and her friends had fun baking and chatting. There were lots of cookies being made, and the oven went into overtime. Clara, Edna, Ruth, Ruby, and their new friend, Edith, made cookie baskets with a sample from each of the ladies' recipes for everyone to take home as a treat, as well as gifts for them to give to their friends. After the baking was all done, the women dressed in beautiful Christmas dresses, as if they were going out on a lovely date. Mrs. MacAfee and her friends loved to dress for a party even more than the girls did. And they did not need to be going on a date to do it.

There they were drinking eggnog, and laughing, and having a wonderful time. Mrs. Bocook was wearing low black heels and a green lace Christmas dress with a beautiful cameo pin. Mrs. Craddick had on a black lace and chiffon dress, with white pearls and black patent leather shoes. Mrs. MacAfee had dressed the most glamorously. She had on a black velvet dress with long sleeves and a black lace collar. The sleeves and skirt were trimmed in black lace as well. Her beautiful red flower brooch was stunning against the velvet. The girls loved looking in and watching the women, who were having a great time. They were totally giddy over the fact that word was out about their party.

Every man in the neighborhood knocked on the door hoping for hot chocolate and cookies. Mr. Bocook had shared with his friends that the women were baking, so they all made their way to the MacAfee home. Ruby and her friends discovered that no matter what age a woman is, there's still a young girl inside of her. Edna, Clara, Edith, Ruth and Ruby cracked up laughing as they listened to the ladies bantering and tittering about the men lined up outside.

After the second wave of men disappeared with cookies in hand, Mrs. MacAfee closed the door and said with a grin, "Man, if I had known baking cookies all night would bring over that hunk of a man, I would have baked every night!"

"Phoebe!" the women exclaimed and then began laughing. More jokes were made among the women, but they grew quiet when the girls entered with more eggnog.

"Now ladies, it packs quite a punch, so you might

want to sip it, or you might be chasing the next man that comes a-knocking," Ruby said with a smile.

Mrs. Craddick said, "In that case, pour me two glasses so I can be ready!"

They all clinked glasses and hooted. The rest of the evening was filled with laughter, good food, and carol singing as everyone gathered around the piano and Ruby provided the music. As the party began winding down and the ladies were leaving, the girls started to clean up. With the last dish put away, the girls told Mrs. MacAfee that they could not remember the last time they had had so much fun. The girls were staying the night, and they convinced Mrs. MacAfee to join them by the fireplace and unwind.

"Aw, girls, I do not know if I have ever laughed so hard," Mrs. MacAfee said.

The girls smiled at her, and then Edna said, "You know, we should thank you as well; we had so much fun being with your friends. You helped make the Christmas season special for us as well."

"I agree. Thank you," said Clara.

"Mrs. MacAfee, it really was lovely to be with a group of fine women," said Ruby. "We learned something tonight."

"Oh? And what was that?"

"Well, for one thing, no matter where you live, men will come calling if there is food around, especially baked goods. The other thing is, no matter what age we women are, we still appreciate a handsome man."

"So true, Ruby!" her friends said in chorus while Mrs. MacAfee giggled.

"Oh, Ruby, if you don't beat all. Girls, she is right. Now you remember this night. Your body might change as you age, but your mind can be as young as you want. Make sure you always have friends that enjoy life, and that means men as well. My words of wisdom. Merry Christmas!" she said as she held up her eggnog. "Now before we retire, I've decided it is high time you girls call me by my first name. I am Phoebe Anne, but you may call me Phoebe."

The girls were touched. "Of course! Phoebe it is."

Phoebe's home became the meeting place on weekends. She would have her friends over, and there would be a cross-generational teatime during which they each learned from one another. The girls had only seen Phoebe and her friends as women who had babies and cooked and cleaned while their husbands worked. They discovered there was much more to them. It turned out that at one time, Phoebe had been a schoolteacher. She told the girls how the rules were different for schoolteachers back then. They had since lightened up a bit but not by much. When she married, she had to give up teaching, as a woman could not be married and teach. It made

Phoebe so mad because a man was allowed to teach and be married. That was when she'd decided to march for women's rights. She had been lucky to have a husband who felt the way she did, but not everyone agreed with her.

Mrs. Bocook had been a midwife in her small town, but when she moved to Chillicothe, there were already several established midwives living there, so she decided to get involved with the church. The girls learned quickly not to assume that all women just married and had babies. These women were actively engaged in their community and loved hearing about what the young women of the day were up to.

Ruby's friends learned that some women were happy with the status quo, but if they became widows, often the last thing they wanted to do was to marry again, as they would have to give up all their land, including their houses, to their new husband. Phoebe explained that she enjoyed her independence as a widow. Whenever the girls left after teatimes, they wondered who had learned more, them or the older generation. The girls grew to admire Phoebe and her friends even more.

They discovered that Phoebe had helped a large number of girls from her generation complete a college education. Ruby and her friends would pick Phoebe's brain for her thoughts on various issues.

The girls found it fascinating to speak to someone who had lived through so many presidents and seen so many changes in her lifetime. Phoebe enjoyed them as well, as they made her feel respected and not old. Ruby felt so lucky that she had met Mrs. MacAfee, or Phoebe, because she made it easier to be so far away from home. Phoebe encouraged the girls to concentrate on their studies and assured them that there would always be time for boys later. Phoebe was never quiet when it came time to share her opinion. She would always let them know that if she were young like them, she would be going to business school and eventually running a whole corporation.

Phoebe invited Ruby's friends, who also couldn't go home for the holidays, to spend Christmas Eve and Christmas Day with them. Phoebe always loved for her home to be filled with people and laughter, and that had not happened in a very long time. Ruby knew she needed them just as much as they needed her.

That Christmas Eve, Phoebe turned on the lights on a tiny tabletop tree in the window for her neighbors to enjoy. She joined the girls in the kitchen, where they were getting out some of the Christmas cookies that they had made for the party the weekend before. Phoebe handed Ruby her special Santa cookie plate that she had used every year with her husband. Ruby placed the cookies on the plate, and the girls put cookies and milk on the table next to the tree. Phoebe then suggested that they should turn in early if they wanted Santa to eat those cookies. The girls smiled and promised not to stay up too late, and Phoebe said her goodnights and headed off to bed.

Once the girls felt sure that Phoebe was asleep, they got to work. They had a surprise for her, and it took almost all night to achieve their goal. The first thing they did was move the tiny tabletop Christmas tree to the parlor window. The girls had managed to hide a full-sized Christmas tree at a neighbor's house. It took all four girls to carry the tree in. They placed an old blanket on the floor so as not to hurt the wood. Then they took an old wooden washtub and put it on the blanket with a bag of soil next to it. Three of the girls placed the tree in the stand while Ruth poured the dirt into the tub. The girls laughed and shushed each other as they tried to keep it straight while packing the dirt tight around the tree so that it stood straight. The girls held the tree while Ruth poured water around it and added more dirt around the trunk to make sure it was secure. They stepped back to observe their work, and they were pleased.

Then began the work of decorating it. That was a sight all by itself, especially in that day. The girls brought out the ornaments they had purchased. Ruby and Clare wrapped red ribbon around the tree while Edna held the ladder and Ruth placed the star on the top. They did not put lights on the tree as they felt it might be too dangerous. They would leave it up to Phoebe to decide if she wanted lights. Once more, the girls looked at the tree, and they were delighted with how it had turned out. They took some Christmas fabric and wrapped it around the base of the tree. The final touch was done, and it was time to enjoy some Santa cookies and get a little shut-eye.

The girls decided to sleep downstairs by the tree, as they did not want to miss seeing Phoebe's face in the morning.

The sun woke them up, and they went into the parlor to wait until they heard Phoebe coming down the stairs and into the kitchen. They could hear her moving around quietly, getting the coffee started and the eggs ready for breakfast. They stifled a giggle and tiptoed out to the tree to wait for her to go into the living room. It was her routine to put on the coffee and then pull open the drapes.

When she came into the living room, the girls cried, "Merry Christmas, Phoebe!"

"Oh, girls! A tree! A big one! When did you do this? I am speechless." She was so touched that tears ran down her face as she kissed each girl and said, "Bless you!"

The girls all hugged her and wished her merry Christmas once more. They helped prepare a big breakfast, which they ate around the tree. They then dressed for church and headed to Christmas service.

It was a Christmas to remember with all the hustle and bustle in the kitchen, each girl making something special from her momma's recipes to bring a little taste of home to their Christmas party. Afterward, they enjoyed opening up the gifts they had bought for one another and watching out the window as children and their families walked past.

Phoebe handed Ruby a package that had not been under the tree, and all the girls' eyes were now on Ruby.

"What's this?" Ruby looked at Phoebe.

"Well, it arrived some time ago, but it was in a box addressed to me. I did not recognize the address, but the letter was charming. A certain beau of yours back home asked me to save it for you till Christmas. Looks like you have been holding out on us Ruby."

All the girls chimed in to agree with Phoebe.

"No, all of you are reading way too much into this. We agreed to be friends. I told you about him already. I have not even spoken to him since I left."

"OK, OK, open the gift," Edna said.

"Well, there is a letter. Maybe I should open it in

private." Ruby grinned and turned away from them, blocking the package from view.

"No way are you leaving us out of this." Edna reached for her elbow and turned her back to face them. "You can read the letter in private; open the gift."

"Well, OK," Ruby agreed and carefully began opening the package. It turned out to be a novel by Irish author Liam O'Flaherty called *The Neighbor's Wife*.

"Seriously . . . a book! He really knows you," said Clara.

"But if he wanted to win you back, he should have sent a necklace or something romantic," said Edna.

"I don't know. I think it is sweet that he knows I would not be able to purchase a book just to read. I think it is very considerate," said Ruby.

"Now, now, girls, leave her alone," said Phoebe. "It was very thoughtful for sure." She started gathering up the crumpled wrapping paper. "Now, let's get back to enjoying the tree, and, I know, let's try some of my apple pie!"

The pie was served up, and all the women settled in to enjoy their time around the tree once more. Ruby excused herself, saying she wanted to call home, but first she made her way up to her room to read her letter. Ruby was excited to hear from Arthur but, at the same time, wondered why she had not thought of him more often. She opened the letter.

Dear Ruby,

Merry Christmas. I hope you have a beautiful one. I ran into your brother at the store when I was home for the weekend. I was happy to hear it all worked out for you. I had hoped to hear from you, but I realized if I was busy with school, you must be just as busy with studies as well. Then later I heard you would not make it home for the holidays, so I decided to send you a little something for Christmas and let you know I think of you all the time. I hope you will call over the holidays. Call collect, as I do wish to speak by phone. School is going well, but I miss you. Call soon.

Regards,
Arthur

Ruby folded the letter and placed it in her top drawer. She had much to think about, but for now, it was time for her to call home. Ruby went back downstairs to the hallway, sat down at the phone table, and dialed. She was very excited as she spoke to all her brothers and even Rilla, who was there with her family. She told them how much she loved them, and then, finally, she had her mom on the phone. They spent extra time talking, and Ruby became choked up. She missed her mom so much. When her mom told her that she was proud of her, Ruby was overwhelmed, and tears rolled down her face in droves.

"Momma, that is the best gift ever, having your approval. I will make you proud, I promise."

"You have always made me proud, my sweet girl," her momma said. And with that, they said their goodbyes.

Ruby put down the phone, still with tears in her eyes. Her stomach filled with knots, but they were happy ones this time. Her mom was not mad; it was the best Christmas ever. That night, the girls returned to their own places, and Ruby spent the evening thinking about how to handle Arthur. She went to bed, as she had decided to chicken out and not call him. Ruby did not want to deal with any surprises he might have had in store for her in regard to his feelings. Ruby knew that without his help, she wouldn't have ever made it to college. Ruby didn't dare to break his heart over the holidays, so she decided to ignore the whole situation, as it seemed to be the easiest way out.

Once the holidays were over, it was back to the books. Ruby never complained about her studies, since she had worked hard to be there.

Ruby was not going to waste one minute of her time. She watched others drop out of the program, as they were more into socializing. What Ruby learned from watching those who dropped out was, if you pay for your own schooling, you appreciate it much more. Then she thought, maybe that was why her brothers were not making the grades as they should have been. They had no idea of the sacrifices their parents had made for them to go to school. One day she was going to do something extra special for her parents, but until then, she would crack the books, determined to make that happen.

Chapter 27

A LOSS

THE SECOND SEMESTER ARRIVED, AND RUBY HAD picked up her schedule at school with her friends so that they could see what classes they would have together. As they sat there comparing schedules, Ruby was also thinking about how far she had come. Ruby had close friends, knew her way around the town, and even knew how to get to the big city of Springfield. She had learned which teachers to avoid and which courses to take to finish her first year, but nothing had prepared her for the new teacher, Mrs. Basey, who was teaching Introduction to Algorithms.

Ruby was having a hard time remembering all the formulas. No matter how hard she tried, she would get so far into them, and then a mental block would happen. The teacher finally called Ruby to her office, and Ruby was terrified.

Ruby had never experienced being summoned to "the office" due to poor grades. Her hand shook as she knocked. Mrs. Basey opened the door and invited Ruby to take a seat.

"What seems to be the problem with your math work, Ruby?" Mrs. Basey asked.

Ruby stammered, a bit surprised at the teacher's harsh approach. She kept firing questions at Ruby and then answering them herself.

"Well, come on girl, speak up," Mrs. Basey said.

Ruby fumbled with her words at first, as she thought for sure she would be interrupted, but this time, the teacher waited for a reply, and that caused her to become even more tongue-tied. Ms. Basey gave her a stern look, and for some reason, Ruby was reminded of her dad, and she knew she needed to get her act together.

Ruby shored up her courage and sat up taller. "Well, I'm not really sure," she began. "I've always worked hard to be good at math, but this course seems to get the best of me." She paused, hoping for some sympathy, or at least some helpful advice.

Mrs. Basey just stared long and hard at Ruby, and then she said, "Look, Ruby, this is a man's world. If you want to be a part of it, part of the new world that women are fighting to enter, you have to get past whatever mental block you have. Do you understand?"

Ruby agreed, of course, but then Mrs. Basey looked right at her and told her she did not believe her. "I thought you would be stronger than this," Mrs. Basey said. "I would not have even bothered calling you into the office except that I heard the story of what you did to get here. That was courageous. That's the Ruby I want to see sitting here in front of me and whom I wish to help."

Ruby was amazed. "Help?"

"Look, Ruby, I believe in you," she said. "I looked at your grades, and you have what it takes to graduate and work as a bookkeeper. Now, I set time aside, and we are going to spend the next thirty minutes going over some problems, and I want to see how you think so I can pinpoint where you are getting stuck. How does that sound?" She pushed her glassed up onto her nose and opened the textbook.

Ruby's eyes grew wide as she watched Mrs. Basey shuffling papers, not really knowing what to do, but she was no longer scared of Mrs. Basey; she saw her in a new light. She was a teacher who wanted all her students to succeed, but especially the girls who were brave enough to take the toughest classes while also learning new technologies. By the end of the thirty minutes, Mrs. Basey had figured out where Ruby was going wrong with her formulas and straightened her out.

Ruby came back to Mrs. Basey's office after school the next day, retook the test she had failed, and passed it. Ruby's confidence grew, and from that day forward, Ruby heard Mrs. Basey's harsh voice as a voice of determination. She decided to keep that voice in her head to remind herself of her own passion for success. Algorithms were no longer a scary, secret math to be afraid of, but a puzzle to put together. She reveled in the feeling of accomplishment that came with each new problem presented and solved to perfection.

With this new wave of confidence, Ruby decided to relax a bit and take some time to enjoy going out with her friends. She had been avoiding parties to concentrate on her studies. During her first semester, she had found herself enjoying football season, as it reminded her of home and all her brothers. She had never thought for a moment that she would miss them, or football for that matter, but there she was in the stands cheering the team on.

Her friend Ruth loved football, or more importantly, she enjoyed the likes of Chris Sparks. He was from a small farming town in Missouri, and he came to CBC for two reasons: first, he could still help his parents with farming, and second, he could play football. He loved it, and Ruth loved watching him.

Ruth was head over heels in love with Chris. He respected her for wanting to continue her education and work before she settled down. Ruby was happy for Ruth but could see that her dream of running a company could change with Chris in her life. But who was she to interfere?

Chris was also great pals with Cal Hubbard, who was considered one of the best football players on the team. It seemed most girls were smitten with him, but Cal did not appear to let that go to his head.

Football season came to an end, and it gave way for Chris, Cal, and Ruth to hang out on the weekends. One weekend, Ruth really wanted her friends Ruby, Edna, and Clara to join her and Chris to watch a basketball game. The girls agreed to go to the game but planned to head home afterward rather than go to the post-game party.

When the phone rang the following morning, Ruby rolled over and put her pillow over her head. She knew Phoebe would take the call. Ruby just needed a little more sleep. An hour later, she finally dragged herself out of bed and made her way downstairs.

"Oh, Phoebe, I am so sorry, I did not mean to sleep so long," she said as she walked into the kitchen.

"It is all right, dear. I figured you needed a little extra rest and decided to let you sleep. Would you like some coffee?" Ruby nodded, and Phoebe poured her a cup. "Have a seat, Ruby. I have some news to tell you."

"Oh goodie, I love news." Ruby smiled as she took the cup of coffee from Phoebe.

"This is not that kind of news," Phoebe said as she took the chair next to her.

"Oh," Ruby said. "What is it?"

"Ruby, there is no easy way to say this, so I am just going to come out with it." She took a deep breath. "Ruth and Chris died last night."

"What? That can't be! We were just with them. You must be mistaken!" Ruby insisted.

"No, dear, I am not." She reached out and took Ruby's hand. "Clara called this morning and told me the news. I decided to let you sleep, as I knew this would upset you."

"But how? What happened? Tell me everything," Ruby insisted.

"Well, dear, I could, but I think you should hear it from Clara. Why don't you call her and let her tell you?"

"No, please tell me what you know. Clara might not want to keep reliving it."

"OK, but I can only tell you what Clara said. Ruth and Chris were out late; I guess it was past midnight. They were driving home, and you know how dark and curvy the roads are. Well, another driver must have lost control of his vehicle and come into their lane. Chris swerved to miss him but ended up in a gully. He died on impact, and Ruth was thrown from the car, but then the automobile tipped over and crushed her. The boys in the other car pulled over and tried to lift the vehicle when they saw Ruth was still alive." Phoebe paused to let Ruby absorb the news. "Are you OK? Do you want me to go on?" Phoebe asked.

"Yes, please . . . I want to hear the rest." Ruby wiped the tears that were spilling down her cheeks.

"They pulled her out, but from what I could gather from Clara, before the boys could even put her in their car to get her to the hospital, she died. They said she asked about Chris, and then she said, 'Never mind, there he is. Chris . . .' She reached her hand out as if to hold his, gave a gentle smile, and died."

"This is not happening!" Ruby sobbed. "It just can't be. She had her whole life ahead of her." Ruby started pacing the kitchen. "Seriously, my dad has always said they need to make the roads wider. When I was little back home, a lot of people were still on horseback, and the cars would swerve and hit a horse. It was a huge mess." Ruby knew she was rambling, but she couldn't stop. "You know, if the road had been expanded, maybe she would still be here." Ruby choked up and began to cry again.

Phoebe gathered Ruby into her arms and held her for a long while until the sobs abated.

"Now, dear, why don't you go give Clara a call? I am sure she is waiting for you."

"Yes, that is just what I will do. Thank you."

Ruby went into the hallway and sat down at the phone table. She looked at the phone and thought if she did not pick it up, then maybe she would discover this was a dream. Finally, she quit staring at it and placed the call.

Clara quickly picked up. "Ruby, is that you?"

Ruby was so surprised with her response, as it was not the proper way to answer a call.

"Yes, how did you know?"

"Because I have spoken to everyone else, so I was just waiting for you." Clara's voice cracked, and she sniffled. "Isn't it awful?" She didn't wait for Ruby to answer. "Listen, I will explain more, but for now, can you get over to my place?" Ruby could hear Clara as she blew her nose. "Ruth's parents got into town just a short while ago. We need to go to the Leeper Hotel, where they are staying. They have already been to the hospital, and the bodies have been released to the funeral home. We need to go and be with them. I told them we would be there for support."

"OK. I just can't believe it. I don't think it has quite sunk in yet. I'm sure her parents are devastated." Ruby took a deep breath. "Do you want to meet me at the end of the block, and we can walk together over to the hotel?"

"Sure. I need to tell Edna to meet us there."

"Good. See you in a jiffy."

Phoebe listened to Ruby's report of the conversation and then told Ruby to get dressed and not to worry about the house or her lunch. There were plenty of leftovers for lunch, and she probably would not want to eat anyway. Ruby hugged Phoebe and quickly ran upstairs, got dressed, and headed out to meet Clara.

The two girls found Ruth's parents in the coffee shop, and Edna joined them. They finished their coffee and invited the girls up to their suite, where there would be more privacy. Ruth's dad charged the coffee shop bill to his room, and they made their way upstairs. Ruby saw Jeb, the elevator operator, for the first time since she had started school, and there was an exchange of hellos. Ruby let Jeb know she would catch up with him later but was happy to see him. Jeb understood, as he knew who the family was and what they were going through. News traveled fast in a small town.

Once in the suite, the conversation was one of disbelief and questioning. Why had she not gone home with Clara, Edna, and Ruby? Why had she been out so late? The questions would not bring her back but seemed necessary to ask, as it all felt like a horrible nightmare.

The girls had been there about an hour when

some other family members arrived, so they decided it was time to go. The family was going to take Ruth's parents to the funeral home to handle all the details. The funeral was the following weekend to give loved ones time to arrive from out of town. Ruth's and Chris's parents decided to have both funerals together, and their children would be buried beside one another.

As Ruth was lowered into her grave, the girls wept for their friend, who'd had so much to live for. Ruby decided then and there that she would never learn to drive. Public transportation was the only way to go. She could hear her momma's voice telling her, "Ruby, be smart with your choices. They have consequences, and life can change in the blink of an eye."

If only Ruth had had that drilled into her head, Ruby thought. *Maybe she would be alive today.* Ruth's death made a significant impact on Ruby, and she spent the rest of the semester glued to her books.

There were days when Ruby would look up at the clouds and feel Ruth's spirit. Sometimes a tear would roll down her face, and once more, she would feel motivated to focus on her schooling. Ruth's death reminded Ruby to not lose sight of what it had taken to get to Missouri, to school, and to make sure she remained focused on her mission, achieved her goals, and graduated for Ruth as well as for herself.

Chapter 28

GRADUATION ... NOW WHAT?

TWO YEARS FLEW BY IN THE BLINK OF AN EYE. IT was 1925, and so much had changed, including Ruby. Her family back home was doing well. Ruby was paying more attention, not just to her studies, but to the world around her—politics in Washington and internationally, and how it was all connected, even with countries so far away. Ruby thought of President Theodore Roosevelt and how he was the first American to win the Nobel Peace Prize for putting an end to the Russo-Japanese War in 1905. She learned how he had made a difference in the world with other global leaders.

Ruby learned about the impact of wars, from the Spanish–American War in 1898 to the Great War from 1914 to 1918. Both had impacted so many families, including her own, and she wanted to understand how politics played into world conflict. So, Ruby began following her dad's routine of reading the editorials and the headlines of local politics every morning. She learned more about the needs of people in Missouri and parts of Kansas from Phoebe, and those conversations were eye-openers.

She was happy that her grasp of mathematics had improved, as it helped her understand the economic discussions that she read about in the paper and heard around town as well as in the classroom. Ruby believed in the American dream, and President Coolidge was living proof. He was a man who had been born into a modest home in Vermont, where his dad was a village storekeeper. His parents did well, and he was able to earn a degree in law before eventually becoming a governor and then president. Ruby reveled in the new inventions coming to be, from traffic lights to the television. It was also an exciting time for women, whose positive impact on society and in the workforce was finally being more widely recognized. The women's movement was gathering momentum. Finally, winning the right to vote had given women the power to have their voices heard. Ruby was reminded that she had been born into the best generation, where women were constantly making inroads into the "man's world."

Graduation day was upon them, and Ruby could not believe how far she had come. As she sat there listening to the commencement speeches, she revisited old memories—dancing in the red-light district, winning dance contests, and, of course, Arthur taking her to the train station. What a journey from saving for her dream to that dream becoming reality! Ruby clapped for Clara and glanced at her brother Zach, who had come up for her graduation and to make sure Ruby was on the train headed home right after.

She looked at him smiling from ear to ear and noticed his strange look at Clara, almost like he was in love with her. *There is no way they have been in contact*, Ruby thought. She knew Clara would have told her if that was the case. So, she dismissed the whole notion that had popped into her head, and she too began clapping very loud for her friend. Many more names were called, and finally, the "Ds" were up.

The president of the school announced her name: "Ruby Pearl Dinsmore!"

Ruby walked across the stage, her face beaming with pride. She took her diploma and shook hands with the college president and several teachers. As Ruby walked down the steps, she saw Zach clapping really hard, and then he gave her a thumbs-up. Ruby knew he was proud of her, which she found so exhilarating. If he was proud, her parents would be too. She took her seat and watched the final group of graduates accept their diplomas.

Afterward, there was a gathering of the graduates in the main hall. Zach came over and congratulated Ruby and her friends. Phoebe, Mrs. Bocook, and the other women came too. They were beaming with pride for the girls. They felt there was a little piece of themselves in the girls' success. The space was filled with graduates, and their energy and excitement for the future coursed through the room.

Eventually, things quieted down, and the graduates and their guests filtered out of the hall. Zach went to grab some lunch and go back to the hotel. Their train would not be leaving until the morning. Ruby had told him she would be busy with her friends, so he had the rest of the evening to himself. He had promised to come by with a taxi first thing in the morning, and they would head to the train station together. Ruby had agreed. She was excited to see her momma.

After the graduation ceremony, Mrs. MacAfee had several of her lady friends over, and they threw a small luncheon for the girls. Mrs. MacAfee gave each girl a special gift, but for Ruby, she had two treasured gifts. The first was her husband's pencil and pen set that he had used to balance his books. Phoebe wanted Ruby to have it to bring her success.

The second was her favorite brooch for Ruby to wear on her first day of work. Ruby was so touched and thanked her profusely.

"Don't be too grateful; it is a selfish gift, actually," Phoebe said. "Because when you wear the pin, a part of me will be at work with you." She smiled.

Ruby hugged her and gave her a kiss. "Of course, you will be in my thoughts every day."

The girls told all the women that without their guidance and support, they probably would not have made it this far. They all enjoyed the rest of the day together before they made their way to pack up and prepare for the next chapter in their lives.

Ruby said goodbye to her college friends. They all promised to write to each other. Clara was going to New York, where she had landed a job, and Edna was staying in town to work at the school as an accountant. She was going to move into Ruby's room and be Phoebe's new boarder. This pleased Ruby so much, as leaving Phoebe alone was not something Ruby had looked forward to.

As Ruby closed the door to the last of her and Phoebe's friends, she turned and gave Phoebe a big hug. Ruby really wanted her to know that without her, that day would not have been possible. Ruby asked her to relax, as she wanted to give the place that had been her home for the past two years one final cleanup. She wanted everything to be in perfect shape for when Edna moved in and took over her duties.

That evening, Phoebe and Ruby spent time reminiscing about the past two years together. It brought laughter and tears, especially the memories of Ruby's wig, hiding from her brother, and their first Christmas together. All in all, the two years together had been good times. Phoebe told Ruby that she had brought her back to life and reminded her of how much she still had to give to the world, to family and friends. Ruby had encouraged Phoebe to dream once more, and Phoebe had inspired Ruby to keep dreaming big. It had been a win-win situation for both of them. They retired early, both happy and a little melancholy at the same time.

The next morning, Ruby woke up and prepared to go to the train station. She said goodbye to Phoebe and promised to keep in touch.

Phoebe gave Ruby one more piece of advice for the road. "Remember what your mom taught you about choices in life," she said. "If you make good choices, you will go far."

"I do believe that, Phoebe, thank you. You've been like a mother to me and a good friend the past two years."

"Well, dear, you always have a place to stay, so please do come back and visit."

The two women embraced one last time.

"I'll do my best."

Then Ruby was out the door and waving goodbye as Phoebe watched her leave in a taxi with Zach. Ruby had saved a bit of money, as she and Phoebe had made a deal that Ruby never told her dad about. Phoebe really did not want someone else in the house cleaning, and Ruby wanted to earn extra money on top of the spending money her dad gave her, so she kept working for Phoebe. Since Ruby's dad paid her room and board, Phoebe paid her in cash. The extra money came in handy at times, besides giving Ruby a sense of independence with her savings.

At the train station, Ruby was checking which platform the train to Tulsa would be at when she heard someone talking about catching a train to Chicago. Well, that got her thinking, and her brain went back and forth: Chicago or Tulsa, Chicago or Tulsa. Her brother had already purchased their tickets, and soon the train would be arriving. The siblings talked as they waited for the train, speculating about what the women in town would be saying in anticipation of Ruby's return.

Finally, it was time to board. Ruby stepped up onto the train with her brother, and they found their seats. They were a little early, so Ruby told him she was going to walk around and see the other cars. Ruby walked away nonchalantly, but once she was out of sight, she quickly went to find her bag in the luggage compartment so that she could get off the train, switch platforms, and board the one bound for Chicago. She had to go two cars up, and just as she was about to pull her bag out, her brother appeared.

"Going somewhere?" he asked.

Ruby just stared at him and shook her head.

"I saw how your eyes sparkled when you heard the announcement for the train to Chicago." Zach laughed. "I know you too well, Ruby Pearl. It dawned on me what you were really up to when you went to supposedly 'look at the other cars.'" He put her suitcase back on the rack. "There is no way I am going home and facing our parents empty-handed."

Ruby walked back to their seats, dragging her feet the whole way, and plopped down. She was disappointed but knew Zach was right. She did not want to hurt her momma again. Chicago would have to wait. The train pulled out, and they were off to Oklahoma.

Their dad was waiting for them when they pulled into the Drumright station.

"Welcome home, Ruby, my college graduate!" Her dad pulled her into a bear hug.

Ruby was so pleased to see how her dad was smiling; he was so proud of her. They put the suitcases into the car and headed home. As they wended their way to Oilton, driving through several small towns along the way, Ruby could see that much had changed. The roads had been expanded; there were more cars and zero horses. They pulled into the new double-width driveway, and Ida Jane came running out.

"Ruby, you are home!"

The sisters hugged one another, and Ruby thought Ida Jane was never going to let her go.

"Ida Jane, let Ruby alone," said their dad. "Give her some room to breathe."

They all laughed, and as Ida Jane let go of her embrace, Ruby saw her momma walk out onto the porch.

"Momma!" Ruby cried and went running to hug her.

Her siblings grabbed Ruby's things, and eventually, everyone made it inside. Henry and Ida Jane had made a huge sign that said, "Welcome home, Ruby, our college graduate!" Ruby was so moved that her eyes teared up.

It was a warm welcome, and the whole family was buzzing. Zach took his sister's things upstairs while everyone was making a fuss over her. Before Ruby knew it, the rest of her brothers and sisters had come over for supper and a celebration. Ruby's parents wanted to have a family homecoming for Ruby, dinner and all. It could not have been a better night.

The entire family together was a dream come true for Ruby's mom. All her kids, their spouses, and her grandkids under one roof.

"Ruby is home!" It was all she could say as she finished up the dishes and then made her way to her bedroom.

Exhausted, Ruby went upstairs and into a new room. She lay down on the bed and stared at the ceiling. For the first time since it had happened, she felt grateful that her brother had stopped her from going to Chicago. She would not have wanted to miss this homecoming for the world. Her whole family was proud of her. It was a dream come true. Ruby fell asleep, leaving the unpacking till morning.

Chapter 29

THE JOB HUNT
AND MUCH MORE

RUBY SLEPT IN AND WAS SURPRISED THE ROOSTER had not woken her. She learned at breakfast that there were no more chickens, nor a rooster to crow in the morning. The eggs were delivered by a neighbor, and her momma never had to feed the chickens again, and no one had to pluck them! Ruby read the paper after breakfast and marked a few ads. She went into the kitchen to help her momma and told her she would be happy to cook dinner one night for her. Zola loved having Ruby back home and let her know that she would enjoy just being in the kitchen and cooking together. So that is what they did.

Lunch had come and gone, and as soon as they got the lunch dishes done and the wash in from the clothesline, it was time for dinner preparation. So, washing the vegetables, cutting, and chopping commenced. A loud laugh came out of Ruby as her momma plopped the plucked chicken onto the counter.

"So, who plucked the chicken?"

"Oh, the young boy Danny, who lives down the street, plucks the chickens for me to help out his parents. No one in this family ever plucks chickens anymore."

"Wow! I never dreamed that would happen. I think you should make Ivy do it just because we had to."

"Oh, hon, you know times have changed," said Zola. "She doesn't need to know how to pluck a chicken. And now with her 'educated' big sister setting an example, she will want to be a college girl too." They both laughed. "Now, let's get busy cutting the chicken up and dredging the pieces in the flour mixture. I hear you've become quite a cook!"

Ruby's apron was still hanging up where she had left it. She put it on and began helping her momma as they got reacquainted. Ruby's momma told her all that had been going on around town and with the family.

That night, the dinner table was filled with a lovely meal. As the conversation flowed enjoyably, Ruby looked around. It was a smaller dinner table, as her married brothers and sisters had gone to their own homes, and her momma had taken one of the leaves out of the table. Ruby even had to be told where her seat was. She had never thought about how life would change at home while she was gone. Of course things would not be the same, but for some reason, it seemed to her that they should. She should have seen the obvious changes the night before, but she had been peppered with so many questions about her college life in a new town that she hadn't noticed.

Ruby's dad was pleased to hear how much of a help Ruby had been to her momma and that her little sisters had only had to set the table. Life seemed to be simpler around the house compared to when Ruby was in high school. There was no one hiding under the stairs, the horses were gone, and even the guns did not seem to be in the hallway anymore. There was a new radio and phonograph, but at least her momma still had her china cabinet, and the family clock was still on the mantel.

By the time dinner was over, it had been settled that James would drive his daughter to Drumright in the morning to look for jobs.

Ruby retired to her new room. Everything had changed. The house was so different. Will had moved out and gotten his own place with Zach. Ida Jane now shared the room with Ivy, and Ruby's bed had been moved to Ivy's old room, which had also become a sewing room for Ruby's momma. That was just one more unexpected change and reality check for Ruby. She was happy her momma finally had more space to enjoy her sewing, which was more of a hobby now, as the girls were wearing store-bought clothes. Ruby thought about how Ivy was now old enough to do the dishes and saw how close she and Ida Jane had become. Why, even Henry had grown up, and he and Thomas seemed to be close as well.

She lay down on her bed, ready to relax and enjoy a new chapter in her book, when she realized she had forgotten how easy it was to hear the conversations downstairs. So, she lay there listening to her parents enjoying each other's company as they discussed their day and was amazed that there was no arguing about her siblings or Dad's work . . . not even money. Children were not running in and out with the doors slamming behind them. It was just the quiet house she had always dreamed of, and now she found it uncomfortable. Ruby lay there wondering what her friends from college were up to. She rolled over, ready to go to sleep, but her brain kept her awake as she thought about how far she had come. She had worked so hard to get there, but she hadn't thought about the reality of what was next. She had not pictured being back in her childhood bed, yet she was glad to be home and see her momma.

Her momma really was everything to Ruby, her approval and acceptance of Ruby's need to be a working woman. She was not sure her mom completely understood, but at least her parents were willing to try. A tiny tear rolled down her face onto the pillow as Ruby closed her eyes and finally fell asleep.

Morning came, and Ruby woke up to the smell of her momma's biscuits! Ruby imagined Zola getting up early, getting the coal stove going, and making biscuits for breakfast. Ruby's momma loved her coal stove. It might have been small and not new compared to some of her friends', but she was not giving it up for anything. Zola had mastered her cooking and timing on this coal stove, and she loved how the house smelled and how the coal stove warmed their home in the winter. It was just perfection, as far as she was concerned, and she did not need the new, high-tech Royal Herald cookstove, no matter who might insist she did.

Ruby joined her momma in the kitchen.

"Take a seat, dear," Ruby's momma ordered. "I made you a big, fat breakfast since you will be gone all day interviewing. I do not want you to go hungry."

Ruby kissed her momma and took a seat in the kitchen. She did not have the heart to tell her momma that it was too early to eat or that she would rather just have a cup of coffee and some toast.

Pretty soon after, the rest of the household was up, and the house was buzzing with people eating, dishes banging, and all the familiar sounds of home, which surrounded Ruby. A warm feeling of contentment took over as she watched her younger siblings, who were no longer babies, do all the chores she and her older siblings used to do. Ruby now understood only too well what her momma always said: "Life changes in the blink of an eye." With that thought, Ruby helped her momma with the kitchen preparations for the rest of the day's meals and then made her way upstairs. Ruby was busy getting dressed when her sister Ivy walked in unannounced and let Ruby know what she had been planning to tell her when she finally came home.

Ivy shared with her sister that she had hurt their momma's feelings and told her she better stay around for a while. Then Ivy took off and ran downstairs. Ruby was so startled by her younger sister speaking to her like that, much less telling her what to do. The baby whose diaper she had changed was now old enough to give Ruby a piece of her mind. It was a shocker, but one Ruby guessed she should have expected to hear, just not from Ivy. Ruby continued to get ready, all the while keeping Ivy's message in the back of her head and knowing she somehow needed to make it up to her momma . . . and her dad too.

It was nine o'clock in the morning and James was ready to take Ruby to Drumright to look for a job before he started his own work of surveying for new streets between Tulsa and Oilton. The drive was interesting to Ruby, as she again noted the road expansion and marveled that there were no horses and so many more cars.

People honked when they recognized each other and gave a friendly wave. It was like there was a whole new form of communication between drivers. Ruby asked her dad to drop her off at the newspaper, so he did, then wished her good luck and drove off.

Ruby walked in and asked to speak to the editor about a job opening. The editor was very familiar with who Ruby was. Word had already spread that she was back in town. He explained to her that he wanted a person with experience and said he was sorry. She shook his hand and excused herself.

Ruby did not expect to be hired off the bat but was hoping that by some small miracle, she would be. She walked a little farther to the Drumright Bank, but still no luck. So off to the First National Bank she went. Even though there was not a job opening listed, Ruby thought she would introduce herself, so if something came open, they would know her skills and consider her.

The accountant at the bank was made aware of Ruby's presence, and he was given the background of who she was: the daughter of James Dinsmore. When he saw Ruby walking out of the president's office, he let her know he was not going anywhere. She smiled and just said, "I am sure you are right, but who knows? Maybe we will work together one day. Good day, sir."

He stood there, wanting to respond, but he was tongue-tied as he watched her walk out of the bank.

Ruby knew she had gotten to him, and she took a deep breath. *It might be a man's world, but I plan on being a part of it.* Ruby looked up the street and saw Bessie's mom's store, Markey Fall. She thought about going in but felt she might get carried away catching up, would lose valuable time, and miss a job opportunity, so she continued on. There was only one more place she knew of that was looking for an accountant, and it was the local telephone company. Ruby chuckled as she remembered when the Dinsmores had gotten their first phone in the house, and she thought about how amazing it would be to work there. Ruby straightened her dress to make sure everything was in place and walked into the office. She filled out the forms and waited to speak to the boss. The secretary told her that one other person had applied for the job and another person was being interviewed, so Ruby would have to wait.

Several minutes passed, which made Ruby feel uneasy. She could hear the two men inside the office laughing. Finally, the door opened. The two men shook hands, and Ruby was ushered in. The interview began, and Ruby felt she was more than qualified, but in the end, the boss said he had already given the accounting job to the gentlemen who had just left. Ruby was startled to learn that she had gone through all his questioning for nothing.

"Don't worry, pretty little lady, someone will want to have a cute filly like you around the office." He patted her hand. "You handled yourself quite well during the interview, so I am sure you will be great at pouring coffee and helping the men out with the number crunching."

With that, he showed her out of the office.

Ruby was not surprised at his statement. She was sure there was more of the same to come. After all, she really was a trailblazer. She walked over to the hotel restaurant. She needed to relax and think about what to do next. Ruby walked inside, and all seemed to be exactly the same, as if time had not passed at all. She was even able to sit by the window at the same exact table she and her momma used to sit at when they had their "girl lunches."

Ruby ordered a cup of coffee and looked at the paper in case there were some ads she might have missed. She looked up from the paper and saw the table where she and Arthur had sat discussing their future. So much had changed.

"Excuse me, Ruby?" Arthur's dad paused beside her table.

"Oh, Mr. Woods, so nice to see you," Ruby said.

"Mind if I join you?" he asked.

"Of course not," Ruby replied, but he had already sat down before she had even completed her reply. Ruby could tell he had something to say to her.

Mr. Woods said that he had heard she was in town. He started going over the history of her and his son and how disappointed he had been to hear about his son's role in her running away to school. He started to lecture her on how she could have learned accounting for free just by marrying Arthur. Mr. Woods continued to give her a piece of his mind and let her know that he would have been more than happy to have had a smart daughter-in-law to teach the accounting part of the business.

"You missed a great opportunity, one that would have brought more joy to both our families and to the community, and not heartache."

He closed by letting Ruby know that Arthur would not be coming home for the summer. He would be taking summer classes. He blamed Ruby for that. Ruby watched him walk out the door, once more astonished that two people now had let her know how they felt about her running away. Ruby sat there thinking about how she had not even considered the consequences of her actions and, in hindsight, that it was very immature of her to have been so selfish. She sat there feeling sorry for herself as she drowned her thoughts in a second cup of coffee.

Stirring the coffee as if the cream was never going to mix, Ruby noticed two nicely dressed men come in and sit down at the table next to her. She sat there trying her best to hear what they were saying. She knew it was all about their business, which she overheard was located in Ardmore, where Healdton Field was located. It just so happened that it was one of the largest oil fields in Oklahoma. It turned out that the men were going to speak to some of the powers that be in Drumright about ways they could work together. This got Ruby thinking, and with that, her dad walked in and motioned to her that he was ready to take her home. So, she paid her bill and caught up with him.

"Well, today was certainly not my day," she said. "But I have some ideas."

"I am not surprised. You always seem to," he said and put his arm around her shoulder. "Let's get home, Ruby," he said. "Tomorrow is another day."

Off they went. Ruby found herself holding her hat and then recalled how she had hung on to her hat years ago to make sure it did not blow away. It was a car ride that had given her the idea to study math, and now she was a college graduate. She smiled and looked at the clouds and gave thanks. Tomorrow would certainly be a new day, just like her dad had said.

Ruby ended up working for the family. She kept the books for the grocery store that her brother Zach was running. She was doing accounting, but Ruby felt she knew so much more. There was no way she was going to complain, though. She owed it to her momma to stay in town and make up for what she had done. But things were not the same. Her sister Rilla had three kids now; her older brothers, Will and Robert, lived out of town and were raising their families. Her sister Ida Jane was engaged to be married to her childhood sweetheart, Thomas, who was graduating from high school, and Henry was a basketball star who was busy dating.

Time had marched on without her in Oilton, and the girls she had grown up with had as well. They did not think much of Ruby for what she had done to Arthur. Apparently, word had spread around town that Ruby had not called him on Christmas after he had mailed her a gift. Of course, everyone knew, as he had sent it from Oilton, and so, as was the way in small towns, everyone knew Arthur was still in love with Ruby. Other girls had tried to win his heart, but they could not compete, and so the girls in town resented Ruby for it.

Weeks passed, and soon Ruby did not smile as much. She heard Drumright would be working with some men from Ardmore, but there were no jobs for accountants in that business plan. She would go into Drumright with her momma to buy fabric, as her momma still enjoyed sewing, and it was lovely to see Bessie's momma. Bessie was in the store every once in a while, but Ruby found that Bessie had moved on too. She was married with two children and found she really had nothing in common with Ruby anymore. Her parents had come down hard on Bessie once they learned that she knew of Ruby's plans and kept quiet. Bessie had told Ruby when they did try to reconnect that it was a hard time for everyone. It took a while for the town to get over what Ruby's friends had done by helping her save money and then run away.

A year passed, and Ruby's parents noticed that the spark in Ruby was no longer there. She was not dating anyone. She did not even bother to read in her favorite spot. She just went to work, came home, helped out with dinner and cleanup, and repeated the same the next day.

Her parents tried to engage her in conversation, even topics she enjoyed, such as politics, but still, they could tell it wasn't their Ruby.

Finally, one evening they called her into the living room after dinner and got right to the point.

"Ruby, it's time for you to leave the nest," her momma said.

Ruby couldn't believe her ears. She was getting kicked out of her home.

Before Ruby could protest, her dad said, "Ruby, you belong in a big city. It is time for you to look for the job you have always wanted."

Ruby could not believe it. Her dad told her to pick whichever city she wanted and start looking for a job.

"Well, I really don't know what to say," Ruby said. "But thank you!" She ran to each of her parents and gave them hugs before sitting back down with a frown.

"What's the matter, dear?" her momma asked.

Ruby sighed. "You know it is easier to go to the city and interview for jobs in person." She looked at her momma and then her father.

They both laughed.

"If you could choose a town, where would it be?" her momma asked. "Maybe Tulsa or Oklahoma City?"

"Oh, I'm sorry, Momma, but no," Ruby said. "Chicago is where I have always wanted to go."

"Then, Chicago it is!" her dad said. "Let's see what the train schedule is, and you must make your way to Chicago as soon as possible."

Zola was not prepared for Ruby to depart so quickly, but James said it would be harder on everyone if they put it off. The next morning, when Ruby woke up, her dad said, "Pack your bags. The train leaves in two hours."

Ruby could not believe her ears. She asked about work, and her dad said the store would be fine. Ruby packed her bags, and this time her momma and dad drove her to the train station. She was Chicago-bound with her parents' blessing!

In the blink of an eye, a decision was made, and Ruby was going to rise again to a new challenge. Her world was about to change once more.

ABOUT THE AUTHOR

 **Diann Floyd Boehm** is an international children's author who lived in Dubai for fourteen years and is now based in Texas. Diann has always enjoyed the art of storytelling and has taken her imagination and has taken her imagination to print so she can share her stories with more children and families around the world.

Rise! A Girl's Struggle for More is Diann's first young adult novel. She is also the author of five children's books, partner published with OC Publishing. One of her books, *Harry the Camel*, was translated into Arabic and won the 2020 Authors Marketing Guild Award for Best Children's Book–Foreign Translation. Diann also started a YouTube channel in 2020 called The Story Garden, where viewers can enjoy the author reading her books and interviewing various authors, highlighting their books.

Her creative flair encompasses the performing arts as well. She performed in musical theatre productions in Dubai produced by Popular Productions out of the UK, and she enjoys making guest appearances on the radio and in-person, where she encourages young and old to embrace their imagination.

Diann is not only an educator, but also a wife and mother of three. She was born in Tulsa, Oklahoma, but grew up in Texas with five brothers. She has traveled extensively to many parts of the world. She has a Bachelor of Education from George Mason University in Fairfax, Virginia, and has taught elementary school both overseas and stateside.

Diann is available for speaking engagements, book signings, and author visits.

Learn more about Diann and her books at:
www.diannfloydboehm.com

OC Publishing
www.ocpublishing.ca/diann-floyd-boehm.html

Amazon
www.amazon.com/author/diannfloydboehm

Interact with her on social media:

Twitter
www.twitter.com/diannfloydboehm

Facebook
www.facebook.com/diannfloydboehm

Instagram
www.instagram.com/diann_floyd_boehm

Pinterest
www.pinterest.com/DiannFloydBoehmAuthor

Linkedin
www.linkedin.com/in/diannfloydboehm

B4R Store
www.b4r.store/diann-floyd-boehm.aspx